LORD FARLEIGH AND MISS FROST

Lord Farleigh *and* Miss Frost

Clairvoir Castle *Romances*
BOOK FOUR

Sally Britton

Published by Pink Citrus Books
Edited by Jenny Proctor of Midnight Owl Editors
Cover design by Blue Water Books
Illustration by Melanie Bateman

Sally Britton
www.authorsallybritton.com

First Printing: November 2022

To the Christmas Elves Who Make This Season Magical for Their Loved Ones, Year After Year.

Merry Christmas.

CHAPTER 1

DECEMBER 1819

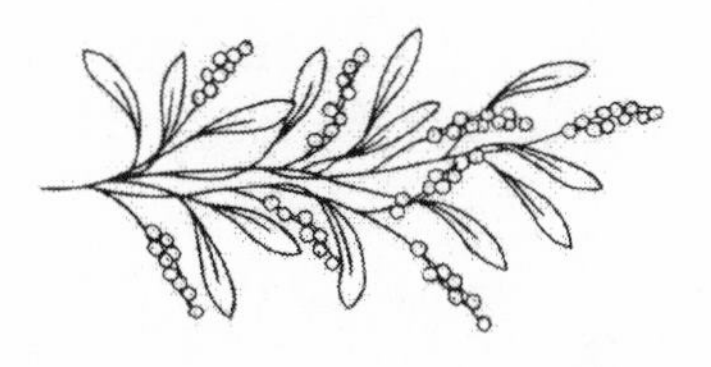

The carriage jolted to a halt—the third stop of the day—when the wheels sunk too deeply into the mud to come out again. Isleen Frost winced while her mother closed her eyes and started whispering in Irish. Isleen's older brother Teague, Baron Dunmore, cast an apologetic smile to his mother. He winked at Isleen, who sat across from him, then gave a gentle tug to their younger sister's escaped curl. Fiona glowered at him, as though holding poor Teague responsible for the state of the road.

"We are nearly there, ladies. This will be the last time we stop. I'm near certain of it." He opened the carriage door, not waiting for the driver to jump down and inform the passengers that they must all climb out again.

Teague did not bother trying to avoid the deep muck. Dried mud already covered his boots nearly to their tops. Isleen looked down at her far less-sturdy traveling boots and winced. The boots were fair ruined.

Fiona grumbled. "This isn't much of an adventure."

They'd tried to cheer Fiona when she discovered she'd spend the holiday away from her friends in Dublin by appealing to her exploratory nature. The ten-year-old wouldn't be happy until she set sail across an ocean or climbed the Alps. She inhaled adventure novels as some would their favorite pastries.

Their brother held out his hands to help Isleen jump from the carriage, then he swung her over to the higher—and dry—rise of earth beside the road. She gave him a thankful smile as she put her hand atop her head to adjust her bonnet. Then she peered uphill, her view filled with trees and not much else.

There was supposed to be a castle at the top of one of these hills. The tree-lined road made it impossible to spy the edifice, though she'd been searching for it through her window since they'd entered Vale of Clairvoir. Apparently, approaching from the south meant the castle hid behind trees until one was only a hundred yards away from it.

Máthair came down the carriage step next, and Teague swung her to the same little rise as Isleen. Neither of them complained, though Isleen could guess well enough what they were all thinking.

They ought to have stayed in Dublin for Christmas and remained in Ireland until Parliament reconvened in January. But when the Duke of Montfort invited an Irish representative to his home for Christmas and Twelfth Night celebrations, folly alone would keep that Irishman from attending.

It took time enough for England to grant any kind of support, thanks to the bickering lords, to have their country's needs met. And the Irish had a long road yet to travel.

Fiona made no such effort to bite her tongue. As soon as Teague had settled her boots on the dry dirt next to their mother, she heaved a large sigh. "Why must it be so wet and mucky?"

"I am not sure mucky is a word, Fi," Isleen said before her mother could respond to the complaint.

Teague spared Isleen a raise of his brows before he tromped to the back of the carriage to help the driver and the secondary coachman push.

Lady Dunmore looked up at the gray cast sky. "At least it isn't snowing."

Isleen avoided adding the word "yet" to her mother's sentence, but barely. Instead, she cheerfully tacked on, "I would take snow over mud."

Her mother hummed with amusement, the sound nearly a song on its own. "And I would prefer flowers over snow. But we take what God gives us, and we're thankful."

"We do, Máthair."

With a gentle smile, her mother warned, "Best not let your Irish show overmuch, dear. Our English hosts won't find it to their liking, I'm thinking."

Fiona snorted. "If they didn't want to hear it, they shouldn't invite the Irish to their home." The little girl wrapped her arms tighter about herself.

A shout drew their attention before Isleen offered her own remark on the unfairness of their mother's directive. Though she quite agreed with her little sister. Why did she have to change how she sounded merely to appease a duke and his family? The English had ground the Irish underfoot for centuries. One would think an Irish tongue the very least of their worries when families from the two countries came together. Still, Teague had made both his sisters promise to behave as the very best of guests.

The carriage lurched forward. "Ah, there we are now." Lady Dunmore clapped her hands. "And hopefully for the last time."

The coachman tipped his hat to them as he came around the carriage. "Ready again, ladies."

Teague walked behind the man, mud now above the tops of his boots. "I'm not certain I ought to climb back in with the three of you. I might get this mud all over your skirts."

"You cannot ride on top like a servant, Teague," his mother protested. "You are a baron, visiting a duke."

"And you are a baroness and two fine young ladies, guests of the duchess." Teague opened the door and then came to fetch his mother to save her from the mud. "I'll not get a spot on your gowns. It wouldn't do to shame you like that, would it now?"

Though she didn't argue, their mother threw a concerned glance over her shoulder to Isleen. The woman had a fair amount of pride. Anything that made them appear less in their esteemed hosts' eyes would sting, whether or not the baroness admitted it aloud. Even if the duke and duchess themselves never let on about such a thing, Baroness Dunmore would feel it keenly.

Isleen waited until her brother returned for her before saying, "I have an idea." He quirked his eyebrows up. "Why not put the blanket around your legs instead of over ours? That will save our gowns from ruin and you from certain shame by riding on top of your carriage instead of within."

"I suppose a filthy carriage blanket would be better than the alternative." Teague answered her grin with his own. "That's a fine idea, Isleen."

She shrugged. "I am an expert at solving problems."

"That you are. Let me solve yours now and tuck you back into the carriage, safe and sound." Teague was a strapping gentleman, thankfully. He handedly replaced Isleen and Fiona back into the carriage before carefully coming in again himself, taking one of the warm blankets and wrapping it around his legs in a way that would prevent so much as a fleck of mud from leaving his boots and trousers for the ladies' skirts.

Fiona pressed her nose against the carriage window, straining to look upward as the carriage shifted to begin a steeper climb. "Do you think this castle will be like the Tower of London?" she asked. "Or more like the Rock of Cashel?"

"Both of those buildings are terribly old, m'dear," Teague said with his head tilted against the back of the carriage. "This castle is newly built upon old foundations. I imagine it will feel modern in all the most important ways."

"You mean there will be water closets?" Fiona asked, rather indelicately.

"Fiona," their mother warned, closing her eyes and shaking her head. "A lady only asks about water closets when she needs one."

"I will certainly need one when we finally arrive," Fiona stated with a grim slant to her eyebrows. "We have been in this carriage all day, bumping along the roads like apples in a cart. What lady wouldn't need a water closet on arrival at a castle with roads like these?"

Isleen had to fight against a laugh as her mother raised her eyes to the heavens, as though beseeching them for patience. Fiona was eighteen years younger than Teague and fifteen younger than Isleen. She'd been a late addition to their family, bringing great joy to their parents, but she'd also been spoiled rather more than was good for her. Thankfully, she had a kind nature overall. The long journey could be blamed for putting her out of sorts.

"We are nearly there, and once you have rested and had something to eat, I think you will perk right up." Isleen gave her mother's hand a gentle squeeze. "We all will."

The carriage's tilt changed as they moved to level ground. Isleen and Fiona moved as one to the windows and looked out. Isleen ignored her brother's amused chuckle; they had arrived at last. The carriage turned, and neatly trimmed hedges came into view. And then, a tower soaring above them, then several smaller turrets, all of them with walls of bright yellow-gold stone. The modern castle, despite its recent build, appeared quite medieval.

What had she heard her brother call the style? Gothic revival. With the blue sky bright behind it, and the green lawns stretching away from the stone walls, she'd never seen a castle look more cheerful. Indeed, it made her think of summer and warmth, even though she wore gloves to protect her fingers from the December air.

"It looks like a fairy tale," Fiona whispered with reverence.

The carriage horses walked with lighter steps up the gravel

and stone drive and into a part of the castle itself. They entered a portico that offered protection from the elements for weary travelers. The sounds of the horses' hooves echoed in the open stone chamber as the vehicle came to a gentle stop.

Suddenly, Isleen felt quite small. Their family home in the country was nothing like this, and the house where they spent most of their time in Dublin could likely fit inside the main tower of Castle Clairvoir with room to spare.

From the outside, the Duke of Montfort's seat of power was as imposing as it was beautiful. What would she find within? Hopefully just enough adventure to keep Fiona entertained but not so much that she traded in being a respectable young woman to be a piratical maiden.

A servant dressed in the duke's livery opened the carriage door and bowed, allowing her brother to step out first and then take each of the women by the hand and assist them down to the ground. Isleen looked up at the long corridor before them, with windows high and bright, shields and tapestries hanging on the walls, along with rows and rows of swords. At the end of the hall, a cannon pointed their way.

Not the most welcoming sight, but certainly a statement of power, she thought, then allowed herself to count the number of liveried footmen and starched-aproned housemaids standing along the corridor. There had to be at least twenty of each, the women wearing dresses that seemed to indicate different statuses among them, and the men all dressed as though they had stepped out of the previous century rather than wearing sensible clothing from their current time. The servants at the farthest end from where they entered were the best dressed, for certain, which marked them high in the household pecking order.

Isleen couldn't help sorting out what she knew of the Duke of Montfort and what this display of wealth might mean. Her brother wasn't a high-ranking member of the peerage. A baron put him nearly at the level of the untitled. There was no need, therefore, to impress or intimidate someone of his status. Add to that his Irishness, and most Englishmen of rank would snub him.

This wasn't a snub. Or a show of power.

Servants at the end of the long walkway came forward to take their wraps, overcoats, hats, and gloves, and Isleen's fingers immediately felt chilled.

It occurred to her as they passed from the sword-covered and servant-lined corridor that the duke and his duchess were putting on this show for an entirely different reason. The only thing that made sense was that they wished to show *honor* to their guests.

At the same moment of her realization, a deep voice boomed through the large room where the corridor had spilled the Irish guests.

"Welcome, Lord Dunmore, Lady Dunmore, to our home."

The duke stood on the red carpet, a tall man with dark hair turning gray at the temples, dressed in a deep green coat and gold waistcoat that made his eyes blaze as green as the Emerald Isle itself. Despite his age, he cut a commanding figure. The floor around the carpet looked like a giant chessboard, black and white marble squares stretched in all directions, and two hearths large enough to roast a pair of boars blazed on either side of the room. The fires kept the room from falling to the low temperatures outside, but they wouldn't warm Isleen's hands from their respective places in the room.

"Thank you, Your Grace." Teague hadn't stopped walking, nor had her mother. Fiona had to give her a poke to the small of her back before she realized she had fallen three steps behind.

Someone giggled, only to be immediately shushed. Isleen kept her chin high and a smile on her lips. Her gaze immediately found the source of the giggle. A boy near Fiona's age stood at the end of the duke's family line. The girl next to him had shushed him, and she smiled kindly when Isleen's gaze met hers.

The duke spoke again, and Isleen forced herself to stop

gawking at the finery like a country bumpkin and pay attention to a man with nearly as much power as the Regent himself.

"I am honored by your acceptance of our invitation, Lord Dunmore. It cannot be an easy thing to spend your Christmastide with near-strangers, though my son assures me he counts you as a friend. Will you introduce your family?"

"With pleasure, Your Grace. We are honored to be welcomed into your home. This is my mother, Lady Dunmore."

"An honor, Your Grace." Máthair's polished curtsy left nothing to be desired.

"And my sisters, Miss Isleen Frost and Miss Fiona Frost."

Isleen curtsied in tandem with her sister, eyes lowered appropriately. They rose again, and her eyes flicked from the duke's to the duchess's kind blue gaze, then of their own accord slid farther to the duke's right—meeting a pair of dark blue eyes that sent a small thrill of surprise down her spine.

A man she hadn't bothered to notice before, except as a form standing in the duke's reception line, stared at her with an intensity she'd call audacious in another man. This had to be the duke's eldest son and heir, the man who had sought out her brother and befriended him during the last parliamentary season.

Lord Farleigh, Earl of Farleigh, future Duke of Montfort. What was his name again? She had thought it odd, since all Englishmen seemed to be called John or William.

"My wife, Her Grace the Duchess of Montfort. My son, Lord Farleigh. My daughters, Lady Isabelle Dinard and Lady Rosalind Dinard, and my son Lord James Dinard. My eldest daughter will arrive this afternoon with her husband, and we will have other guests to introduce you to soon enough."

The duchess offered a warm smile. "It is wonderful to have your family here for the Christmas celebrations. I hope you enjoy your time in our home. I know it can be difficult to leave your own when there are beloved traditions to honor."

"It is a delight to be here, Your Grace," Máthair said with sincerity. "Thank you for thinking to invite us."

Fiona shifted her weight from one foot to the other, and Isleen quite suddenly recalled her sister's carriage conversation regarding water closets. She tried to subtly take her sister's hand to offer a squeeze, the only reminder she could give to exercise patience when a duke and his family stood on such ceremony to welcome them.

Her gaze wandered as those bearing titles continued to make the usual sort of conversation people would upon introductions and welcomes. Suits of armor stood between pillars above the staircase that led up and into the castle. Banners hung from the ceiling above, along with a large stag's head and old shields bearing crests she'd never seen before. Flanking the large fire-places were men dressed as servants, but in less eye-catching clothing than the livery the footmen wore, and she wondered briefly at their purpose.

The ceiling stretched high above her.

Quite suddenly, someone cleared his throat at her elbow.

Isleen had grown inattentive again in her admiration of the architecture, which meant she had no warning that the duke's family meant to escort hers to the guest wing where they would stay. Wasn't that something far beneath the duke's status? Surely, a servant leading the way would be perfectly acceptable.

But the duke's son, with those deep blue eyes he inherited from his mother, tilted his head forward. No smile touched his lips as he held his arm out to her. "Miss Frost. May I escort you upstairs?"

Isleen saw in an instant that the duke himself already led her mother to the first step of the elegant staircase, with her brother escorting the duchess, which left her to be on the arm of the heir, while their younger siblings followed behind.

"Of course." She laid her hand upon his forearm. "Thank you." Belatedly, she forced a tight-lipped smile. He must think her backward and strange, to catch her gawking at his family's entryway as though it were the king's own palace. She'd been in grand places before, but had apparently hidden her awe much better.

Already she had failed. She hadn't wanted to give anyone in the duke's family reason to think less of her own. Isleen ground her teeth together and plotted her way out of the poor first impression she'd given the heir to the duke.

SIMON HADN'T MEANT TO STARTLE MISS FROST, BUT SHE'D not been paying any attention to the flow of conversation around her. Which amused him, somewhat. Most young ladies, when introduced to his family and to him, pretended that every word flowing from a member of the duke's kin was as intoxicating as it was fascinating.

And here, Miss Frost had practically ignored them all.

Perhaps she had another game in mind. Most single women he met had one plan or another to gain his attention or—in less honorable circumstances—his father's.

"Do you like the castle?" he asked, his tone flat and eyes forward rather than upon her as he spoke.

Simon Dinard, Earl of Farleigh, knew his duty when his parents invited guests into their home. Especially with these particular guests. His father had wanted to meet Lord Dunmore ever since the man's appointment to the House of Lords.

Simon had a duty to his parents' guests, to see to their comfort. And to escort Miss Frost from one room to the next until a lady of higher rank arrived at the castle. Or until his brother-in-law and best friend, Sir Andrew, arrived to take over that duty.

Miss Frost must have heard something of his suspicions in his tone. She tilted her chin up and offered him a smile with a lot of teeth.

"I find I do. It won't be difficult to enjoy our stay, given the beauty of the castle. I understand your mother had her hand in its design. I hope she will not mind sharing how such things came to her mind as a fireplace without a chimney."

He blinked and glanced down at her. "Not everyone notices that. You have keen eyes, Miss Frost." Was it his mother she wished to impress for social gain? It was a lesser-used tactic, but he'd seen it before.

She gave a tight nod. "Have you been to Dublin, Lord Farleigh?"

"Yes. I spent the better part of a year at our family's holdings in Ireland. Dublin is where I first met your brother." The abrupt change of topic didn't put him off the scent. He'd know soon enough if she meant to be more than a well-behaved guest.

"Then you know how grand the cathedrals, castles, and estates are where I come from." She raised her chin a notch. "I can admire the work that goes into creating fine buildings, both ancient and modern."

"So it would seem." He couldn't keep the amusement out of his voice this time. She would speak to his mother, then, and hope to win the duchess's favor. That would be amusing, if he happened to be there when his mother decided to put the girl through her paces. But he could offer her a fair warning. "It will delight my mother that you have an interest in architecture. She never tires of the subject. Though many young ladies who attempt to speak to her about it soon find themselves overwhelmed."

"As most would, I imagine." She seemed unruffled, and perhaps unaware of the fact that he was on to her. As she continued to speak in a self-assured tone, his pace slowed. "Ladies are not trained to recognize the differences in limestone and granite, or whether the columns of their garden follies are Ionic or Corinthian. I, myself, have only found a recent interest in the subject when I discovered how closely art, fashion, and buildings follow such things as religious transformation or the transference of political power."

Simon took a moment to sort through her words, then stopped completely in his tracks. No one noticed that he and Miss Frost had ceased moving. His parents were several steps farther down the corridor of the guest wing, in the middle of their own conversations.

His younger siblings had already turned a corner to take Miss Fiona to the nursery rooms, where most children stayed until they were old enough to sit with the adults at dinner. Isabelle had only just claimed that right, but she'd still take any nursery guests in hand until she was presented at court.

He opened his mouth to respond to her, then closed it again. And couldn't help frowning. He'd never heard a woman of her age speak of "the transference of political power."

No one saw the way Miss Frost stared up at him, her eyebrows raised in challenge. Her eyes themselves, a shade of brown so dark it reminded him of rich earth and black coffee, sparked with indignation. As though he had offered her some sort of insult.

"The Irish are capable of producing well-educated women, my lord," she said, her voice soft so it would not carry past the two of them. "You needn't worry that I'll falter in conversation with anyone. Even a duchess." Her directness startled his next words out of him.

"That isn't what I meant." And then he wanted to kick himself. Because her head canted to one side, and she narrowed her eyes at him.

He'd thought her only interested in impressing his mother, or him, but she seemed to hold no interest in gaining anyone's regard at that moment.

"Then what did you mean?"

He jerked his chin upward, resetting his posture. Women didn't talk to him like that. At least, most of them didn't. He supposed his sisters did, and Emma, who might as well have been a fourth sister to him. Must he admit to Miss Frost he'd been certain she meant to set her sights on his mother for her own gain?

That wouldn't be polite or acceptable coming from a gentleman, let alone a duke's son.

"Lord Farleigh?" she repeated, expression unchanged. Her determination to catch him out on his poor manners rankled, but with good reason. She was in the right. "Will you not clarify what you meant?"

"It was nothing of importance," he said, then added before she could question him again, "We have fallen behind the others. I am sorry for delaying your rest, Miss Frost."

Her expression clearly shared that she knew his excuse for what it was—a diversionary tactic.

"I am perfectly content with our pace, my lord." Then she turned away, letting her eyes wander the walls as he walked with her down the corridor past portraits of ancestors and thin tables covered in candlesticks, flowers from the hothouse, and small treasures from his parents' travels.

Her genuine interest in her surroundings made Simon wonder if he'd miscalculated in his assumptions. Miss Frost might not have any interest in him or climbing higher up the social ladder. Considering what Simon knew of Lord Dunmore, it wasn't so difficult to imagine his sister sharing a similar disposition.

"Are you not eager to see your quarters?" Simon asked, keeping his gaze ahead. "My mother chose your room herself."

"How kind of her." Miss Frost sounded not in the least impressed.

Had he offended her? In the first quarter hour of their acquaintance? He couldn't recall ever managing such a feat before. "Your rooms overlook the gardens, I believe."

The woman nodded once, and when she responded her tone remained cool. "That sounds lovely."

Yes. He'd offended her. Though not with his actual unvoiced

thoughts. She had taken exception to his challenge of her knowledge. And bristled up like a hedgehog.

They arrived at the guest wing as his parents turned and walked toward them, having seen their other guests settled in comfortably. His mother's eyebrows were raised, but his father appeared his usual steady self. The duke rarely gave away his thoughts by his expression.

"Ah, here you are, Farleigh. Miss Frost. We worried you'd gone astray," the duchess said with a teasing smile.

"Miss Frost expressed her curiosity in the castle's construction." Simon forced a smile. The woman at his side might be daring enough to speak to him so coldly, but surely she wouldn't offer even a sliver of insult to his parents.

"Oh? Have you an interest in building design, Miss Frost?" the duke asked, and Simon tried to detect whether his father harbored the same suspicions about Miss Frost that Simon had.

"Only in so far as it relates to culture and history," she answered with a prim little smile. "I could never design such a construct myself. I was a woeful student in mathematics, which I know plays an important role in architecture. I enjoy studying the history behind such works."

Simon had the rare surprise of watching his father's most genuine smile appear in front of a complete stranger. When the duke lifted his eyebrow at Simon, he remained uncertain of what had impressed his father.

"I find the influence of culture on a building's creation quite interesting, too," the duchess confided. "We must make time to converse about such things while you are our guest, Miss Frost."

"I would enjoy that, Your Grace."

"Simon, let us leave your mother to show Miss Frost her room. I have need of you elsewhere." The duke bowed to the women, and Miss Frost curtsied low as Simon and his father took their leave.

As soon as they were safely away from the women, the duke spoke. "You aren't usually distracted by our guests, son."

"She wasn't distracting so much as disquieting," Simon answered, forcing himself to match his father's posture and gait. He'd tried to imitate the duke's walk and the way he held his broad shoulders since childhood. Even now that they were of the same height, Simon couldn't match the duke's purposeful stride.

"Really? In what way?" the duke asked. "She seems an ordinary enough sort of young lady."

Black hair, brown eyes, and fair skin might sound ordinary, Simon supposed. But there was more to Miss Frost than that. Her heart-shaped face and slim build were enough for most men to declare her pretty. Simon admitted such with ease, though not out loud to his father. But there was something more than that. A fire in her eyes that set her apart.

"She is quite forthright," Simon said at last, unable to think of a better way to describe the effect she'd had on him. "And I have the feeling she is not easily impressed."

At this, the duke chuckled, and Simon could've sworn his father muttered, "The lady's most worth impressing never are." The duke quickly changed subjects, however. "Your sister and Sir Andrew arrive in a few hours, returning with your grandmother. Emma comes with her ambassador the day after next. Do you think you can manage the amusement of our more youthful guests until then?"

"Of course, Father."

"Excellent." They were going to the library, and the duke's personal office. Simon didn't ask why, and his patience was rewarded the moment they stepped inside. Two members of the duke's guard waited within, standing at attention.

Captain Rockwell had served under the duke for decades, beginning his place as a guard to the duchess. The younger man standing beside him, Sterling, was the most likely candidate to one day take Rockwell's place. Sterling had spent the majority of his time on duty watching after the now-wed Lady Josephine. Now he acted as second in command.

"Rockwell, Sterling. What have you to report on our new arrivals?"

The duke didn't mean the baron's family—but the servants. The baron's servants had arrived earlier that morning as was typical;, generally, servants from other households poured into the castle ahead of their employers. Most of them would never know or guess that the duke employed a number of trained soldiers whose purpose was to protect the family and castle from all threats, within and without.

In Simon's lifetime, they'd only needed that kind of protection a handful of times. In the last year, with the political unrest that had led to a violent and deadly massacre in Manchester three months before, the duke had grown more serious about the guards' place in his home.

"Nothing stands out as unusual at this point, Your Grace," Rockwell announced. "Though it's early days yet. Most of the servants will keep to themselves until they're more comfortable in the common areas."

"And you, Sterling? What have you to report?" the duke asked.

Rockwell commanded all the guards, but Sterling possessed a natural charm that made it easier for him to form new friendships with other servants. "I agree with the captain, Your Grace. There are no signs of trouble as of yet."

"Thank you. I'm most concerned about the male servants," the duke added, "and their political leanings. If anyone has connection to the Lancashire movement, I want them watched carefully." In the days since the St. Peter's Field incident, more than one man had sworn that the politicians of England would have vengeance visited upon them.

It didn't matter that the duke was one of the few who championed the people's needs. He was still a duke, and a strong symbol of noble rule over the people. Political agitators had attacked the duke's carriage, with the duchess inside, during the summer.

The duke dismissed the guards after asking a few more questions and ensuring they had what they needed for the coming weeks to see to their duties. That left Simon and the duke alone in the office.

"Simon. Keep your eyes and ears open too, son," the duke said as he relaxed into the chair behind his desk. "I cannot shake the feeling that we have not seen the last of violence. Our people are desperate, in many respects."

"Yes, Father." Simon let the weight of the duke's trust settle on his shoulders. All his life, he'd trained to one day take the reins from his father. The duke's family, lands, estates, and political responsibility would all fall to Simon, though he hoped it would be decades yet before he took his father's title. "But we can hope for a quiet Christmas."

"With Josephine and Emma back under the castle roof?" the duke asked, one eyebrow cocked upward. "Unlikely."

Simon chuckled and took a seat across from his father. "You have missed them."

"I have." The duke steepled his fingers together before him. "Do you think our Irish guests will feel at home during the celebrations? It has been a decade or more since I spent a Christmas in Ireland. I confess, I cannot remember much of the traditions I experienced there."

"I am certain they will enjoy our English hospitality, Father." Simon tapped the arm of the chair as he spoke. "I can ask Lord Dunmore what we might do to help his mother and sisters enjoy their time here. Perhaps incorporating some of their traditions with our own."

"A good idea. I am pleased with how well your friendship has progressed with Dunmore. He is an intelligent man, but not too solemn to enjoy a conversation."

"Andrew will like him," Simon added with a grin. "Dunmore

has a keen sense of humor, so I feel the two of them will get on well."

At his father's request, Simon had made a point of searching out and befriending the baron in order to extend this invitation to Castle Clairvoir. Simon knew what was at stake, politically, and he knew what his father expected of him. He'd agreed to keep Lord Dunmore and the elder of his two sisters amused, at least until Josephine arrived to take charge.

He'd genuinely come to like Lord Dunmore. The man had a good head on his shoulders, didn't show a temper, and had a sense of humor that made him easy to be around. Simon hadn't imagined the sister might be the same. His own sisters and he were nothing alike in temperaments.

Simon rose to take his leave. "If you have need of me, Father, I will be in the saloon."

"Simon?" his father called as Simon's hand touched the door handle.

He turned to face his father.

"Good luck with Miss Frost."

Given the way his father smiled at him, Simon thought it best not to question what the duke meant. His father rarely teased his children, but it was best to leave off speaking about any single young women. Simon kept his response to a mere bow, then went on his way.

Good luck with Miss Frost. He was a duke's son. He didn't need to impress anyone. Nor did he need luck. Especially where a temporary houseguest was concerned.

Simon had too much else to worry about. Miss Frost was the least of his concerns.

CHAPTER 2

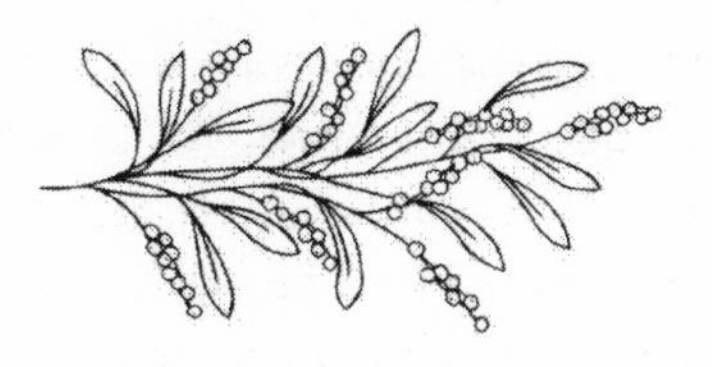

Isleen's annoyance with the handsome and—Arrogant? Smug? Proud?—irritating Lord Farleigh diminished somewhat as she rested in her well-appointed guest bedroom. By the time she rose to prepare for dinner, the Irish woman had sorted him out.

She, not the lordling, had equated his indifferent tone and treatment with her place of origin. He hadn't said a word against Ireland. Nor had Teague made it seem as though either the duke or his heir were prejudiced against Dubliners.

She slipped into the gown Darrie, her maid, had pressed for the evening. Admiring the fabric even as she eviscerated a certain nobleman in her thoughts.

Lord Farleigh had stated that *young women* were overwhelmed by his mother's knowledge of building. He hadn't actually said anything directly about her Irishness causing an intellectual lack. Though casting dispersions on her sex certainly did him no credit. Men thought themselves so clever when they put women down, and it always disappointed her. A man like Lord Farleigh, with such a clever mother, ought to know better.

Obviously, the man needed work when it came to his view on female intelligence. Since that wasn't her responsibility—not in the least—Isleen dismissed the earl from her mind and focused on pleasanter things.

Isleen wore a gown of deep blue, the material thick and warm despite her bare arms. The gloves laying on her dressing table would help, at least until dinner. How they kept rooms in a castle warm in winter, she couldn't guess. The duke likely spent a small fortune on coal and wood.

Arriving at the castle weeks ahead of the Christmas celebration meant that Isleen's family needed to incorporate themselves into the daily routines of the duke's household. It meant their personal servants had to do the same.

"Are your quarters comfortable, Darrie?" Isleen asked her maid while the younger woman helped twist her hair upward and back into a cascade of spiraling curls. "If you need anything changed, you have but to tell me."

"Everythin' is nice enough, miss. They put me in a room with Lady Dunmore's maid, and that Lady Wycomb's maid, too. The three of us will get along fine." Darrie was only eighteen, but she had quick fingers and a kind disposition that Isleen had always liked. Mrs. Walsh, her mother's maid, had a stern disposition. Isleen had rejoiced four years ago when her brother had finally deemed it time for her to have her own maid.

"That doesn't sound too terrible."

"Tis not." Darrie tucked a sprig of baby's breath into the curls. Then changed her mind and took it out in favor of a pin with a pearl on the end. "Your brother's man settled us in with the servants right quick. There's so many lords and ladies, and the duke, duchess, and duke's own mother, all with servants that have their own places at the table. It's more than I could keep track of."

Even the servants sat down in an hierarchal order when they took their meals. Something many saw as natural order, she saw as rather useless. They were not hens, to peck each other into line. But she smiled at her maid through the mirror's reflection.

"I'm glad O'Neal is looking out for all of you." Darrie was

shorter than Isleen, and slight of build, but the girl had the same fight in her that most Irish females possessed. She wouldn't let anyone mistreat her. "I hope you make new friends while we are here and enjoy whatever you can of the countryside. It isn't like Dublin, where you can slip out to the pub with ease."

"It isn't, miss. I told Mrs. Walsh we'd have done better to bring mountain climbing equipment with us to get down and up to the castle again." The maid giggled, and Isleen couldn't help grinning as well.

"Thank you, Darrie." Isleen rose from the dressing table and picked up her ivory-colored gloves. "Now I'm away to eat with the English. I shouldn't need any help tonight, so take your evening to do what you please with it."

Her brother and mother waited in the corridor to walk with Isleen through the castle, led by a liveried footman through twists and turns until they came to a sitting room where members of the duke's family waited. Sarah, the duke's mother and dowager duchess, immediately welcomed Isleen's mother to sit with her and the younger duchess at a set of chairs near the fire.

The duke's eldest daughter had arrived that afternoon, and Lord Farleigh had already introduced them. Lady Josephine Wycomb, called Lady Josephine because her birth rank was higher than her baronet husband's, had immediately struck Isleen as an interesting individual.

"Ah, Miss Frost," Sir Andrew, Lady Josephine's husband, greeted her first. "Thank goodness you are here. Please, come sit beside my wife and speak to her of books. I cannot discuss *The Modern Prometheus* with her to her satisfaction." He shuddered. "I find it too grim a tale, to be truthful."

"I prefer *Ivanhoe* myself," Lord Farleigh added from where he stood beside a large window. The sky behind him was dark as though it were midnight, though the clock had yet to strike seven.

Isleen had settled in the seat next to Lady Josephine, as bidden, and so faced the lord as he made this declaration. Teague took an unoccupied chair to her left. When she exchanged a glance with her brother, he was smirking.

Did he mean to encourage her to enter the debate?

"*Ivanhoe*?" Isleen would not, of course, admit that she also liked that book better than the grimmer *Frankenstein*. "Are you a romantic, Lord Farleigh? Or merely fond of tales with Robin Hood and tournaments?"

Isleen pressed her lips together over her sharp tongue. No one here knew her well enough for her to exercise her wit. Especially when her tone held an edge for the duke's eldest son and him alone.

Lady Josephine laughed lightly, and Isleen forced a smile as the lady spoke for her brother. "It cannot be the romance he favors. Simon isn't the least bit interested in the longing sighs of heroes for their fair maidens. Are you, brother?"

The earl shrugged one shoulder and smirked at his sister. "I would have said the same of your baronet, yet he turned traitor to bachelorhood the moment you gave him leave to court you."

The banter the three of them exchanged testified of a long friendship. Though Sir Andrew and his wife were newly wed, the baronet possessed an easiness with them that could only be born of a long acquaintance.

Sir Andrew's grin turned crooked. "I cannot let you blame Josephine for my defection. Not entirely. Bachelorhood is quite dull, it turns out. I much prefer married life."

"Do you hear that, Dunmore?" the duke's heir asked, one eyebrow raised. "This traitor thinks our lives dull."

Teague raised both hands in an attitude of defense. "I have no wish to argue against matrimony, Lord Farleigh. And I would never dare tell a lady she is wrong on such a subject." He nodded deeply to Lady Josephine. "You have my support in your argument, my lady."

"There you have it." Lady Josephine grinned in triumph. "Bachelorhood is dull, matrimony is the highest order of life, and you, my dear brother, would do well to note such a thing as truth."

Lord Farleigh groaned and rubbed at his forehead, as though vexed by his sister's words. Strangely enough, it was to her he seemed to address his next question. "Why is it when people you know marry, they must go about insisting everyone else do the same?"

Isleen related well enough to that and spoke before she thought better of it. "My dearest friend in Ireland married at the beginning of summer. She has taken every opportunity to point me toward eligible bachelors ever since." She shuddered theatrically. "And while she is a perfect companion in almost every respect, her attempts at matchmaking have horrified me."

"There, you see." Lord Farleigh crossed his arms as though Isleen's words settled the matter. "Leave those of us still unfettered to find our own way, Josie." He drew himself up. "And if I prefer Ivanhoe actually doing something about the troubles he faces, rather than Victor Frankenstein, who spends the whole of his novel moping about the problem *he* created, that is my right."

Even Isleen could see the spark ignite in Lady Josephine's eyes, and the lady drew in a breath before releasing a slew of words in support of the *Frankenstein* novel. Teague's jaw dropped open at one point during her literary lecture, her husband propped his chin in his hand and listened with a crooked smile as though he adored every word that came out of her mouth, and her brother bristled with impatience.

Or so it seemed. Until he made eye contact with Isleen when Lady Josephine spoke about the true moral of the tale, and Isleen caught the glimmer of amusement in his eyes.

The man actually enjoyed his sister's diatribe.

"Now, dear wife," Sir Andrew said when she paused for breath, "you make excellent points on the fallen state of man. None of us can argue with you when it comes to literary matters. Not if we hope to win."

"I am not arguing," she countered. "I am stating my views." Then her cheeks pinked, and she turned with wide eyes to Isleen. "I am terribly sorry. This all started with asking you for *your* opinion. I have prattled on most self-indulgently."

"I have not minded," Isleen assured the younger woman. "I'm fascinated. I suppose I must admit that I didn't enjoy *Frankenstein* during my first reading. Now you have given me a reason to try the novel again."

Lord Farleigh's low chuckle preceded his dry statement. "I would not willingly torture myself that way a second time."

What had happened to the man he'd been during their last interaction? He no longer acted coolly or with indifference. Around his friends, he appeared relaxed. Amused. Not the least bit prideful or even aloof.

"Pay him no attention," Lady Josephine said, giving Isleen's hand a pat even as she narrowed her eyes at her brother. "We two will have fascinating literary conversations while he is still trumpeting about Robin Hood and Friar Tuck."

Before anyone could respond to Lady Josephine's comment, the butler declared the table ready for them to dine. The shuffle began as the ladies each accepted escort through to the next room, except for Isleen.

The duchess had explained earlier in the day that they had invited the rector, to keep the numbers even, but he had sent his regrets rather than acceptance. An uneven table might have made other hostesses miserable, but the duchess had seemed troubled for Isleen's sake alone.

But Isleen didn't mind following at the tail of the procession, without escort. She'd never given much merit to the sillier parts of society's traditions. What did it matter, who entered a room first or last? It simplified things when everyone was of nearly the same rank.

The duke escorted his mother, his son escorted the duchess,

which meant Teague escorted Lady Josephine, and Sir Andrew gave his arm to Isleen's mother.

When Isleen took her seat, she found herself next to Lord Farleigh, who sat at his mother's right hand. She slipped her silken glove from one arm and then the other, laying them across her lap before taking up her spoon.

The feast laid out before them would be considered modest by the wealthiest members of Society, but Isleen couldn't help feeling rather impressed. Chestnut-stuffed pheasant, glistening rolls, jellies, roasted vegetables in many hues, and more stretched from one side of the table to the other. Boats of gravy and plates of butter were within easy reach of everyone, and the food still steamed as though it had arrived from the kitchen at that exact moment.

She hoped the kitchen staff ate after the family. Otherwise, the food might well go to waste.

Lord Farleigh served Isleen from their nearest platters, then answered a question from his mother. He was quite attentive to both of them before serving himself. Once his own plate was full, he turned toward Isleen with a determined gleam in his blue eyes.

"I hope you didn't mind our literary argument, Miss Frost. My sister and I have had a long history of reading the same books merely to debate them later. Her friend, the former Miss Arlen, and Sir Andrew also took part in those battles. We forget ourselves in company, from time to time."

"I found the conversation stimulating," she admitted with a tiny lift of one shoulder.

Holding Lord Farleigh to the first impression he made no longer seemed fair. Especially since she had made a poor presentation, too. First by gawking, and then by challenging his opinion of her quite rudely. Seeing him interact with his sister and friend had made him far more likable. And deserving of another chance.

"You never told us which of the two novels you favor. If I promise not to reveal the secret to anyone else, will you confide it to me?" The tilt of his head to one side betrayed his curiosity, and one corner of his mouth crept upward.

Perhaps he was much friendlier than she had thought.

"I think it best I not declare a favorite, as I am so new to your household, I have no wish to pick a side until I know what both have to offer."

"Are you a politician, like your brother?"

"No. Merely cautious in declaring my allegiances." She gave attention to her meal when Lord Farleigh's sister asked him a question from across the table.

Whatever the duke paid his cook, it certainly wasn't enough. Every bite of the meal was delicious. A variety of sauces made the tenderest fowl rich to the taste while rosemary, thyme, and hints of spices she didn't have names for made the roasted vegetables as much a treat as the fruit-flavored jellies.

The conversation flowed freely around her as the duke's family spoke with informality of the happenings at the castle and the nearest village, Lambsthorpe.

It was amid the general chatter that Lord Farleigh leaned closer to her to say, in that same low voice as before, "Miss Frost? I hope you don't mind my presumption. Earlier today, I think I said something that made you cross with me. If that is the case, I apologize for it."

An heir to a dukedom—apologizing to *her*? She nearly choked on the bite of potato in her mouth. She had to cover her lips with her napkin while looking at him askance. Yes, she had misjudged him.

Once certain no unladylike coughing fit would take hold, Isleen answered him. "I think I was cross when I arrived at your doorstep, my lord." The admittance cost her nothing and was the truth. "We had traveled a long way, and I was more sensitive than I had reason to be. I likely didn't make a fair impression on you, either."

The man's smile remained somewhat crooked. "As a gentleman, I will insist you made the very best of impressions."

"Come now, my lord. We both know I leapt on every word you said like an antagonized house cat. You were making conversation, and I took your remarks as a critique of my education."

"Ah, is that what happened?" He seemed genuinely surprised, confirming all the more how horribly Isleen had misinterpreted him. "I didn't mean to do such a thing, Miss Frost. I would never question a lady's education or intelligence in that way."

Isleen stared at him a moment, sorting through their exchange from earlier that day. "Then what, pray tell, were you trying to get at? I feel even more at sixes and sevens with that conversation."

He blinked, and the man's face turned a shade more red than before. It was a good thing Isleen's mother sat at the other end of the table. She'd be mortified to see how easily her daughter had put a future duke to the blush.

Simon hadn't expected Miss Frost to continue asking forthright questions. More the fool him. Even in a cherrier disposition, she wasn't one to let a thing be said without fully understanding its meaning. It was a trait he'd normally admire, except as the one under her scrutiny, he felt terribly uncomfortable.

If only the ladies would rise at that moment to leave the men to their pipes and brandy. But everyone around them continued to chat merrily with their plates still more full than empty.

He couldn't leave her question unanswered. But it wasn't right to answer in a way that would make her uncomfortable, either. "I was merely trying to remain aloof," he said at last.

Her eyebrows drew tightly together, creating a small crease between them. "Aloof? What a strange thing to be when welcoming a guest."

He could leave it at that. He knew he could turn back to his plate and pretend he had nothing more to say. But the downward turn of her lips and the disappointment in her tone acted as pricks to his conscience.

"An unmarried, lady guest," he corrected. "I hope you do not think me arrogant, Miss Frost. You see, I am used to fending off the attentions of eligible women when they visit my family's home."

Her delicately curved eyebrows went upward at once, and her dark eyes widened while her lips parted. "Oh—oh dear." Then she sucked in a quick breath that momentarily worried him. Was she about to cry? But—no. She covered her mouth to stifle a *laugh*.

The pretty Irish woman was laughing at him.

His pride took the hit gracelessly, and he felt heat in his cheeks in a way he hadn't in years and years. The little colleen had made him *blush*. A thing reserved for damsels and youths with cracking voices. Not for a man grown, and certainly not for the heir of a powerful dukedom.

"What is the joke?" Josephine's question popped the bubble of humiliation Simon had created for himself.

He looked at his sister, completely speechless.

To his surprise, it was Miss Frost who answered. "Your brother is merely making his case for Ivanhoe, my lady. He has a rather clever way of looking at Friar Tuck that amused me."

Josephine's eyes narrowed in Simon's direction. "It isn't fair to sway her when I cannot have my say as well. Miss Frost, you mustn't allow him to cheat like that."

Miss Frost gave a sharp nod as she affected a serious expression, her eyebrows drawn together again, though not as tightly as before. "I will change the subject of our conversation, Lady Josephine." Then she smiled at his sister, as though they were all playing a game together.

Simon forced his own grin, and his sister dismissed him with a tilt of her head before returning to her conversation with their mother.

When the woman at his side spoke again, it was with a lowered voice. "I am sorry for that, my lord. I didn't laugh at you, merely at my own suppositions. I genuinely thought you considered yourself my superior in more than birth. I am rather on the defensive here on English shores, as most Irish folk would be."

"Oh." Really, what could he say to that? "I am...relieved."

"I assure you, Lord Farleigh, I have no plans—matrimonial or otherwise—for you during my stay at Castle Clairvoir."

Nothing had ever mortified him quite like Miss Frost's calm assurance. How he must have sounded to her—the arrogance and presumption. Before he could offer up a defense for his earlier statement and assure her he didn't think every woman he met had designs on him—even though most did, he felt certain—Andrew took Miss Frost's attention in a conversation about horses.

As Simon listened, he realized she knew just enough on that subject to converse as intelligently as she had on the other topics they had spoken about. The woman slid easily from one topic to the next, well-versed to a degree that made her conversation flow easily and her questions intelligent.

The chatter continued around him, along with the clinking of crystal and cutlery as people enjoyed the meal, none of them guessing the sudden shock that had befallen the heir to the castle in which they sat.

Simon used his fork to push a purple carrot from one side of his plate to the other, though his appetite had fled. Then he hid behind his wine glass for a moment before pretending an interest in his mother and sister's conversation.

Despite what Miss Frost had claimed before, she had all the makings of a perfect politician. She reminded him a bit of his father's ward, Emma. Emma took an active interest in politics, theater, and literature. She was the perfect wife for her ambassador husband, and he'd heard many accounts of how well she had acted as hostess at the embassy where she and her husband resided.

Lord Dunmore was lucky to have a sister such as Isleen on his side.

Simon had stumbled today in his hosting duties, and that stung his pride. His father never made such a fool of himself; Simon had thought his days of blundering over words in conversation long behind him.

At nearly seven and twenty, awkward social moments ought to be squarely in his past. And yet, here he was. How had one misinterpreted conversation with a woman demoralized him so?

When the women rose from the table a short time later, he still hadn't found a satisfying explanation.

With Miss Frost gone, Simon had a direct line up the table to see Sir Andrew and the Duke both staring at him, somewhat expectantly. He cleared his throat. "I beg your pardon, Father. I haven't been attentive to the conversation. Did you ask me something?"

Lord Dunmore glanced between Simon and his father, seeming more confused than expectant.

The duke's mouth twitched briefly, as though he wanted to smile but fought the urge. "I asked what you thought of Miss Frost. She and Josephine seemed to get along well."

Andrew chuckled. "They allied against Simon within moments of coming together this evening."

Folding his arms, Simon cut a glance at his best friend. "You didn't come to my defense, I noticed."

"I have plenty of my own debates to win with my wife, Simon. I don't need to take part in yours." His grin was far cockier than usual. Marriage hadn't changed Andrew's playful nature or his high opinion of himself. Though it had made him a great deal happier, for which Simon was grateful.

"Wise words for a new husband." The duke poured brandy into a glass and offered it to Andrew. "If Josephine is fond of Miss

Frost, she will do all she can to make her feel at home. I hope that puts you at ease, Dunmore."

"It does, Your Grace." He relaxed into an easier posture. "I looked in on Fiona before dinner. She seemed pleased with her welcome by your younger children."

The duke's smile warmed. "Good. I hope we give her a holiday she will fondly remember." He had a soft spot for children, Simon well knew. His father had always made a point of treating children, his own and any others he came upon, with respect and as though their words and feelings had value.

Though the conversation moved through other topics that Simon ought to have paid attention to, especially given his place as heir, his mind stayed snagged on Miss Frost's words. Rather like a wool scarf might stick on a protruding door handle, causing distress even if it did not cause damage.

Why had the idea of setting her cap for him caused such mirth? And why did it bother him? People took him seriously. They always had. Even his own family treated him with respect when he stood as the heir to his father's title. His grandmother rarely even called him by his Christian name, insisting it was more appropriate to use his title.

Somehow, and without looking like an even greater clod, he wanted to understand what had made his way of thinking so very absurd to the pretty Irish woman.

CHAPTER 3

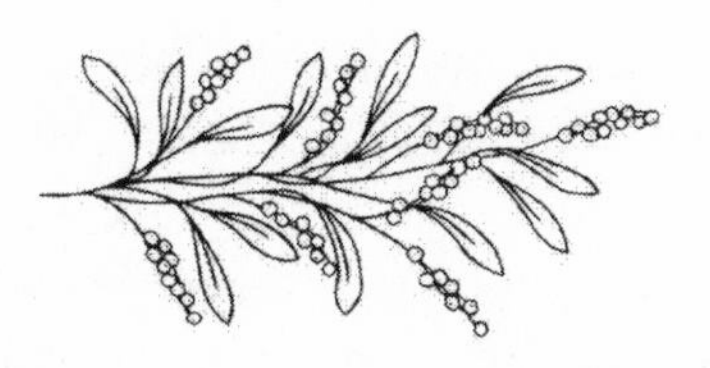

At eleven o'clock the next morning, Josephine dragged Simon out of the library and down to the main floor. "I will not give this tour with Andrew," she said as she pulled him along. "You know how he likes to make up stories about our ancestors, and I cannot listen to his joke about Great-Grandfather Charles and the beagle again."

"I thought you and Andrew couldn't get enough of one another's company," Simon said, by way of complaint that he had been pulled away from a book.

"Oh, I adore him. Do not mistake me on that matter. I merely do not wish our poor guests to bear witness to his ridiculous antics. If Emma had arrived already, I would ask her to join us. But as she is not here, and Mother has the headache, so I am left with you."

"You flatter me," he said, the words dry of all sincerity.

They had arrived at the divided stair, and he could hear the voices of their guests in the guardroom where they had met the day before. Josephine pulled him to a stop, pretended to wipe his shoulders free of dust, then nodded once. "Yes, I suppose you will have to do."

Simon glowered. "You realize I am doing you a favor, Josie."

"Of course I do. But do you understand the favor I am doing for *you*?" she asked, nose wrinkled.

"Whatever do you mean?"

"You stared at Miss Frost most intently last evening after dinner, and you two seemed quite cozy during the meal. Speaking in low voices so the rest of us could not eavesdrop upon your conversation."

Simon took his sister's arm and pulled her farther away from the staircase, then whispered with urgency, "What are you talking about? Miss Frost? Surely you do not think I desire more time in her company than—well—than any other guest's."

"Your attention was quite pointed," Josephine said, matching his tone. "And she is quite pretty. One has only to watch her eyes when she speaks to see how intelligent she is. Why are we whispering?"

"Do not play matchmaker, Josie. Please."

"Matchmaker? Me?" She pulled away from him, placing a hand over her heart. "Simon Dinard, you were *staring* all night. If you do not wish for people to get ideas in their heads, then perhaps you ought to do a better job minding your manners. And I did not say you must wed the woman. I merely think you both might amuse yourselves with a harmless flirtation. You are obviously out of practice."

That took him aback, and he caught one of his great-great-grandmother's portraits from the corner of his eye, looking rather as though she scowled at him. Even his ancestors thought him lacking that day.

"I am not out of practice. Flirting shouldn't be something people need to practice."

"That shows how little you know." Josie held up a hand to forestall his next aggrieved words. "I am finished discussing the matter. Our guests are waiting for us." She brushed the skirts of her gown free of imagined dust, then squared her shoulders and spoke like a general giving orders. "Now. We have a tour to give, and you are coming with me, even if you aren't any good at flirting."

He followed his sister down the staircase to the marble floor. The baron, his mother, and both his sisters waited. And James was there, too, for a reason Simon couldn't fathom. The duke's youngest child wasn't likely to behave himself on a tour without growing profoundly bored.

Miss Frost stood between her younger sister and James, her expression serene, while the children on either side of her appeared displeased. Miss Frost wore a gown with long sleeves and made of a soft blue material.

The lighter color made her dark, glossy hair stand out. Today, her black curls were sensibly looped about her head in a style likely meant to mimic a Greek statue somewhere or other. A few curls remained loose at the nape of her neck and her cheeks, framing her face.

Fires burned in the hearths of the great entry hall, though they were lower than the day before, and men-at-arms dressed as footmen flanked both fireplaces. Hanging above the mantel on one side was a pair of swords. On the other, the fireplace didn't appear to have a chimney at all, something Miss Frost had noticed straight away. His grandfather had cleverly designed the piece to move smoke through the floor and out of the castle another way. His mother had always liked that feature and happily puzzled guests with it.

"I am delighted to show you the castle," Josephine said, her smile bright and tone full of warmth. "It is the dearest place in the world to me, and since you are to be with us until Epiphany, you ought to know all my favorite corners. There is every chance we will not finish before tea, but we can always resume the tour tomorrow if need be." She continued on, sketching a brief history of the castles that had come before the one their mother had built, the baron and his mother listening with attentiveness.

Simon stood next to his younger brother. Nearly eighteen

years separated them in age, but he still got on well with the younger chap. Simon kept his tone low as he asked, "How did you get involved in this?"

James scowled up at his brother. "Mrs. Robinson says my hosting skills need practice."

For some reason, Simon's gaze darted from his brother's up to Miss Frost's. He caught her watching him from the corner of her eye. "It would seem Fiona and Lord James both have lessons to learn today."

Miss Fiona crossed her arms over her chest and made a "hmph" sound, as though annoyed by her sister's words.

Ah. James and their youngest guest had likely had a tiff of some sort. Mrs. Robinson, the governess, had sentenced them to the tour as a form of punishment.

She was a clever woman.

"A good, long walk through the castle is the surest way to make friends of enemies," he mused aloud. When Miss Frost blinked in confusion, he gave a shrug. "They will be too tired to continue their argument by the time we come to the end."

Though Simon had never measured the distance himself, he knew well enough that to walk the castle from one end to the other was taxing. Peeping in all the rooms could easily make the tour's steps equivalent to a mile's walk. With this in mind, he prepared to offer his arm to the baroness—but she had already accepted her son's escort.

Josephine still had a job in mind for him. "Farleigh. Will you please see to it we do not lose anyone along the way?" She looked pointedly at their little brother, who continued to pout.

It would be just like James to slip away the moment he thought he could. Likely into one of the family's secret passages, too, so they couldn't call him back. The little scoundrel. Simon didn't bother hiding his grin from the boy. "I am happy to be the rearguard."

James appeared mutinous but said nothing.

Thus they began the expedition, going through the most public rooms of the house one by one. In each room, Josephine took a moment to point out an item or feature of interest. "This is the portrait gallery, of course. Here you see an original painting of King Henry VIII, by Hans Holbein. His Majesty gifted it to the Earl of Montfort..." Or "This is my father as a child, painted with his father's favorite dog, named Brick." "This wallpaper is hand-painted silk." And "This is the room where the Regent stayed last summer." And into the room from the evening before. "This is the Long Gallery. You saw it last night, but now you can make out more details. Such as the tapestries, gifted to my mother by Louis XVI of France."

James groaned from his place several feet behind Miss Frost and Miss Fiona. "This is tedious."

"I think that is the point, at least in regard to your purpose on the tour," Simon whispered back.

"Does anyone care about all our furniture? They're just chairs and pictures."

"I know. But it is something to look at, isn't it?"

Ahead of them, Miss Fiona tugged on her sister's sleeve and then whispered, none-too-quietly, "I'm bored."

Her older sister shushed her. "Mind your manners, Fi."

Then they came to the statue of the Three Graces—three nude, feminine forms meant to depict Greek goddesses. A tasteful piece, most thought, but James fell into a fit of giggles as Josephine gestured to the piece to talk about the artist who had created the statue, as well as several Greek-inspired figures in the gardens.

Miss Fiona's nose wrinkled as she stared up at the statue. Then she looked at her sister. "Why haven't they put on any clothes? Wouldn't they be cold?"

"Saints, Fi. It is *art*." Miss Frost cast a glance over her shoulder at that moment, and her gaze made contact with his own. She smiled at him, rather indifferently, he thought, and shrugged. She mouthed the word, "Children."

He gave a sharp nod and gestured with one hand to James and mouthed back, "I know."

They shared commiserating smiles, then continued to the next room. By the time they made it through the library and down two more long corridors, then into the smaller, private dining room, Lady Dunmore had either reached her limit for the day or else decided to take pity on the others in their party.

"Oh, my dear Lady Josephine, I am afraid I must beg a rest. This is such a beautiful castle, and your family's treasures are extraordinary. I think we will have to continue on tomorrow, though I have several questions to ask. Do you think your mother would discuss her thoughts on some of her decor decisions? I would not dare to presume upon her time."

"Mother would be delighted to discuss anything to do with the castle," Josephine assured the baroness, leading her to a couch to sit and converse.

Though Miss Frost stepped forward as though to follow her brother, mother, and Josephine, she stopped when James heaved a dramatic sigh.

"Finally. Come on, Fi. I'll show you a shortcut back to the schoolroom."

The little girl drew herself up, looking remarkably like her older sister. "You *cannot* call me that, Lord James. It isn't mannerly of you."

"Why not?" the boy asked.

"She hasn't given you leave to use her Christian name," Simon reminded his little brother, cuffing him lightly on the shoulder. "One doesn't call a lady by such familiar terms without permission."

"Oh, that." James scoffed. "Listen, you can call me James. But don't call me Jim. I had a tutor who did that once, and I hated it. If you don't like Fi, I can call you Fiona, but Fi saves time." He used his thumb to indicate the door behind them. "But if you want to get out of here before they make us look at even more furniture, we should leave while Josephine is distracted."

Simon checked to see how Miss Frost was taking this strange conversation and found her biting her lip, her eyes dancing with amusement. Why was she only cheerful when he wasn't speaking with her? Puzzling woman.

"Fine," Miss Fiona said with a put-upon sigh. "If you try to scare me with ghosts in the attic again, I'll call a banshee down on you."

At that, Miss Frost gasped. "Fi, we do not jest about such things."

She shrugged. "He told me his great-grandfather haunted the attic and cellars and would chain me up in the dungeon if he caught me out after midnight."

As ridiculous as that tale was, Simon had a difficult time sounding disapproving. Even though it fell to him to take his brother to task. "James, is that how this started?"

The boy shrugged, quite unconcerned. "Castles without ghost stories are boring. And we don't even have a dungeon."

"That is beside the point." It was no wonder, Simon thought, that the governess had banished the two children from the schoolroom. Mrs. Robinson was a saint to put up with his brother's antics. Now an Irish girl was threatening them with a keening, ghostly creature that heralded misery and death.

"Doesn't matter," James said, taking Miss Fiona by the hand. "Come along, Fi, before Simon lectures us too." He gave her a tug, and with a mighty sigh, the girl followed him out the doorway and into some other mischief.

Miss Frost stepped beside Simon, watching the two run down the corridor.

"Should we go after them?" she asked, laughter in her voice. "Or trust that he will not find an attic in which to lock her up? Of course, she's as likely to pretend at laying a fairy curse on him as anything."

"If she is as feral as he is, I cannot see any harm in them disappearing together."

"Can you not?" Miss Frost canted her head to the side and eyed him with obvious amusement. "Even if they are not a threat to each other, imagine the havoc they could cause in a castle this size."

His lips twitched. "Shall we go after them?"

"I think we must take our chances on them behaving themselves." Her smile reappeared. "Lord Farleigh, you differ greatly from what I thought when I met you yesterday."

"Oh?" Simon looked down at himself, then up again at her. "I feel the same as I was then."

"You struck me as rather pompous," she said without hesitation. "And then quite presumptuous, at dinner."

"Ah, you are speaking of when I implied all females had ulterior motives when in my company." He wouldn't blush. He refused to. He tucked one hand behind his back and squeezed it into a fist, willing himself to act as a man instead of a flustered boy. "I acted the part of a pompous bore, and I apologize for that. My intention from this time onward is to be a good host. Nothing more."

"Mm." She joined her hands together before her and wandered toward a pedestal, upon which sat a large vase. The vase was from Siam, the majority of its surface a soft jade color with gold embellishments in a concentrated lattice pattern. "This is a pretty thing."

"An admiral gifted it to my father after visiting Bangkok."

Her lips quirked upward. "Here now, are you as knowledgeable a guide as your sister?"

"It is my duty to know the province of every stray piece of furniture and curiosity in this castle."

"Because it will one day be yours to govern and care for."

"Indeed."

Her expression softened, though her eyes remained on the

vase. "That is an enormous responsibility. Not only the knowledge of things, of course, but all the people associated with your lands and titles. It is no wonder you take your position so seriously. Lesser men would break under that weight."

A discomfiting tightness at his throat made him want to loosen his cravat. She wasn't wrong. Every time he looked into the future, a heaviness pressed upon his mind and heart. There was still so much to learn.

At Simon's age, his father had already inherited the title and had made a name for himself in the House of Lords. Simon carried the barest fraction of the ducal burden, and already his knees buckled under the strain.

"There." Miss Frost's gentle tone pulled him from his bleak thoughts. "There is the man I met yesterday. All seriousness." He found her dark eyes trained upon him, her eyebrows lifted.

Josephine's voice pulled Miss Frost's attention away. "Miss Frost, we have not yet seen the library. Your mother must be allowed to rest, of course, but I would be happy to show you where you might find a book or two. If you need a way to pass the time. Do you have an interest in seeing the library?"

"I do." Miss Frost turned away from him, and as she approached his sister, Simon considered her words.

All seriousness. Lesser men would break under the weight of his future. All of it would be his to govern and care for.

No longer needed as a secondary tour guide, Simon yielded to his sudden impulse to flee and left the room without looking back.

Had anyone dared address him about what was to come when he inherited? Not really. Except for a few ill-informed ladies who thought bringing up the fact that his father's death would make him a powerful man would somehow endear Simon to them.

No one talked about what it would mean to him, personally. Simon's father prepared him for his future role, of course. The duke hadn't explicitly stated, "I will die, and you must carry on as

I have," But it was implied in every interaction. *Had always* been implied.

His father loomed large in Simon's mind, as the duke did in life. He was as complex a man as he was powerful, and he wielded his influence with the same precision as a master swordsman would a rapier.

No matter how he tried, Simon remained in the duke's shadow. Trying to mimic a man he loved and admired. Yet fear remained, and haunted his dreams, that he would never achieve the standard set by Gregory Dinard, the Duke of Montfort.

CHAPTER 4

Two English duchesses, a Sicilian contessa, an Irish baroness, a baronetess, and a mere Irish miss sat together in the Elizabethan Saloon.

Isleen smiled at her lap. There ought to be either a joke or a mathematical equation at hand. Though she had sat in company with ladies of varying titles before, it had never occurred to her how often those of even higher status had to remember whom outranked whom.

"Miss Frost, I hope you are not sitting in a draft so far from the fire," the dowager duchess said rather than asked.

"Thank you, Your Grace. I am comfortable here." As the lowest-ranking member of the women's party, Isleen needed only to remember she must defer to everyone else. And speak when spoken to.

"Would you like a shawl, Miss Frost?" Lady Atella, wife to the Sicilian ambassador to England, had arrived the day before. The duke's household welcomed her and her husband as family, and the cheerful contessa wasted no time in acquainting herself with Isleen. "There are dozens of hidden shawls, tucked in nooks and crannies all over the castle, at the ready."

Isleen smoothed the arm of her gown down to her wrist. "I am quite comfortable, though I thank you for your concern." She exchanged a glance with her mother, who sat directly opposite the dowager and near the hearth. The current duke's duchess sat in the chair beside hers.

The duchess held a sketchbook while Isleen's mother worked on needlepoint.

Lady Josephine rose from her place beside her grandmother to flank Isleen's other side, bringing with her the scent of jasmine and oranges. That put the three younger ladies on the opposite side of the rug from the others, giving them the ability to converse without their elders hearing. None of them had objects to keep their hands busy, though Isleen had been offered several little projects should she wish for them.

The younger girls had accepted an invitation to join the adults, too. Mrs. Robinson, the governess, had her two female charges and Fiona with her on the rug opposite the duchesses. They were all working at embroidery.

Fiona had a mutinous look about her, but at a warning look from Isleen, concentrated her efforts on her needle and thread.

Conversation was the order of the day for Isleen's set.

The two ladies on either side of her spoke with easy familiarity, soliciting Isleen's comment often enough that she didn't feel out of place. They were both excellent hostesses, a trait she would expect in a duke's daughter and ambassador's wife.

The subject turned to plans for the Christmas Eve ball, still weeks away.

"I wish there was a way to gather and preserve the greenery prior to Christmas week." Lady Josephine plumped a cushion and settled it between her and the stiff arm of the couch. "It always takes ages to wrap it up in ribbons or balls to hang in all the corners."

"Children and servants do the most work, as you well know." Lady Atella's hands stayed settled calmly in her lap, folded atop one another. "And your mother plans on bringing a tree indoors again."

"A live tree?" Isleen couldn't help repeating the odd notion. "Are sprigs of holly and pine boughs not enough in this part of the country?"

Lady Josephine giggled. "Not when you're a duke in a castle, Miss Frost. My mother and father were at the palace in 1800, the year Queen Charlotte brought in a tree as tall as my father. There were gifts tucked in its branches for all the children. My parents didn't start the tradition here until one prince came for Christmas a few years ago, but we've had progressively larger trees in the ballroom ever since."

"Bless me, why would anyone want a tree indoors?" Isleen tucked a stray lock of black hair behind her ear. "Does it not cause a right fine mess?"

"A very fine mess," Josephine agreed. "But it makes up for it in fun. We string ribbons from branch to branch and hang sweets and toys in the branches. Then we put the tree back outside and the gardener plants it in the ground the moment he can."

"It is rather like the tree attends a party before going out to join its family."

From several feet away, Fiona chimed in. "I would rather have a party out with the trees than bring trees inside to one of our boring parties."

Máthair calmly gave a more powerful *look* toward Fiona than her older sister could manage. "You best mind your manners, dove, or you will stay in the nursery for the best of the festivities."

That made the little girl duck her head. "I apologize, Máthair."

"I cannot say I blame Miss Fiona for her feelings." The duchess tucked her pencil behind her ear in a very un-duchess-like way before passing her sketchbook to her mother-in-law for her opinion. "I promise we will do our best to amuse all the children, Miss Fiona. Isabelle and Rosalind help us plan the children's parties every year. I am certain they will include your ideas. Will you, dears?"

"Yes, Mama," both young ladies said, smiles upon their faces.

Lady Rosalind, the younger of the two, bounced a little in her chair. "It will be ever so much fun, Fi. You will see."

At last the little Irish colleen responded as she should to her betters. "Thank you, Your Grace. Lady Rosalind. I would like that." Her cheeks blazed scarlet, but she smiled as she lowered her gaze to her work.

Lady Rosalind patted Fiona's hand and started talking with cheer about the games they had played the year before, kindly distracting Fiona from embarrassment.

In a lowered voice, Lady Josephine murmured to Isleen, "Your sister is a force, Miss Frost. I quite like her."

"As do we, when she minds her manners."

At this remark, Lady Atella grinned brightly. "We were all her age once. And you haven't heard anything until you are at an event with James. Last year, after a recitation for guests, he had a frog in his pocket that took up a performance of its own. His Grace had to fight to keep from laughing."

"A frog?" Isleen couldn't imagine the stoic duke responding with humor to such an event. Then again, she did not know him very well. "What did your elder brother think of that?" She put the question to Lady Josephine, tipping her head to one side. "I cannot imagine someone as serious as he is being best pleased with his brother's games."

"Simon?" Lady Josephine blinked, then frowned. "I cannot recall him acting put out by it. He used to be as mischievous as James. He and Sir Andrew were always running about the castle, playing jokes on people and performing the oddest pranks."

"They have done little of that in years." Lady Atella picked up a biscuit from the table before them, laden with treats of various sizes and sweetness.

"Simon hasn't," Lady Josephine corrected. "Andrew is still

determined to act the part of a jester whenever the opportunity presents itself." She spoke with affection rather than disapproval, which made Isleen wonder at the nature of her relationship and history with her baronet husband.

Lady Atella tapped her finger on the arm of the couch. "I suppose that is true enough. The last thing I remember Simon having his hand in was that time he moved all the mistletoe in the castle in the middle of the night." She shared an exasperated smile with Isleen. "We had spent hours the previous day finding the right spot for each kissing ball, large and small. All our plans for handsome gentlemen hinged upon that mistletoe being precisely where we put it."

"He laughed for hours," Lady Josephine added, her own smile at war with the furrow of her brow. "I suppose we can laugh about it now, too."

With her imagination struggling to picture the serious-natured earl laughing for more than a few minutes about *anything*, Isleen edged the conversation in a different direction.

"I have never understood the appeal of mistletoe. It isn't native to our Irish trees."

"No mistletoe in Ireland?" Lady Josephine blinked. "But why not?"

"Perhaps it is the wrong climate for it," Lady Atella said without concern. "What do you mean, Miss Frost, by the appeal of mistletoe? It is a long-standing tradition to hang it in halls. Likely because it is one of the few green-leafed plants we have access to in winter."

Clarification on that point was simple enough to offer. "As a decoration, it doesn't bother me in the least." Though why people wanted a sprig of something that acted as a parasite inside their home, she didn't quite know. "The kissing beneath it is what puzzles me."

"You object to kissing?" Lady Josephine sounded oddly disappointed by that notion, and Isleen couldn't help a small laugh at that.

"I do not. Rest assured on that count." Though it had been ages since anyone had stolen a kiss from her lips. She brushed the unwanted thought aside.

Isleen glanced at her little sister, then leaned closer to her two new friends and lowered her voice. "I object to the idea that if I am caught beneath it, any strange man might make free with my person, taking a kiss I might have no wish to give." She shuddered. "It sounds like the very trap it is."

The two married women exchanged a wide-eyed look. Lady Atella spoke with some hesitancy. "I haven't ever thought of it that way. We have always been in company with gentlemen. People the duke trusts."

"Or the people around you have known that His Grace wouldn't allow ill treatment of you. Perhaps, as you were both under his protection, you were spared the unpleasantness of unwanted kisses." Isleen shouldn't need to point such a thing out, but the other women appeared rather surprised by the idea.

"Yet another privilege of having a duke for a father," Lady Josephine said aloud and sighed. "Andrew is forever pointing out to me here or there how much I was protected from. There is so much I never gave thought to, and it stings my pride when I realize how blind I could be."

Isleen understood the sentiment well enough. "We are all sheltered in ways we do not understand because we are loved. When we learn something new about the world around us, we adjust and move forward with our new knowledge." She had not meant to lead them to such a melancholy place. "Tell me, now that you are married women, do you still stand beneath kissing balls at Christmas?"

They exchanged glances and Lady Josephine laughed. "Oh, Andrew would be quite put out if he wasn't the one standing next to me if I did."

"Luca would certainly prefer it that way." Lady Atella played with the edge of her shawl, running the fringe between her fingers as she gave the matter some thought. "Can you imagine the look on his face if anyone else attempted to kiss me?"

They giggled like schoolgirls, and Isleen let the conversation pass into other avenues. Still, her mind lingered on the last time a man had kissed her, years and years ago. That hadn't been a cheery press of lips at a party. No, it had been a kiss goodbye. A kiss that neither of them had known would be the last they shared.

Six years felt like an eternity at times. Especially in moments like these, when the people around her were so happy and bright. Yes, Isleen had ceased mourning her lost love. And she was ready to move forward. Had been ready for some time. Yet she hadn't met another man that made her feel half the adoration Sean Hurst had inspired.

Sometimes, she feared she never would.

CHAPTER 5

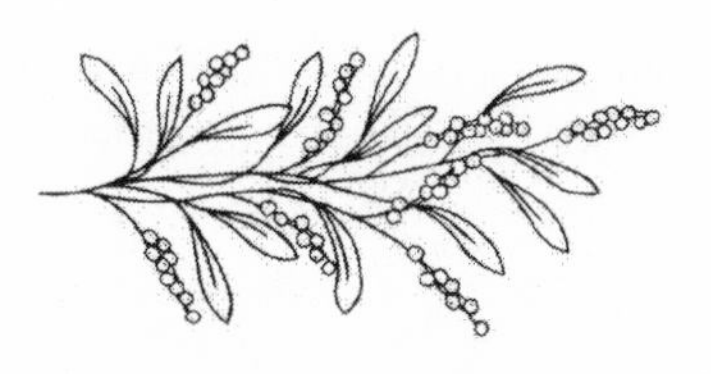

Simon expected to have a less combative evening with men near his own age present at Clairvoir. The arrangements on the third evening of the house party meant they had a completely balanced table.

Lambsthorpe's newly installed vicar, Jonathan Wood, attended this time. That meant the duchess had a perfect number of ladies to men at the meal. All the men but the duke were less than five and thirty, while half the women were well over forty. But age and eligibility mattered less this evening than the appropriate amount of hes and shes.

The young earl sat to the right hand of his father, across from his grandmother, with Emma and Lord Dunmore between him and the somewhat troublesome Miss Frost. Not that he viewed her as a troublemaker, of course. However, conversation with her seemed to lead him into dangerous territory.

When the entirety of the meal passed without any debates on his end of the table or the other, Simon breathed a sigh of relief.

His father, the vicar, Simon, Luca, and Andrew remained behind at the table while the women went into the next room to begin the evening's conversation. The separation of men and women at this point after the meal had confused Simon when he was younger. Now, however, he realized it was an opportunity for men to engage in something their ladies wouldn't approve of: making terrible jokes at each other's expense. At least, that's how Andrew used the time.

"I have had the most entertaining conversation with Miss Frost this evening," he said, leaning back in his chair in a way that would have made Simon's grandmother rather cross. "She told me about an Irish Christmas tradition. On Christmas Eve, when families in Ireland go to bed, they leave the table laden with bread, seeds, raisins, and milk. And they unlatch the door. To feed poor wanderers. Can you imagine? Leaving a great big place like this castle in such a way?"

The duke had crossed his arms, a pipe in hand. He looked to Lord Dunmore. "I imagine the noble houses in Ireland wouldn't be likely to leave their homes unlocked, either."

"Some do, to keep with tradition." Lord Dunmore poured himself coffee and added a splash of dark amber liquid. "But there are alternatives to leaving the household proper open. Sometimes a table is laid outside, or in an outbuilding."

"Ah, yes." The duke gave his pipe a puff. "I recall one Christmas the duchess and I were there that we did something similar. We filled a table at the nearest church with bread and crocks of milk and cream. The priest watched over it that night."

"It is a fine idea," Mr. Wood said, a thoughtful gleam in his eye. "We gather all sorts of things to give to the poor and needful on Boxing Day. Putting a feast out to give people more for their table come Christmas morning isn't something I had considered before."

"They also light a candle and put it in their most prominent window on Christmas Eve," Andrew added. "Miss Frost said it was a way to welcome Mary and Joseph when they cannot find a place at the inn. I can't think we do a thing to honor those two specifically."

"The candle is for more than that," the vicar said, eyebrows furrowed. "We studied the Irish resistance to Anglican conversion at University, of course. The lit candle used to be a way to signal to Catholic priests that the house was a safe one for them to perform mass."

Simon's gaze flicked toward Lord Dunmore to see what the Irish politician's reaction was to the subject of the Penal Laws. The baronet shifted in his seat and lowered his eyes, his jaw tight.

The duke made a soft sound of interest. "Perhaps that is how it began, Mr. Wood. Though our Catholic neighbors have nothing to fear from us now, practicing their religion in the open as they wish, there are still many ways our fellow countrymen look down upon their faith."

"Reform comes too slow for many in Ireland," Lord Dunmore said, tone even and quiet. "My family is Protestant, or I would not hold my seat in the House. But many of my closest friends and farther-flung kin are, and will forever be, of the Catholic faith and traditions."

A heaviness settled over the table, and Simon wished he had Andrew's knack for saying the exact right thing to lighten the mood. But even Andrew's humor seemed blocked by the topic. The duke released a deep sigh.

"We will set things to right, Dunmore. Public opinion stands behind the Catholics more and more. There are calls for reform."

There were also calls in the streets for blood from those who took part in the protests and the massive crowds of working class; they demanded change to tax laws, to their representation in the government. And not enough men in power were like the duke, working for the good of the people under his care.

Luca, a practicing Catholic, had this far remained silent. As an ambassador from the Kingdom of the Two Sicilies, he often walked the delicate boundary between political views. His king was technically a Hapsburg, and a Protestant. Luca had married Emma Arlen, the duke's ward, in an Anglican ceremony, likely disappointing many people from his homeland.

When Luca spoke on this subject, he did so with the barest of smiles. "When good men are in power, the government works for its people. Regardless of their religion, education, or class."

"Then let us hope more good men enter both the House of Commons and the House of Lords in future," Simon said, lifting his glass.

Andrew did the same. "I can drink to that."

"I can, too." The baron lifted his cup. All the men raised a glass to a better future for England.

After the cups lowered again, the duke rose from his chair. He left his pipe on the same silver plate on which the footman had brought it to him. "We should join the ladies. Their gentler sensibilities will go a long way toward putting our hearts and minds at ease."

Once in the saloon his mother favored after dinner, Simon found his favorite chair near the windows. The saloon's green-papered walls and rich, gold accents, familiar in their beauty and comfort, eased what was left of the tension from the after-dinner conversation.

The furniture in this long room was gathered about in small clusters. A table with four chairs, another with six, awaited anyone who wished to play games. Chaise lounges were across from couches. A writing desk stood along one wall. A large fire burned in the hearth with mirrors above and across from it to reflect the candlelight from wall sconces and the chandelier hanging above.

The rug on the floor was enormous, in the same pinks and greens his mother favored. Bowls of white roses from the hothouse were scattered upon tables, making the room smell sweet and fresh.

Simon turned to the chair nearest his, a comment rising to his lips that Andrew would appreciate—but Andrew hadn't followed Simon to the far end of the room and the darkness of the windows. He had stopped at the chair of his wife, Simon's sister, to whisper in her ear while she grinned.

No one had followed Simon.

Luca, like Andrew, stood next to his wife. As though even their brief parting had been too much for him. The duke had taken up his chair next to the duchess and held her hand in his, fully attentive to whatever it was she said to him. And the rector sat on the couch between Simon's grandmother and Lady Dunmore.

The Earl of Farleigh was alone in a corner.

Marriage had certainly changed things for his friends. While he didn't begrudge them their happiness, Simon hated feeling left out and alone. His position as his father's heir already left him without many true friends. Too many wanted Simon's ear for their own gain or popularity. He never quite knew who to trust when Andrew wasn't there.

He had been fooled a time or two by men who acted one way in his presence and another the moment he left the room.

Simon sighed and tilted his head back against the chair, turning his eyes upward. In the dim candlelight, the murals on the ceiling weren't easily visible. But he knew them all quite by heart. They were all domestic scenes of women and children, frolicking in meadows, leaping across streams. Idyllic. Peaceful. Completely unlike anything he'd ever experienced.

A lilting voice broke through his thoughts. "Have you grown tired of company already, my lord?"

Simon opened his eyes and shot to his feet, as one must when a lady approached. But Miss Frost had already settled in the chair next to his, leaving him to tower awkwardly above her while she fussed with the blue and green shawl around her shoulders. He retook his seat, looking to the chair where she'd been when he entered the room.

"No, Miss Frost," he said, recalling her question. "It would be a sorry thing if I tired of a month-long house party on the third day of the occasion."

"My thoughts precisely. Of course, a month of having guests in your home cannot be wholly comfortable, either." She smiled at him, somewhat sympathetically, he thought.

"A castle this size makes it easier. We need not be on top of one another every moment."

"True enough. Your sister tells me there are even secret passages for traveling from one side of the castle to the other, without being seen."

Josephine ought to know better than to speak of such things to an outsider. Simon shrugged, as though the subject mattered little. "I suppose they are useful to servants in that way."

Miss Frost raised her eyebrows at him, but her smile stayed in place. It seemed she was in a pleasant mood this evening. Perhaps not having him as a dinner companion had helped. "Sir Andrew told me at dinner that the two of you practically grew up together."

"We did." He fidgeted with the cuffs of his coat, then laced his fingers together before him, elbows still on the arms of the chair. "Andrew even stayed the year with me in Ireland when I visited our estate there. He was with me when I first met your brother."

"It is a good thing, I'm thinking, to have a friend as close as that. I am afraid I cannot boast of the same. Though my brother puts up with my company most of the time." She looked away from Simon, her gaze taking in the others in the room. "Your sister and her friend are lovely."

"They have a close attachment, too." Simon considered that fact as his sister and Emma held a book between them, their heads bent close together while their husbands spoke with each other.

"We are lucky in our friendships. Is there anyone in particular you will miss while away from Dublin, Miss Frost?"

Her gaze met his, and a trace of sadness appeared in her dark eyes. "A few very old friends of the family is all. Most of my closest friends are married and spend their Christmas season in the country, or in England with their husbands."

"Ah." He studied her again, for the first time wondering exactly how old she was. And why she was unmarried. She was pretty, with those soulful eyes and rich, shining hair that looked soft as silk in the candlelight. Older than his sister, he would guess.

"Five and twenty."

Simon's mouth popped open without him meaning for it to, then he said, "I beg your pardon. I didn't mean to pry—" And he was certain he hadn't asked her age aloud. A gentleman asking a lady's age? Absolute rudeness. He'd admonished his little brother for it only the day before.

"You didn't," she assured him with a smirk. "It was an easy enough thing, to know what you were thinking. I am five and twenty, and unpromised. Because you wondered about that, too."

Presumptuous. That's what she was. Yet he couldn't deny her words. "I apologize for being so easily read, Miss Frost."

She waved aside the apology. "Age isn't anything to be ashamed of, to my way of thinking. It is merely a number, and if we are lucky, we will count many years instead of few."

"That is a philosophical way to look at it."

"An honest way, too." Miss Frost mimicked the way he sat with her elbows on the arms of the chair and her hands clasped before her. "What was your favorite thing about Ireland when you visited?"

The abrupt question made his mind halt a moment in confusion before finding the right path in their new conversation. "My favorite thing? I spent most of my time in the country, at our house in Donabate. But when we visited Dublin, the journey was always enjoyable. The land is breathtaking."

That answer satisfied her, given the way her smile softened. "I have always found my homeland beautiful. The people are what I enjoy the most, though. The talking and the singing, the story-telling. I never passed a dull evening among friends in Ireland."

Josephine had approached as they spoke, Andrew with her. "Will you tell us some Irish stories while you are with us, Miss Frost?"

Andrew let his wife sit on the short sofa across from Simon and Miss Frost's chairs before collapsing with far less grace onto its other side. "Irish stories?" He shook his head. "They are all about some white-headed warrior named Finn, if memory serves me right."

"Finn McCool," Simon said at the exact same time as Miss Frost said the same in Irish, "Fionn mac Cumhaill." She exchanged a look with him, and he shrugged somewhat sheepishly.

Josephine laughed. "If this Finn person made an impression on Andrew and Simon both, his stories must be exceptional."

"They are the legendary backbone of Ireland," Miss Frost confirmed with a nod. "Much like King Arthur is here in England."

Andrew lifted both his hands to speak, waving his fingers about as he said in a false-whisper, "Including the idea that Finn McCool never died, but fell asleep in a cave surrounded by his immortal warriors. One day, he will awake and defend Ireland in the hour of its greatest need."

The Irish woman laughed and shook a finger at Andrew. "You best be careful, Sir Andrew. More than one fight has started in the name of Ireland's greatest hunter and warrior."

"Luca," Andrew called over his shoulder, unfettered by any worry of manners at the moment. "Luca, are there any Sicilian legends about warriors who never die?"

The ambassador tucked his hands behind his back as he approached, his expression thoughtful. "You remember I was taught primarily by monks, do you not?"

"Truly?" Miss Frost leaned forward, her eyes wide and expression one of fascination. "What a unique upbringing."

Luca shrugged. "Aside from the fact that they did not hold with such superstitions, you must remember that my country's history dates back to the days of the Roman Empire. One could argue that Hercules is our best example of an undying hero."

"I'd forgotten about him," Andrew said, turning the right way around again.

"How could anyone forget Hercules?" Luca stood behind Andrew and Josephine's couch, his expression curious.

"Arthur, Finn, and Hercules. Wouldn't they get up to trouble if they all turned up at once?" Josephine's eyes sparkled. "You must tell me all about your Finn McCool, Miss Frost."

"If you wish." Miss Frost looked up at Luca. "I have heard stories about Lord Farleigh and Sir Andrew's youth, causing mischief. Was there any of that for you, my lord, surrounded as you were by monks?"

"Not as much as I liked," the conte answered with a grin. "My wife says I am lacking in embarrassing childhood stories."

"Sadly, he is." Emma had arrived, too. Simon's quiet, dark corner had transformed quickly into the most crowded portion of the room. "Luca, will you bring a chair for me?"

"Of course, *amore mio*." He came back a moment later with a chair. He settled it next to Miss Frost's, then fetched another for himself.

"There are any number of stories I could tell about these two," Josephine said, gesturing to Andrew and Simon. "And possibly a few about us." She pointed to Emma and herself.

"Like the time Simon slid down the banister and his grandmother caught him at the foot of the stairs?" Andrew's sly grin appeared. "One of my favorite stories. He turned seven shades of red before settling into a ghostly white while she lectured him on the proper behavior of a future duke."

Years of hearing that story and reliving his grandmother's indignation protected Simon from a blush at that very moment as all eyes turned toward him.

"I was eleven," he said by way of explanation. "And that was the very last time I slid down a banister."

"Compared to you, James never faces any sort of consequence to his more adventurous behavior," Josephine pointed out. "None of us did, really."

Andrew chuckled while Simon shifted uncomfortably in his chair. His friend waved his hand in the air with a flourish. "The heir is held to higher standards."

Miss Frost looked at Simon with pursed lips. "That explains why you seem so stern all the time, Lord Farleigh."

"Me?" He sat up straighter. "Stern?" Surely not. He had been a well-mannered host. He had smiled at her. Even attempted a jest a time or two. "I am not stern."

The word itself conjured up images of his grandfather's portrait on the wall, a scowling headmaster, and his father's Captain of the Guard, Rockwell. Those old men were stern. He was merely...proper. Respectful.

"I am afraid I must agree with Miss Frost," Luca said, taking his wife's hand in his. "You have always struck me as a serious man. Despite your age." Luca was only five years Simon's senior. That certainly didn't sound flattering coming from him.

"You used to be a lot livelier than you are now," Andrew added. Whose side was he on? "You aren't nearly as much fun as you used to be." The traitor.

"I *am* lively," Simon retorted, then winced at how sullen he sounded. "My status as my father's heir requires I conduct myself with dignity and respectability. That is all."

His sister turned against him next. Ever since marrying

Andrew, she'd become quicker to tease and jest, though her sense of humor was dryer than his.

"It sounds as though you think a duke's offspring should be the dullest person in company." Josephine put her chin in her hand and made a show of studying him while her eyes sparkled with mirth. "Dear me, I hope I am not expected to behave that way. I will disappoint everyone terribly."

How had everyone turned against Simon in the five minutes since they had sat down with him? He glowered at Andrew, feeling his friend was the most to blame for this sudden attack on his character. His friend smiled with complete innocence.

Andrew looked pointedly at Miss Frost. "I suppose he isn't all bad. It is more the idea that he doesn't wish to make a spectacle of himself."

Simon opened his mouth to give a retort, but Miss Frost spoke before he could. "I can understand that motivation. Having anyone stare at me for less than flattering reasons is off-putting."

"What would a less than flattering reason be, precisely?" Josephine asked.

Almost as though she and Andrew were working together. Driving the conversation to a particular point that Simon could not yet see. But no. That was ridiculous. He had obviously spent too much time studying his father's military books. Why else would he get the feeling he was being led into an ambush?

"Oh, well." Miss Frost's fair cheeks darkened to a soft pink hue. "When we spoke of mistletoe before. That is a distinctly uncomfortable situation for a lady to be in, I would think."

Isleen hadn't the faintest idea why the conversation had turned on her. She'd thought Lord Farleigh's friends wanted to draw him out. She needn't be involved in whatever scheme they were concocting.

Except Lord Farleigh turned toward her, one of his eyebrows cocked upward. "You do not hold with the mistletoe tradition?"

"I haven't ever taken part in it," she admitted with what she hoped the others would see as a confident smile. "Mistletoe doesn't grow in Ireland, and I have never celebrated Christmas anywhere else."

"But you would object to someone stealing a kiss beneath a kissing ball?" Lord Farleigh seemed flummoxed by her reluctance, and she couldn't help bristling.

"It is still called *stealing*, which would imply a kiss not freely given." Then she turned to Josephine. "You cannot tell me that there is any other point in the year in which one would think it an acceptable pastime to go around kissing women merely because they stand beneath a certain *plant*."

That confounded them for a moment, and Isleen thought she'd won her point across.

"But it is tradition." Lord Farleigh still stared at her with bemusement. "One doesn't go about wearing masks unless invited to a masque ball. That particular behavior is reserved for the right time. So too are mistletoe kisses."

She had never sat among a group of men and women discussing the topic of kissing to this extent. Perhaps it was all well and good for them, who knew each other or were connected via their marriages. But Isleen shifted uncomfortably, then met Lord Farleigh's gaze.

"The man being lectured for his lack of frivolous behavior hardly seems the right person to take me to task for disliking a holiday tradition."

"I am perfectly capable of being frivolous."

"And I am capable of taking part in a tradition, ridiculous as it may be." But that didn't mean she *wanted* to take part in it.

"A wager, then." It was Sir Andrew who said the words, yet Isleen was staring at the earl when he reacted to his friend's words. Lord Farleigh turned pale, and his eyes widened, then his eyebrows came down sharply as he turned a hard-edged smile to his friend.

"What did you say, Andrew?"

"A wager," Lady Josephine answered for her husband. "What a wonderful way to begin the month. We will issue a challenge to the both of you."

"I am not one to gamble," Isleen said, trying to understand the gleeful light in Lady Josephine's eyes. She looked to Lady Atella to see a similar expression.

"We never wager with money," Sir Andrew said with a wave of his hand, dismissing the monetary notion entirely. "That would be quite dull."

"All your wagers are dull," Lord Farleigh said, between clenched teeth.

Lord Atella chuckled and leaned back in his chair. "I would not say that. My introduction to your family consisted of wagers. For boat races. Horse races. A puppet theater."

Isleen very much wanted to follow that trail of conversation. Puppets seemed safer than whatever they were discussing at present.

"Here are the terms," Sir Andrew said, steepling his fingers together. How had they come to having *terms*? "We challenge our dear Simon Dinard, Lord Farleigh, to put aside his fears of frivolity and embrace the ridiculous during this month. If he fails —meaning, we catch him acting the part of a bore without reason —then he pays the forfeit of making a fool of himself at the Christmas Eve ball."

The reaction of Lord Farleigh's friends to this idea was far too appreciative. And supportive.

Lady Atella's gentle smile turned into a wide grin. "What a delightful challenge."

"This is ridiculous," Simon muttered as he slouched forward to rub his forehead. "I do not agree."

"Oh, but you will. Because Miss Frost will determine whether or not you succeed in your challenge. And if you do, her forfeit will be to knowingly stand beneath the mistletoe at the Christmas Eve ball until she has been kissed."

"I will not." Isleen sat up a little straighter.

"Are you saying you do not want to hold Lord Farleigh, heir to an English duke, beneath your Irish heel?" Lady Josephine asked, batting her eyelashes at Isleen. "Think of telling all your friends the tale when you return to Dublin."

Curses. An appeal to her Irish pride was the quickest way to obtain her agreement. How had Lady Josephine guessed at such a thing? Isleen narrowed her eyes and looked for the first time to where her brother sat, on the other side of the room, next to their mother.

He met her gaze, as though he had been watching the proceedings from afar, and winked at her before turning back to his conversation with the duke and duchess.

Had her loving brother set this whole thing up? He knew how she felt about the English and their opinions about the Irish. What if he had a hand in this? What if it was his attempt to teach her a lesson?

She looked to Lady Josephine again. The challenge in the woman's eyes made it difficult to deny the appeal of being an earl's keeper for nearly an entire month.

"Let me see if I understand you," Lord Farleigh said, before Isleen had quite thought everything through. "I agree to act more like this imbecile"—he pointed at Sir Andrew—"until Christmas, and if I succeed, then Miss Frost must give in to our English customs and kiss someone beneath the mistletoe?"

"Yes. A completely harmless forfeit, all things considered." Lady Josephine's innocent smile had returned. Isleen believed what it conveyed less than ever. Though the lady added, "We will not allow it to be anyone truly horrid, Miss Frost. If the idea truly horrifies you, you could name a different forfeit."

"And it is up to Miss Frost to decide if Simon upholds his side of the bargain," Sir Andrew added with a smug tip of his head. "Miss Frost, if you think he fails at this, Simon must do something especially ridiculous in front of all the duke's guests on Christmas Eve."

"He detests singing in company," Lady Atella put in with an air of helpfulness that Isleen certainly didn't appreciate.

"And what do all of you get out of this?" Lord Farleigh asked, glowering at everyone. "Besides watching me make a spectacle of myself."

"That alone is enough," Lord Atella said so quietly Isleen almost didn't hear him.

Lady Josephine leaned against her husband's shoulder. "We receive the pleasure of watching you enjoy the Christmas Season for the first time in years."

Lord Farleigh looked to Isleen for the first time in what felt like ages, and she stiffened her spine beneath his gaze. He appeared tired. Perhaps defeated. And when he spoke to her, his voice was low and deep.

"They will not relent until we agree. Are the terms favorable for you, Miss Frost? Do you wish to be my keeper for the rest of the month?"

He leaned closer while speaking, over the arm of his chair, and she leaned in too, the better to hear him.

They were mere inches apart.

A trickle of warmth began in her belly and moved outward as she stared into his blue eyes—warmth that had nothing to do with the almost intimate tone of his voice.

No. It had to be satisfaction. The idea of bossing around a future duke satisfied her immensely. Of course she would do it.

"I do," she said at last, the two small words sealing her fate to his for the month of December. "I have spent limited time in your company, but I think you will find it quite difficult to behave frivolously."

"You will have to give him lots of direction," Sir Andrew stated, and Isleen abruptly remembered they weren't alone. That four others stared at them with varying expressions of interest and delight.

Why did she have the feeling that she had just been tricked?

CHAPTER 6

Isleen didn't speak to her brother about the odd wager until the next morning. She had turned in earlier than he had the evening before. Finding a moment alone with him wasn't all that difficult; she trapped Teague in an alcove with an alarmingly life-like marble cat before he could leave the guest's corridor.

Considering his part of the wager may have included betrayal, Isleen approached him gently. "Did you put your English friends up to playing a joke on me, brother?"

"I did not," he said, easy-as-you-please. Then he bent to look closer at the marble tabby. "At least, whatever joke they played wasn't my idea. But when Lady Atella asked what might provoke you, I may have mentioned you have more than a touch of the usual Irish pride." He poked at one of the marble cat's fangs.

"Stop playing with that." Isleen crossed her arms. "What if that tooth breaks off? You'll be buying the duke a new one."

Teague snorted but withdrew from the statue. "Lady Atella assured me she didn't mean any harm."

"But they did plan my part in their little wager." Isleen rubbed briefly at her eyebrows, then paced away from her brother. "I have to think their scheming has more to do with the earl than it does with me."

"I never found out what their plans were. Will you tell me the whole of it, Issy?" He only used her old pet name when he wanted something, and she never begrudged him for it. He was a good brother. When he wasn't telling people how best to rile her.

Isleen sketched out the details of the wager, and what it meant for the earl if he lost. Her brother's eyes and grin widened in equal parts until he laughed.

"Faith, 'tis a grand joke. They'll have you following Farleigh about, ensuring he makes a fool of himself. And you'll enjoy every moment of it, will you not?"

She sniffed. "I will indeed." Then she fixed her brother in place with a most serious glare. "So you do not think I have reason to worry? There isn't anything in this that is dastardly?"

"It isn't a play, Issy. There aren't any villains here." Teague held out his arm. "Come, let's have breakfast. Sausage, eggs, toast, and ham."

"Did you fight a giant in your sleep, to make yourself that hungry?" Isleen took his arm. "We might need to warn the duchess that you intend to empty her larder."

"I can't imagine such a thing is possible. Have you seen the size of the kitchens?"

"No, none of my tours included the servants' areas." They started down the stairs, a beautiful rich blue carpet muffling their steps. "I find it strange that yours did."

"It wasn't so much a tour as it was a liberation mission."

"Liberation?" she scoffed. "And what was down there to be liberated? Catholics wanting the vote?"

He laughed, then coughed away the sound. "The jam and rolls might well have been Catholic. You never know."

"Sacrilegious. That's what you are, Teague Frost."

"Not so, sister dear. Hungry. That's what I am, almost always."

A panel of the wall a few steps ahead of them opened, and Isleen had the unfortunate reaction of squeaking and jumping backward in her surprise. From the concealed doorway, Lord Farleigh stepped out into the corridor.

"I apologize for startling you, Miss Frost."

"I was not startled," she retorted quickly, then felt her cheeks warm when both the earl and her brother looked at her with confusion. "Merely...taken aback."

"Ah." Lord Farleigh smiled a little and pushed the door closed behind him. Making it appear rather like a wall again. "Then forgive me for causing so unpleasant a reaction."

She bit her tongue before she could say something else ridiculous.

"Where are you coming from, my lord?" Teague asked, smiling as though earls popping out of walls was a common occurrence.

"There is a spiral staircase behind the wall—mostly used by servants, but it was more convenient than going down to the ballroom staircase or the chapel spiral. The family's private rooms are above the small dining room."

Isleen took in the earl's appearance, looking for a hint of change in his clothing or person for the start of the wager. He looked as perfectly dressed as he had the day before. "Are you as eager for your breakfast as my brother?"

"More so that I am eager to stay out of everyone else's way. If I came down the corridor at the same time as my former best friend, he would likely insist I slide down a banister or perform some other sort of foolishness." Lord Farleigh's grimace made her wish there was a banister at hand at that very moment. "I will not have the wherewithal for that sort of spectacle until I have had breakfast."

Isleen tried not to smile. He seemed quite discouraged in that moment. "I suppose I can understand that. But you know, my lord, you did not have to accept the wager at all."

"Why *did* you agree to the thing?" Teague asked, head cocked to one side. "How did they persuade you?"

"I will happily tell you at the breakfast table." Lord Farleigh gestured to the remaining length of the corridor. "If we can make it before Sir Andrew steals all the bacon." In as practiced a movement as breathing, the earl extended his hand to Isleen. "May I take you in, Miss Frost?"

She accepted without thinking, taking his arm as naturally as he offered it. The corridor was wide enough for the three of them to walk abreast, so the escort shouldn't matter or be necessary. The man had impeccable manners. She could say that much for him.

They were not the first to the table. Lord Atella already had seated himself, and he sipped at a cup of steaming coffee with the newsheets in hand. He rose when they approached and bowed. "Good morning, Farleigh, Dunmore, and Miss Frost."

"Atella." Lord Farleigh pulled her chair out for her before circling the table to take a seat directly across. Her brother sat down in the seat beside hers. "Is your lady exercising her privilege today?"

Married women often took their breakfasts in bed and at their leisure. Isleen sometimes wondered if she would use the hours of the morning in such a luxurious manner. When and if she ever married.

"She does not plan to leave her room until she must." Luca's smile turned crooked. "In London, she is awake before I am to see to the staff and all the social aspects of her role. I do not blame her for taking advantage of her stay here."

The business of preparing plates and cups, of exchanging small pleasantries, took up several minutes before Teague brought up his question from the corridor. "Well, Farleigh? Why did you agree to a wager that, no matter what, will see you behaving in a less than dignified manner?"

Lord Atella smirked and pulled his newspaper up higher until

Isleen could no longer see his expression. She frowned. She hadn't thought the count had seemed all that interested in the wager. Perhaps he had a greater part in the scheme than she suspected.

Did everyone in the earl's life wish to see him make a fool of himself?

"I know Sir Andrew and Josephine too well to fight them on something like this. Apart, they were stubborn. Together, they are formidable." Lord Farleigh cut slices of fried potato even smaller on his plate. "Before they wed, earlier this year, Andrew rattled around telling everyone I was far too serious. So this complaint of his has gone on for nearly a year."

Teague winced. "That is a long time to hear the same complaint."

"Precisely. And it comes from a good place, I suppose. Andrew is my oldest friend."

"He is worried about you." The realization came to Isleen all at once, and almost as a relief. Here she had thought she was taking part in some sort of torture. While the idea of telling Lord Farleigh what to do had pleased her, there had remained some discomfort that his friends were playing a mean-spirited joke on him. That this wasn't the case relieved her more than she thought it would. "This is his way of encouraging you to enjoy yourself."

"Precisely. And he somehow convinced my sister and our other friends to support him. Which tells me they might share his concern." Simon pointedly looked at the newspaper shielding the Sicilian count. "Have I guessed rightly, Atella?"

The count didn't even lower the paper but spoke from behind the newsprint. "I cannot hear anything from behind this paper."

Isleen bit her lip to keep from laughing. What an interesting group of friends. Lord Farleigh was quite lucky to have so many people worrying over his well-being.

But why had they included her in their mischief?

"That is as good as an admission," Lord Farleigh said with a confident smirk. "And I will prove that you have all worried over nothing."

Lord Atella turned a page in his paper, saying nothing in return.

Teague hummed, impressed. Isleen poked at her smoked ham and frowned down at her plate. She didn't ask her question of the count or the earl. Perhaps they had chosen her as his keeper because it would give her something to do, or it was a way to include a guest in their amusement. There wasn't a malicious reason for it, she felt certain, and that was all that mattered.

After she swallowed another bite of breakfast, she tilted her chin up and looked directly at Lord Farleigh. "I still intend to take my role seriously, my lord. If you pass up an opportunity to be light-hearted and merry, I will see to it you pay your forfeit."

And then Lord Farleigh did something she hadn't entirely expected. He allowed a slow, warm smile to alter his expression into something she would call flirtatious on another man. "And I will do all I can, Miss Frost, to see that you are standing beneath the mistletoe on Christmas Eve."

A chill went down her spine at the same moment heat built low in her belly. The conflicting sensations made her shiver, and she hastily turned her attention back to her plate. Hoping no one saw the effect Lord Farleigh's words had on her.

Men such as him had no right to be both attractive and infuriating. It made them far too interesting to study. Doubtless, driving women to such curiosity about him only added to the earl's opinion of himself.

Except—except she really hadn't seen any evidence of arrogance beyond their first impression of one another. Because he had thought she would be like other women vying for his attention. A man in his position had every reason to suspect the intentions of those around him, she supposed.

Isleen couldn't let him have the last word on the matter, though she let it rest while Teague and Lord Farleigh took up another topic of conversation. Lord Atella joined them, expressing concern over the rising grain tariffs. Sir Andrew came into the dining room and immediately piled his plate full of bacon and roasted vegetables. Last of all came the duke, and they all rose until he took his seat.

"Miss Frost, I must apologize. I forgot my younger daughters would take breakfast apart, since we have guests. And all the married women have remained in their rooms. Apart from your brother, I hope these ne'er-do-wells have behaved themselves." He looked pointedly at his son and Sir Andrew.

"Each has behaved as he ought," she reassured the duke. It surprised her how relaxed she felt in his company, given his rank. The man had such a fatherly, kind way about him. She glanced at Lord Farleigh, mentally comparing the two, only to find that he had gone stiff all over and his expression appeared stern.

"Excellent." The duke turned his attention to his son. "Farleigh, your mother asked that I remind you of the letter you promised to write to your cousin, Thomas. She seems to think you will forget."

Though the duke remained perfectly relaxed, his son did not waver in posture.

"I will not forget, Your Grace. I will see to it directly after breakfast."

Isleen rose from the table and hastily told the gentlemen not to rise with her. "I am looking in on my sister. Thank you for a most excellent breakfast, Your Grace. And the fine company, my lords."

She left the room, her mind circling around the strangeness of Lord Farleigh's reaction to his father. Surely, there could be no ill will between father and son. At least, none that the duke seemed aware of. She had sat through enough uncomfortable dinners with people who pretended to like one another to sense when that was the case.

Lord Farleigh could not be intimidated by his father, surely.

But something was amiss.

Perhaps the earl's friends had the right of it, and he needed a reminder to be less stern. And it was up to her, to some measure, to ensure he had every opportunity to act a little silly.

Isleen needed a few ideas. And the schoolroom seemed an excellent place to get them.

CHAPTER 7

Although uncertain what he'd expected, being left alone by Miss Frost surprised Simon. He'd felt certain she would begin her torture of him at breakfast, flexing her power over him in some small way. Especially after he had told her and Lord Dunmore his suspicions about his friends' motivations.

Andrew didn't bother to hide his disappointment over the waste of an opportunity. "I thought Miss Frost had more spirit than that. She didn't seem interested in commanding you at all."

They had left the breakfast table together, leaving Luca, Dunmore, and the duke discussing the future of Parliament and which seats needed filling in the House of Commons. Simon and his father had already had the same conversation, and Simon had a letter to write to the cousin nearest him in age.

"What did you want her to do? Order me to skip about the table while my father enjoyed his morning toast?" Simon had a dozen places to choose from for letter writing. The question was whether he wished to undertake the task in private.

"That would have been amusing. I dare say your father would have had a laugh."

Simon winced. "Then I will be grateful you chose her rather than yourself as my keeper."

Andrew seemed to speak more to himself than Simon, keeping pace with his friend out of long-habit. "I did not think she was cowed by your position, nor enamored with your title, in a way that would keep her from making some truly glorious demands."

That made Simon chuckle. "She certainly isn't intimidated or charmed by me. I told you what she said during the castle tour."

"Indeed. That is what made me think she would be perfect for my plan."

"Exactly how long have you had this 'wager' planned?" Simon put all the skepticism he could muster into the last word as he turned again.

"Hmm? Who said I planned it?"

"You did. Just a moment ago."

"Oh. Well." Andrew shrugged. "Not long, in that case. It all sort of came to me. Recently."

They were making for the Regent's Gallery, the largest room in the house. It was one-hundred-thirty feet long, narrowing to fifteen feet across on both ends, with a semi-circle in the middle. From the outside of the castle, that middle portion looked like an enormous tower, three stories from ground to top. Inside, at the widest part of the room, from the wall to the "tower" window was thirty-five feet.

It was several rooms in one, if one were being honest. There were multiple fireplaces. Several collections of chairs and sofas arranged throughout for sitting. Tables for cards or conversing or taking tea. And a writing desk at the end nearest the door that led to the family chapel.

Simon made for that desk, barely taking in the room's grandeur. Their family spent a lot of time in this large room. James, when he was smaller, used to ride his hobby horse from one side to the other, galloping about while the family cheered for him. This was where they held family recitals. Lounged about after dinner, when there were no guests, or entertained themselves with books or drawing. Together, but busy with individual pursuits.

It was Simon's favorite room. The enormous windows faced south, letting in the most light possible throughout the year.

"Perhaps Miss Frost is only gathering her thoughts," Simon said, taking his seat at the elegant writing desk. He opened the small cupboard to withdraw pens and ink, and the drawer for paper. "She may yet satisfy your mercenary daydreams."

"Let us hope." Andrew clapped Simon on the shoulder. "I'm off to see if Josie is risen yet, then I'll meet you for our ride in an hour."

As his friend walked away, lightness in his step and humming an absurd tune, Simon repressed a shudder. His sister and best friend, wed. And it was now within Andrew's rights to stroll into Josephine's bedchamber—

It didn't bear thinking upon. Indeed, though happy for them, he put a lot of effort into trying to forget they were married.

Likely a juvenile response. And Andrew would have a laugh at Simon if he suspected anything about it.

Simon dashed all thoughts of his friend and sister out of his head and gave his attention to the letter. Mr. Thomas Childwick, fourth son of the Earl of Hixham, was a first cousin on his mother's side. And a genuinely good chap.

Family gossip held that he wanted to leave London's social whirl in favor of a quieter city. Simon's mother had another theory. True, Thomas had always been quieter in nature than his brothers. But he also lived in their shadows. The eldest would one day be an earl, the second son held a high rank in the military, the third waited for a living to become available to be a vicar, and the youngest was abroad on his Grand Tour. That left Thomas without a place of his own.

Simon sympathized with his cousin. Despite being the eldest

son, he, often as not, felt overshadowed. But not by elder siblings. By his father.

He broke the tip of his quill when he pressed too hard against the paper. Cursing quietly, he used a cloth made expressly for that purpose to clean the mess before it ruined his letter. Then he tossed the cloth down on the table and ran his hands through his hair.

Not caring that he would undo his valet's work.

Feeling as he did wasn't fair.

His father likely wasn't even aware of Simon's difficulty. It had started at the beginning of the year. Or perhaps even before that, when Simon returned from Ireland.

He trimmed a new pen and tried to focus on the words his cousin needed. Words of encouragement. Of promising that things would get better. He suggested a change of scenery. He invited his cousin to Clairvoir for Christmas, as his mother had suggested. Indeed, he said all the best things one was supposed to say to a man struggling to find direction.

He said all the things that he had been telling himself.

He dropped the pen and leaned back in his chair.

Maybe Andrew and the others were right. Maybe he did need to find a way to reclaim some of the joy in life. Yet how did one embrace frivolity of any kind knowing about the chaos constantly held at bay by the government? How could he waste a moment in mischief when a single illness or dark moment could take his father away, leaving Simon to carry a mantle far too heavy for him?

Hours later, after posting his letter and his ride with Andrew, Simon had come no closer to finding answers to the what-if's that plagued him. At the end of the long afternoon, he climbed the stairs up to the top floor of the castle to prepare for dinner.

Barely outside the family's corridor, a strange sight caught Simon completely off guard.

Kneeling before a chair, dressed in her own evening finery,

was Miss Frost. She appeared to be studying the arms of the chair —which was a rather impressive piece of workmanship, all things considered, even if he hadn't ever actually seen anyone sit on the furniture.

The reason people would pass by that particular seat had to do with the arms. They were six inches wide, but not smooth or padded. Not curved, either, where one might easily rest an elbow or forearm upon them.

Miss Frost looked up from her place on the ground and smiled at him. "Whose idea was it to carve massive, scaled fish and waves into the arms of a piece of furniture?"

"William I of the Netherlands." Simon knew perfectly well how odd the declaration sounded, though watching Miss Frost's eyes widen was worth sounding off-hand. "He sent it as a gift, along with a few other odds and ends. My father is some distant relation and supported His Majesty in creating a sovereign nation."

"That entirely explains the chair." She held her hand out and he took it quite naturally, helping her come to her feet. "A king wouldn't have a practical view of furniture, would he? No one would ever wish to rest on that to take the weight off their feet." Her eyes sparkled as she made the comment, and Simon chuckled in response.

They stood quite close, and he still had hold of her hand. "I have heard a maid complain about dusting it. The carving is quite intricate, and the gray settles deeply in the grooves."

Why was he talking about dusting? It ought to be the farthest thing from his mind, given the delightful way Miss Frost's eyes danced in the fading sunlight.

"A person should consider the way dust gathers before commissioning furniture." Her lips curved upward. "May I have my hand back?"

Simon released her fingers immediately and stepped away. What had come over him? He had to get hold of himself. "My apologies, Miss Frost. Was there something you needed from my family? A question for my mother, perhaps, or Josephine?"

"I need nothing from them. I am waiting for you, my lord."

"For me?" His chest tightened, and he held onto his breath a moment longer than usual before releasing it in a question. "Why?"

Her pretty smile turned into a wide grin. "I have come with instructions for dinner."

His excitement withered into dread. "Oh? What sort of instructions?"

"Your dress for the evening." She waved her hand at his person. "I am told a neighbor named Mr. Hepsworth is coming to dinner, with a wife and daughter to help balance out the table. Is he anyone of importance to you?"

Slowly, Simon shook his head. "Not especially. The family is often invited to keep company with ours. Their daughters are near in age to my sisters."

"Grand. Then it ought to be easier to follow my instructions. Tell me, what is the brightest color coat you own? And have you a purple waistcoat?"

Simon swallowed. "Purple?"

"Lilac will do in a pinch. And something red, I think, if you can manage it. But no dark blues or greens. And no brown or black, either, where we can help it. How large is your largest stickpin?"

It seemed Miss Frost might yet uphold Andrew's hopes for merciless torture, after all.

The hearth in the Elizabethan Saloon burned bright, and candles set about in the room helped add to the warm and cheery setting. Isleen stood apart from where the women near her in age sat, all of them discussing the Christmas Eve ball though it was yet weeks away. She kept her fan moving, wafting already cool air into her face while her neck prickled with nerves.

Ever since leaving Simon with his instructions on dress, Isleen had questioned the wisdom of her idea. Who did she think she was, telling an heir to a dukedom to dress like a fool? What madness had possessed her?

The madness of children. A half hour in the company of her sister and Simon—Lord Farleigh's—little brother had led to the idea she had thought of as brilliant only hours ago.

Lord James had told her all sorts of things, with little prompting, about his brother. "Simon hates purple. But Grandmama keeps commissioning purple things for him because she thinks it looks good on him." And he'd told her, "Simon doesn't care about fashion. He dresses like a vicar all the time." Then her little sister had come into the game, describing a caricature she had seen drawn with a man who wore his shirt-points so high they had nearly obscured his eyes.

Perhaps it was Lord James's fault that Isleen had started calling the earl by his Christian name. Only in her own thoughts, to be sure. She would never say it out loud. Ever.

The duke's deep voice carried across the room. "Are we all here? Where is Farleigh?"

As though summoned by his father's voice, the doors to the saloon opened. Two footmen in livery each held one handle, perfectly dressed and coiffed. Lord Farleigh stood between them, wearing enough bright and bold colors to put a peacock to shame.

Isleen's jaw had fallen open, and she shut it with an audible snap before hiding her blush behind her fan. Oh, dear. Mortification had overtaken her on his behalf.

What had she done?

Simon Dinard, Earl Farleigh, wore a a coat in a shade of mint green more suitable to a pastoral water-coloring than a real article of clothing. Beneath the coat were *two* waistcoats. The purple, as requested, with a second, golden yellow waistcoat peeking out. His trousers were *velvet.* And deep green. His cravat was snow white, as befitting dinner, but it was enormous and *frilled.* A stickpin larger than Isleen's thumbnail flashed bright red.

And he wore a quizzing glass on his chain.

With the room utterly silent at his appearance, Isleen wanted to sink into the floor. Or leap from the window out into the cold night air—if only she knew how to fly.

Simon, wearing a singularly bored expression, took up his quizzing glass and pretended to polish it a moment. Then he strode into the room and directly up to his father and mother, where they sat together on a settee. He bowed deeply.

"I apologize for my tardiness, Your Graces. I had some trouble with my dinner preparations."

A loud snort made Isleen jump. She turned to see Sir Andrew biting his gloved knuckle, shoulders shaking. Tears in his eyes. Lady Josephine, at his side, appeared horrified. Lord Atella was staring at the ceiling and fighting a smile. Lady Atella had placed a gloved hand over her mouth.

Máthair and Teague appeared rather stunned.

Mr. and Mrs. Hepsworth had turned still as statues, and their daughter gaped openly at the man she had, moments ago, told the room at large she found the very picture of nobility. The two gentlemen dinner guests, the young vicar and a local schoolmaster, Mr. Sprague, appeared somewhat bemused.

It was the dowager duchess who broke the silence. "You still appear to be having that trouble, Farleigh. But I had rather go into dinner than sit here and discuss your regrettable foray into fashion."

That snapped everyone to attention, and as the dowager duchess stood, so, too, did the rest. In due course, the line formed by the ladies' ranks as the men escorted them into dinner. Isleen was far enough back from Simon, who led his mother, that she couldn't hear whatever it was the duchess had leaned in to whisper to him.

Isleen wound up sitting directly next to Simon, who was in the middle of the table from the duchess's right. On Isleen's other side was Mr. Hepsworth, who didn't seem at all inclined to give attention to anything other than his well-laden plate.

Simon turned to her with a pleasant smile but had the nerve to hold his quizzing glass up to his eye. "Miss Frost. I hope you find the meal to your liking."

"I do," she said softly, resisting the urge to sink beneath the table. "And yourself?"

That was when she saw the glint in his eye. A knowing, dangerous sort of light that gleamed more than twinkled and promised retribution. "Yes. Though I had not expected just how much I would enjoy it."

They were not talking about the meal.

Lord Atella sat directly across from Isleen, and perhaps he had overheard their conversation. "I am glad to hear it," he said. "This is a similar menu to the one I prepared last year. Do you remember, amore mio?"

Lady Atella laughed, the sound light and polite. "I will never forget, though I am thankful we did not make the pasta this time."

"I have never heard this story," Miss Hepsworth, sitting on the other side of Simon, said happily. "Will you tell it, Lady Atella?"

"After dinner," the contessa promised. The conversation broke into pieces again, and Isleen dared to look at Simon from the corner of her eye.

Oh dear.

His clothing really was absolutely terrible.

Isleen had to hastily raise a napkin to her lips to smother a hysterical inclination to giggle.

CHAPTER 8

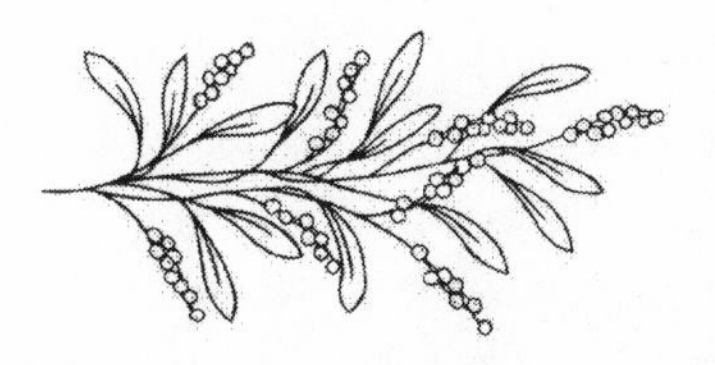

Though most considered the weather too cold in December for outdoor painting, Isleen had decided to brave the temperatures despite the chill in the air. The sun was out. The sky was blue. There wasn't much of a breeze. Surely, she could manage an hour or so in the gardens with an easel and watercolors.

After, she would join the party of people going to Lambsthorpe to explore the village. The party included everyone in the castle under the age of thirty and over the age of twelve.

Which meant Simon would be there.

Though the rest of the previous evening had passed without incident, apart from the jests Sir Andrew made at Simon's expense, Isleen intended to stay out of Simon's way as much as possible.

Darrie had looked at Isleen as though *she* had been the one wearing the purple waistcoat when Isleen spoke of her plans to venture out of doors. In the end, the kindhearted maid had insisted not only on wrapping Isleen up in several layers of wool, but on coming outside with her mistress.

"A fine thing it would be if you'd no one to warn you when

your nose turns blue." She had put her brown wool coat on and followed Isleen out into the winter sun.

They were on the south side of the castle, where the light was best. Isleen turned her easel so she faced the castle itself—ramparts, towers, and all. It didn't take long for her to get its form, as she focused less on details and more on general shapes. It would be pretty-ish when she finished, though hardly a worthy copy of the grand building.

She'd seen several paintings of the castle hanging up inside and knew well where her own skill would rank. But she enjoyed the time spent in art, even if she wasn't the best water-colorist in Ireland. Or, she supposed, in Great Britain.

After a time, she became aware of Darrie speaking in a quiet voice to someone else. A male someone. She listened, though her focus remained on the brush in her hand. She wore fingerless gloves, but hardly needed them. With the sun shining on her back, it wasn't nearly so cold as she'd feared it would be.

"Yer mistress is a fine painter, miss."

"Thank you. But you should see how well she does when the sun shines warmer than this."

"Ah, you're one of the Irish what's been invited for the month. I've never spoken to an Irish girl b'fore."

"You have not? We talk the same as anyone else, to be sure."

"Exceptin' you've a way with your words. Sounds like you're near-singing 'em."

"That's a bit of flattery if I have ever heard it. You ought to take yourself off to your work, if that's all you've come for."

"I am workin', miss. I'm a gardener, and these here hedges need some attention."

Isleen finally sneaked a look over her shoulder to see the man speaking with her maid. He wasn't a large fellow, and looked young. Perhaps he had spotted Darrie and thought he would take the chance to flirt with a pretty girl. Approaching when the maid was with her mistress was quite bold, though.

She faced forward again. She peered over the top of her easel and froze.

Lord Farleigh was coming down the sloping green grass toward her, dressed for the weather, walking stick in hand, and frowning into the sunshine.

Botheration.

She hadn't thought he'd come outside, even if he saw her through one of the castle's many windows. Yet here he came, marching like a field marshal ready to do battle.

She ducked her head and painted faster, as though that might somehow defend her from what he might say next.

He stopped directly beside her. "Miss Frost."

"My lord," she said, narrowing her eyes and leaning closer to her painting, pretending to work on a minute detail atop one of the towers. It did have an exceptional stained glass window she wouldn't mind seeing up close. "It cannot be time to visit Lambshorpe already."

"Not quite yet, no." He didn't sound affronted. But then he asked, "Are you avoiding me?"

"If I were, I would be a fool to admit it." She still didn't look at him.

He sighed heavily and turned to face the opposite direction from her. "You there. Whorton, isn't it? You are the stable master's son."

"Aye, my lord." The gardener sounded sulky, even though Simon had addressed him civilly. Ah, perhaps he knew he had mis-stepped in coming so close to a guest. It impressed her that Simon knew the man's surname at all.

"I'm told the gardeners are all at work at the pond today, getting it ready for the first freeze."

"Aye, my lord. I was just headed there. Good day."

That explained the sulkiness. He had been caught where he shouldn't be. But who had bothered to tell the duke's son what the gardeners were up to? She hadn't imagined a family as highly placed as the duke's would bother to know someone so lowly as a gardener.

"And you must be Miss Frost's maid." Simon's tone completely changed when addressing Darrie. He sounded much kinder. "How good of you to accompany your mistress out into the cold. What is your name?"

"Darrie, your lordship." She saw Darrie bob a curtsy, then twist her gloved hands together. But the maid appeared otherwise at ease.

"Darrie, that is a charming name. You know, Darrie, I had always thought using watercolors outdoors was more of a summer pursuit than an autumn undertaking."

Isleen winced and dropped her brush into the little pot of water she had put on the stone wall she stood beside. "Darrie, would you be so kind as to take my things inside? I think I am finished for the day."

"I will, miss." Darrie curtsied, darted a quick look at Simon, then winked at Isleen.

Oh dear. Her maid had entirely the wrong idea about Simon Dinard if she was winking when he couldn't see. Isleen would correct any false assumptions the moment they were alone in her quarters.

Simon remained standing still, eyes on the gardens stretching out and down the hill of the castle in a gentle slope. Isleen stood beside him, silent and a touch uncomfortable. Only when she heard Darrie's steps leading away did she speak.

She tried to sound bold. Airy. Careless. Anything but nervous. "No purple waistcoat today, my lord? What a pity. The color suits you so."

"Did you think so?" The question sounded light. Perhaps even amused. She dared look at him from the corner of her eye, and she caught the edge of his smile.

A *smile.* Not a smirk, or scowl, or wince. Just as she had thought before, his looks only improved when his lips turned upward. What else could anyone expect, given the handsomeness of his parents? Some things truly weren't fair.

She caught him looking back at her, his smile curving higher, and she hurried to avert her gaze to a distant treetop. "Perhaps a dark blue would be more favorable."

"Royal blue is my favorite color."

"Is it now?"

"Yes."

"Ah. Mine is emerald green."

"Could it be anything else, when you're an Irish girl?"

"Woman."

He cocked his head to one side. "An Irish woman. I stand corrected."

She nodded once, sharply, and released a shaky breath. "Well now, my lord, we know each other's favorite colors."

"A sound way to begin a friendship."

She looked up, and up a little more, to study his profile. He was quite tall. But then, so was the duke. Her brother was quite average when it came to height. What must it be like, to always be eye-level with most people's heads? She nearly asked him. Instead, she asked something more impertinent.

"Is that what you're up to? Trying to make us friends?"

"Have you any objection to such a thing? You are rather embroiled in a wager made amongst the people I hold dearest in the world. That gives you a sound step in that direction."

That creeping warmth came over her again. The one that always seemed to happen when the two of them were near one another for more than a moment. Did he feel it, too?

"A friendship with a future duke is nothing to sniff at, I suppose."

He laughed outright that time, a sharp, quick laugh that seemed to surprise him as much as it did her, given the raise to his eyebrows and his wide grin. "When you put it that way, I sound like an excellent catch. Or a rung in a ladder that would take you right to the top."

Ah, yes. They'd tread this ground before. When he'd mistaken her for one of his eager admirers.

She smiled through her wince, understanding him better now. There was reason enough for his caution. "I'd rather not think of people as things to be stepped on, my lord."

"Not even someone like me?" A hint of something else colored his voice. Made the humor sound melancholier than it had a moment before.

Perhaps he was used to people seeing him as nothing more than that rung on a ladder. As a duke's son, any relationship with him was desirable. He was quite near the top of all things English. The man could probably visit Carlton House or any other important home in England with no notice or invitation needed.

"Not even you, my lord," she answered gently. For a bare moment, she wished to reassure him. Offer him compassion. A man of his position and power needed neither of those things from her. Remembering that pulled her back to more reasonable thoughts. "Of course, if you offered me your hand to climb atop a horse, I'd gladly give you a step then. But otherwise, I'd rather keep my feet on firm ground."

She had to lighten the moment again. Serious topics were dangerous if she wanted to maintain a respectable distance between herself and the handsome English lord. Which she must, or else find herself in danger.

In danger of what, she'd rather not consider. Gossip, for certain. Though she had never much cared for what people thought of her. But there was another danger. One that she could feel coming ever closer whenever he turned his handsome blue eyes upon her.

His smile returned. "Did last evening go according to your wishes, Miss Frost? Did I make enough of a fool of myself?"

"No one there thought you foolish, though your grandmother

seemed to doubt your choice of dinner attire." She sighed, as though harassed. "Obviously, changing your manner of dress isn't enough to test your dedication to—as your friend puts it—enjoying yourself more."

"Andrew's definition of fun and mine are quite different." Simon examined the walking stick in his hands, his thumb rubbing at the silver top where she spied a large letter S. For his first name? Usually, men of his status carried around a symbol of their title, or the first letter of their title. His would be an F for Farleigh, or an M for his future place as the Duke of Montfort.

He saw her looking and held the stick out to her. "Would you like to see it?"

"Oh." Isleen raised both hands to ward off the offer, but instead found him placing the fashionable cane into her hands, which immediately dropped beneath its weight. It was much heavier than it looked.

"Careful," he warned, helping her catch it, his hands sliding close to hers along the polished black surface. His gloved hands brushed her bare fingers, and a shiver went through her. Once he seemed certain she wouldn't drop his strange accessory, he released the walking stick and stepped back a pace, clearing his throat as he did.

Was she not the only one effected when they stood that near? That trail of thought led to madness, for certain.

She turned the cane round in her hands, then held the head of it up to study the silver S. It wasn't set in the metal, but stood out from it, like a raised stamp or seal. "Is the S for your Christian name?"

"Yes. Simon. My father gave it to me as a gift before I left for Ireland."

"Why is it so heavy? The wood cannot be this weighty on its own."

Simon folded his arms across his chest, and the sleeves of his great coat pulled tight against his shoulders. "Make a guess."

There were only a handful of things it could be, given the man who carried it. "It must conceal something." She took the handle in one hand, held the length of it with the other, and gave a twist.

A quiet "click" was the only sound it made, and she raised her eyebrows in alarm and held the thing out to its owner. "Did I break it?"

He laughed softly as he accepted it from her. "No. Merely unlocked the secret." Then he pulled the handle and wood apart by no more than four inches, but it was enough for her to catch the shine of metal and a sharp edge.

"A concealed blade," she whispered, and tales of daring bandits and spies flooded her mind. "But why ever would you have need of such a thing?" And why had he shown her the secret?

"Why indeed." He slid the blade home again and, with a quick twist of the handle, she heard another soft click. "As you might know, Miss Frost, not everyone in Britain has a love for my family or the peerage." His smile was sad again. "I have reason enough to forgo the frivolity my friends enjoy."

Isleen couldn't let him linger on his morose thoughts. "While there is truth in your words, my lord, this is the very time and place to indulge in a little merriment."

"Hm." The sound was a hum of noncommitment. "Would you care to take a walk through the gardens before we go to Lambsthorpe, Miss Frost? Since we are already both outside. Is that merry enough for you?"

Isleen stuck her chin out. "It is not, my lord. In fact, I have another challenge for you."

His forehead wrinkled as he frowned down at her. "You do? So soon?"

"You forget, my lord, that I have no wish to lose. My only sure way to win is to set you on as many tasks as I can think, as you must turn down at least one if I am to avoid my fate beneath the mistletoe."

His eyes smiled even if his lips did not. "You are determined to avoid a stranger's kiss, aren't you?"

She let the Irish of her soul seep into her simple answer. "I am, and so I will."

"You better tell me the worst of it then." He tucked the walking stick beneath his arm. "What are you demanding of me today?"

He wasn't upset with her after the night before. For his silly clothing and the way people looked at him. His pride hadn't driven him to anger. Which meant she could try out the other things she had dreamed up after her foray into the schoolroom.

"Nothing too difficult, I can promise you that." She couldn't help grinning up at him, and he had the good sense to appear uneasy. The poor man. She almost felt sorry for him.

Almost.

CHAPTER 9

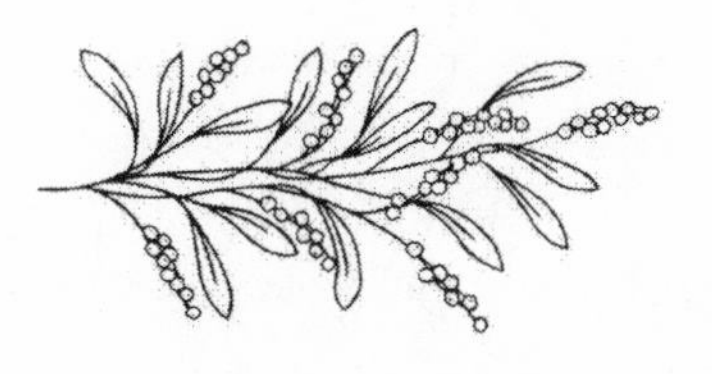

Simon waited, already on horseback, for the others to join him for their visit to Lambsthorpe. His black hunter waited patiently beneath him. The horse had already been well exercised with a morning ride. The trip down the hill and to the village was a mere stretch of the legs for the athletic creature.

But Simon's thoughts kept him fidgeting.

Miss Frost had somehow discovered yet another of his weaknesses, and she knew how to use that weakness to her advantage in their foolish wager.

Poetry had never been Simon's strong suit in his studies. First a tutor, then later schoolmasters and professors, had challenged him to write poetry. Not because he had a talent for it, but because all English schoolboys were expected to understand the creative arts. What better way to understand Shakespeare, Donne, or Wheatley than by forcing busy-minded youths to create their own versions of sonnets? Even if the meters were dubious and the rhyming scheme horribly skewed.

Matters hadn't been helped when a schoolmate of his had given him the *Manipulus Vocabulorum*, a two-hundred-year-old rhyming dictionary.

His Cambridge professor had not expressed the amusement that Simon had hoped for. But Andrew had laughed long and loud after reading the poem Simon had written. A poem about a maiden's eyes of 'green' and a particularly robust 'spleen.'

"Andrew," Simon muttered aloud, and the horse flicked its ears at him. Of course, Andrew had to be divulging all of Simon's secrets to the Irish woman. Well, Simon would have his revenge. Josephine wasn't above playing pranks on her husband, and he had plenty of ammunition to give her from Andrew's school days. "Then we will see if he finds it funny."

If the carriage driver heard Simon's muttering, he gave no indication of it.

Still, Simon pressed his lips together over all the words he wished to say. Dukes and future dukes didn't talk to themselves.

Voices echoed from the pre-guard room out into the December air. At last, the others had gathered. Luca, Emma, Andrew, Josephine, Isabelle, Rosalind, and Miss Frost came out together. The five ladies would ride in the carriage, while the two remaining men had their horses waiting to ride alongside Simon.

And hopefully, no one was in a talkative mood.

Luca and Andrew helped their wives, Miss Frost, and Simon's sisters into the carriage before they came out to mount their horses where the grooms waited.

Andrew came up beside Simon immediately, eyebrows raised to where they nearly disappeared beneath his hat. "What's this, Simon? Already outside? I didn't know you had such enthusiasm for a shopping trip."

"Not so. If I could, I would gladly skip." There. He'd done it. He'd made his first rhyme. And if it was slightly awkward, Andrew didn't seem to notice. He only chuckled and looked over his shoulder.

Rhyming. Why did she have to choose rhyming?

Luca joined them and nodded to the road. "Let us be on our way, gentlemen."

That didn't require any sort of response from Simon, so he nodded and nudged his horse forward. They managed to ride quietly until midway to Lambsthorpe when Luca started asking questions.

"Last year, I was not here for the first snow. When does that usually happen?" he asked, his Sicilian accent as evident as ever.

"Sometimes as late as January," Andrew answered. "But we've had a few storms and snowfalls around Christmas. Simon, when did we get snow last year?"

Simon did not grit his teeth. But searched quickly for a word. "December the twenty-eighth, if my memory is clear."

"Yes, it was after Christmas." Andrew sighed. "The children were happy it came before New Year's. James left a window open in one of the guest rooms—you should have heard the housekeeper's dismay over finding a snowdrift inside the house."

Luca chuckled. "It seems your brother gets up to mischief of every kind."

A strained smile was Simon's best response for a moment, but Andrew changed the topic before Simon thought up an acceptable rhyme to comment on that. *Only respond if you must*, he reminded himself.

Their party's arrival at Lambsthorpe did not set the town astir. Lambsthorpe was as old a village as the site of the castle, and it had always been inhabited by the families of those who owed their livelihoods to first the Earls of Montfort and then the dukes. It also served as the central place for all farmers and families within a five-mile radius to socialize, visit the market and shops, and attend church.

Even for all that, the village was small. A square of greenery with one large tree took up the center, with a main road and a second, smaller road on either side. In years past, the green served as a place for people to keep livestock safe and sound, where someone could always keep an eye out for thieves.

These days, the green was a place to have picnics and snowball fights when the weather changed.

Simon had always loved coming to the village. The people were familiar enough with the duke's family to not be overawed by their position in society, which meant Simon and Andrew could misbehave and still be taken to task by the local baker.

The village bustled with people today. In and out of shops went men and women from all rungs of society. Simon and the other men dismounted before the inn and public house, which was the best place to tie their horses.

The women waited for Luca to open their carriage door, and he helped each of them step onto the street.

Simon exchanged a look with Sterling and the other two guards who had accompanied them. Sterling gave a nod. He would move the carriage out of the way of the main road, and his men would follow the ladies at a discreet distance to keep an eye on everyone.

Josephine and Emma would both be aware of the extra precautions taken, but Miss Frost would think the servants remained at hand to carry parcels and whatever bits and bobs the ladies purchased.

"Are you men going to wander off to do your own browsing?" Josephine asked, approaching Simon and Andrew to take her husband's arm. "Or will you come with us to tell us how much certain fabrics and ribbons become us or match our eyes?" She fluttered her eyelashes at Andrew, who grinned unashamedly at her.

Miss Frost appeared at Simon's elbow, smiling at the exchange. "They make a lovely pair." Then she raised her eyebrows, though she did not once look at him.

He sighed. Of course she would test him. At least this was an easy one. "Yes, one can't help but see their affection and stare."

Her lips pursed. "Is that the best you can do?"

"I am terrible at poetry. I thought you knew." She had fixated on the challenge quickly enough. Andrew *must* have told her. "I wondered who told you." There. That rhymed too.

She started to snicker, then cut off the sound with a light cough. "Dear me. Well now. Remember, the moment you are caught, you must pay a forfeit."

He gritted his teeth and nodded. Surely she did not need him to rhyme that. But she smiled up at him, the look full of false innocence as she batted her eyelashes, her dark eyes flashing with humor. Oh, she expected a response.

"Miss Frost, I am a man of my word, therefore you must give me some credit."

She smirked. "That was a close one. Good luck, my lord."

The women had decided to step into Wilson's, a shop that contained bolts of cloth, hosiery, and everything related to gloves, hats, sewing, and anything else having to do with fabric. The men went across the way to the apothecary, who also sold tobacco, tea, and sweets.

The room smelled of herbs and wood polish, orange oil and tobacco. A heady mix of a thousand scents, some potent and some soft, filled the air so thickly that Simon always expected to see a fog creeping across the floor.

The shopkeeper and apothecary, Mr. Foster, hurried around his countertop to meet them. "Ah, welcome, my lords, Sir Andrew. What a pleasure to see all of you. How may I be of assistance today?" He looked directly at Simon when he asked.

"My father is out of his favorite pipe tobacco, to his dismay," Simon said, wincing.

"Ah, we cannot have that. I will send up an order at once." Mr. Foster withdrew a notebook from the pocket of his coat. "What else, my lord?"

"A variety of sweets for the school children, to calm the hoard." This was ridiculous. He felt heat rising up his neck. Someone was going to notice.

Mr. Foster nodded and made the notation in his notebook. "And anything for you, Lord Atella? Sir Andrew?"

Luca asked after mint pastilles; Mr. Foster would measure and fill a tin for him. Andrew asked after something with ginger in it.

"Ah, for something particular? Passing nausea, perhaps? Upset stomach?" Mr. Foster went behind his counter. "As a tea or a sweet? I find the sweets excellent in the moment, and tea better to take in more serious cases. Either way, ginger is an excellent way to calm a stomach."

"Some of both then, please. On my account, but have it sent to the castle. Except—perhaps a small tin of the pastilles as well?"

Mr. Foster shuffled about, measuring and tutting to himself while the men waited. He put their purchases in bags and tins and made several notations.

As they were the only three in the shop, they had the apothecary's full attention.

"Are you feeling unwell, Andrew?" Luca asked while they waited.

Andrew was studying a row of glass bottles filled with various small seeds. He answered somewhat absently. "Josie ate something that disagreed with her. Merely trying to ward off any other difficulties."

Luca made a hum of understanding. "How has it been, having her settle in at Bytham?"

At this question, Andrew turned on his heel and grinned at them. "Josie has said it's wonderful, and I have every reason to believe her. Instead of the army of servants someone like Her Grace would have to command, she has a small platoon of loyal men and women. She is free to entertain as often as she likes, which is almost never, and she spends most of her time in my office at her own desk. It seems the quiet life suits her best."

"I find the opposite is true for Emma." Luca chuckled and tucked his hands behind his back. "She flies through the rooms of the embassy every day, arranging parties, welcoming guests. I have told her she need not do so much, that we need not entertain so often, and she only laughs and plans another ball or dinner." He grinned with obvious pride. "Our home is always alive with people, and I think we are both satisfied. That is the right word?" He looked at Simon as he asked.

Simon winced and shifted. "It seems to fit, from what I just heard."

"Sounds like you're more than satisfied," Andrew put in. "It sounds as though you two are happy."

"Ah, yes. Happy is better." Luca grinned and seemed ready to speak again, but Mr. Foster took that moment to drop a final tin on the surface of his counter.

"Here we are. The small things you may take with you now, my lords and sir. I will send the rest up to the castle right away."

With the highest rank among them, it fell to Simon to answer for their little group. "Thank you, Mr. Foster, for your assistance and lack of delay."

From the corner of his eye, Simon saw Andrew cock his head to one side. Simon picked up the small pouch of sweets for the children and tucked it into his coat pocket, then shifted out of the way for the other two to pick up their filled tins.

Then he hastily led the way out the door.

"Where to next?" he asked. There were no rules against him speaking first. Miss Frost had only said he had to rhyme the last word someone else said to *him*.

Luca pointed down the lane. "The stationers, I think. I must purchase more ink."

"As must I." Andrew glanced to the shop where the women doubtless still perused ribbons and buttons. "Onward, men."

Simon had a moment to relax. Perhaps Andrew's look hadn't meant a thing. Except, the moment they stepped into the shop, he picked up a bottle of ink. "Ah. What think you of this, Simon? It looks purple."

Simon completely froze.

What in thunderation rhymed with *purple?* Simon opened and closed his mouth.

Luca stepped up to them to examine the glass bottle. "Why would you wish for purple ink? It seems unusual. Does a color like that have a particular purpose?"

So relieved was he not to have to rhyme the word purple, Simon answered perhaps too quickly. "It isn't a color for which I need a surplus."

Andrew put the ink bottle down on its shelf with more zest than necessary, making the other bottles clatter and the poor shopkeeper wince. "Ah ha! I knew you were doing something strange. Is this something to do with our wager?"

The forfeit might be worth it if he could stop speaking with such absurdity. He crossed his arms over his chest and glowered at his closest friend. "You ought to know, handing my life over to a near stranger."

Luca had caught on and laughed aloud. "I hear it now. How long has this been going on?"

"Since an hour before our trip had begun." Simon had to alter his pronunciation to make that one work, but he didn't much care anymore.

At this admission, Andrew started laughing. "Rhyming. How clever. You were always a terrible poet in school."

Simon looked out the front window, his mind already on his forfeit. That didn't stop him from his accusatory words. "I'm surprised you didn't pick up on it sooner, since you gave Miss Frost the idea."

"However would I have done that?"

When Simon looked at Andrew to challenge the question, he knew at once his friend meant it.

Andrew wore a curious frown, as he studied Simon. "I had nearly forgotten about that rhyming dictionary incident. Though it was exceptional. Remind me to tell you of it, Luca. You will appreciate the story."

"If you did not tell her, then who did?" Simon rubbed the back of his neck above his collar and cravat. "It is an odd challenge to issue without knowledge of my history."

"Not really," Luca said with a shrug. "Every woman I know has a favorite poet. Perhaps that is where she found her inspiration. A general love of verse." Then he clapped Simon on the arm. "I must find my ink. Excellent attempt at rhyming, my friend."

As he walked away, Simon dropped his arms to his sides, and he looked out the window again. No sign of the ladies. They were all still inside. And one of them would now ask him to do something else ridiculous.

"There is more to it, isn't there?" Andrew's tone was positively joyful. He was enjoying Simon's torture, even if he hadn't masterminded more than the initial wager. Which Simon still doubted his friend came up with alone.

"A forfeit, paid as soon as I was discovered. I had hoped to at least make it to dinner."

"Better see to it, then." Andrew laughed again. "What will she do to you this time?"

A nervous coil wound itself tighter in Simon's stomach as he thought on the triumphant grin Miss Frost would soon wear. And the feeling wasn't entirely unpleasant.

That thought startled him.

How daft must a man be, to look forward to interacting with his tormenter? Granted, not all taskmasters were as lovely as the dark-haired, fair-faced Isleen Frost. A man, any man, would enjoy her company. Not only for her wit, but for her pleasant manners, her fine features. And—and why was he cataloging her good qualities like this?

"Simon?" Andrew's voice came vaguely from behind him. "Are you feeling well? You look...addled."

That was the right word for it. Miss Frost's ability to disconcert him multiple times, while still appealing to his sensibilities, had addled his brain. He answered Andrew in as unconcerned a tone has he could. "I am perfectly well. Merely preparing myself for Miss Frost's next devious instruction. I had better report my failure to her, to get on with things."

He made his departure swiftly, giving Andrew no room to speak.

"I must find the ladies. I will catch up with you both soon." He walked out the door and cast one helpless glance up at the cloudless sky before he stepped into Wilson's shop. Heaven help him, going into the den of women. Especially with a triumphant Isleen inside.

Isleen held two fans in her hand, one of mint-colored lace and the other a cream-colored fabric with hand-painted evergreens on one side. She didn't necessarily *need* a new fan, but with the upcoming Christmas Eve ball, having a new one for the occasion would be lovely.

"Which do you think is softer?" Josephine asked, having appeared at Isleen's side, holding out two scraps of fabric. "Emma says the cotton will grow softer with washing, but this muslin is more what I am used to sewing."

"It's what the intended purpose is that matters most, I'm thinking." Isleen had taken off her gloves when they first started their exploration of the shop, to better handle the tiny buttons she had sorted through. She felt both pieces of fabric with forefinger and thumb. "Hm. Lady di Atella is right about the cotton. It will grow softer with time. I think it must be sturdier than the muslin, too."

"I might need to get both, then." Josephine bit her bottom lip and wandered away, swatches still in hand.

The bell over the shop door rang, and Isleen reflexively turned toward the sound.

Swiping his hat off his head, Simon Dinard walked into the shop that was—predominantly—filled with women. The exceptions to this were the footman who had accompanied them, standing in one corner, and the shopkeeper.

Simon stood still for a moment at the edge of the room, looking about. There were shelves everywhere, even in the middle of the store. And tables piled with goods, including elaborate hat stands. Ribbons hung from rods attached to the ceiling.

The room was a jungle of muslin, ribbons, and feathers.

The women in the shop became aware of Simon as his gaze landed on Isleen and stopped. Her stomach flipped as he charged forward, not taking his eyes off hers as he marched through tables and seemingly ignored everyone and everything else.

Somehow, having him storm toward her like a lion ready to pounce made her blush.

"Miss Frost." His tone was firm, the words quiet. "I owe you a forfeit."

She gulped. Then stuttered out, "Ha-have you been discovered s-so soon?" Bumps raised along her arm as she failed, quite miserably, to sound amused.

"Yes. I have." He leaned closer, his voice going lower still. "What will you do with me now?"

Her jaw fell open. Never had any man said such a suggestive thing to her. Given his glower, he did not at all mean the words the way they had sounded to her addled mind. Which meant she had interpreted them entirely wrong. Without reason. *Oh dear*.

Her throat tightened, making it impossible for her to answer his question. Even if her mind hadn't been lost to confusion. Words were altogether impossible. Rather, she caught herself studying his eyes. The brightness of them. The way his long nose set so perfectly between those eyes. And how very nice his mouth looked, despite the curious tilt to one side...

Emma appeared at the man's elbow, a tight smile on her face. "Simon? What are you doing to poor Miss Frost?"

"Asking her a question," he answered, not moving an inch. At that moment, Isleen finally saw the flash of his smile—those lips she had studied turned upward, but only just. Of course he wasn't angry with her. He was playing up the emotion for his friends. Letting them think he resisted all their attempts at enlivening his life.

"You are making a scene, more like," Emma whispered. "You look like you want to eat her."

Isleen swallowed. Yes, that interpretation of his expression felt right. The man looked as though he might bite her, or taste her, or...or something terribly ungentlemanly.

That admonition took hold of him, and his eyes widened. Simon rocked back on his heels and let his smile stretch freely. "I beg your pardon, Miss Frost. Did I make you uncomfortable?"

Not as uncomfortable as she was about to make him. "The apology isn't necessary, my lord. However, I have an idea for how you can make it up to me."

She reached into her reticule and pulled out a slim volume of poetry. She had brought it for this very moment. "Choose one of these to memorize and recite later."

With a distrustful look, he took the book from her and read the words embossed on its cover. "'The Poetical Works of the Late Thomas Little.' What is this?"

"Thomas Moore's book of poetry." She grinned up at him with more confidence than she felt, having a moment before been certain he *did* want to taste her. "I think you must enjoy it. He is, after all, an Irishman."

"And when is my recitation?"

"I haven't decided." She tipped her chin up. "In the meantime, perhaps you could help me decide something else."

His eyebrows drew together sharply, and he took another step away from her before tucking the book into his coat. "What would that be?"

"Should I get this fan, or this one, for the Christmas ball?" She snapped both open and held them out for him to inspect. And she appreciated the defensive effect they had, keeping him back.

Simon stared at her, incredulous, and Emma looked between them with obvious confusion.

"The one with the trees," he said. Then bowed to both women. "We will meet you for tea in half an hour, ladies." He left the room, nodding politely to the clusters of shoppers as he went. The bell chimed again as he opened it and went out into the bright autumn day.

"You had better call me Emma from now on," the lady beside Isleen said.

"Really? Thank you. But why?" Isleen put the mint-green fan back upon the table. "Why now, I mean."

"Anyone who can make Simon act like that, in public, is worthy of friendship." Emma picked up the fan that Isleen had discarded and turned it over, not meeting Isleen's gaze. "I haven't seen him wear anything other than a dignified mask when in public. Not for years, anyway. I think we had better keep you close, Miss Frost."

At this, the Irish woman released a shaky laugh, a thrill of happiness rolling through her. "Please. Call me Isleen."

A friendship with the countess was exactly what she had wished for, but the way it had come was rather disconcerting when she thought on it. As she paid for the fan that Simon had picked out, studying the painted trees, her heart skipped with worry.

What did it mean, that she had caused Simon's mask to fall in public? It signified something to his friend. Something that had made her grow fonder of Isleen with immediacy. And the way he had acted, as though he had forgotten or did not care that the other customers in the shop had watched their interaction with wide eyes.

Had he meant to embarrass her? Or had she, somehow, truly done something worthy of note? The puzzle troubled her more than she liked. Even after they had enjoyed tea as a group, conversation flowing easily. Simon didn't give her a single look of significance. Which bothered her still more.

Perhaps it hadn't meant anything, that strange interaction in the shop. Isleen certainly did not spend a moment trying to discover why that conclusion disappointed her.

CHAPTER 10

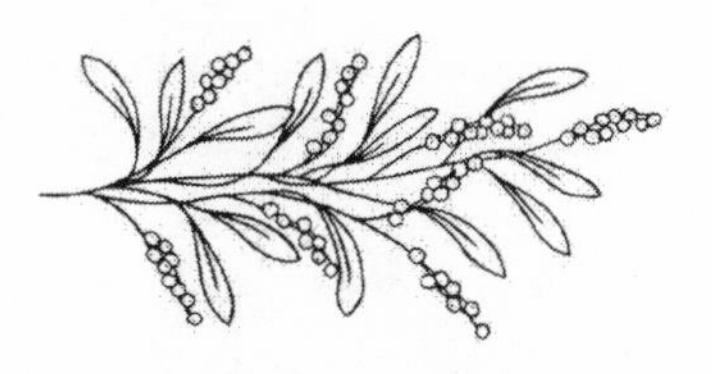

An enormous sneeze shook the schoolroom as Isleen opened the door. The sound, unexpected and loud as it was, startled her into placing her hand over her chest. "Goodness, me. What goes on in here?"

The children sat around a table, books before them, and they looked up at Isleen with varying expressions of boredom. The children's schoolroom overlooked the front terrace and down into the duchess's gardens, with the large windows Isleen had grown used to seeing in the rest of the house. This kept the room bright and welcoming, as did the various things on tables and shelves. Books, a dollhouse, miniature soldiers and animals, a beautiful globe, colored paper and ribbons, small canvases of works by the children.

It was quite lovely.

"I beg your pardon, Miss Frost." Mrs. Robinson's voice was muted, her nose obviously blocked. She sniffled with a handkerchief pressed over her face. "Ever since that walk in the wind yesterday, I have not felt entirely well. But we are managing, are we not, children?"

"I suppose," Lord James grumbled.

Fiona closed her book. "I think Mrs. Robinson ought to rest, but she keeps denying herself so much as a cup of tea."

"Oh, fiddlesticks." Mrs. Robinson put one hand on her hip. "There is nothing wrong with me. The wind stirred up too much dust, is all—" She cut herself off by turning around to sneeze into her handkerchief again.

"You see?" Fiona said, crossing her arms. "She needs a nap. You would make me take a nap, wouldn't you, Isleen?"

Lady Isabelle closed her book, her delicate fingers resting on its cover. "Mrs. Robinson, you are being dreadfully stubborn. And we do so love you. Won't you rest? If only to make us worry less." She was certainly the oldest and most mature of the children sitting around that table.

"I think I must agree with Lady Isabelle." Isleen came all the way around the table, standing near the governess. Mrs. Robinson had a caring way about her, and she had done well taking Fiona and Lord James in hand. Isleen could certainly take time out of her day to show the woman kindness. "Why not pop into your room for a nap, Mrs. Robinson? I can look after the children for an hour or two."

"Oh, I couldn't possibly allow you to do that, miss." She sniffled again. "You are a guest. And the children are my responsibility."

"Very true. But I came to spend time with my sister, and there is no need for both of us to be here. Please, Mrs. Robinson. I can keep them entertained. And when you wake, you will be right as rain. I am certain of it. Of course, you must take tea before you rest. Why don't you see to that while I settle in with the children?"

Mrs. Robinson hesitated again, but finally nodded. "All right. But no more than an hour. I will fetch my tea myself. And if you need anything, fetch me at once, if you please." She pointed to the doorway that led to the nursery, and through it to her room.

A governess was never far from her charges, even when sleeping. Isleen's heart went out to the woman. Whether she held her position out of necessity or for the joy of it, Isleen did not know. But it could not be an easy position. Even in a place with employers as considerate as the duke and duchess.

As soon as Mrs. Robinson had gone, Isleen pointed at the books on the table. "Is anyone still wanting to read?" The remaining open books snapped closed, and four pairs of eyes were on her. She laughed, and said with a merry voice, "I thought not."

"What are we going to do now?" Lord James asked, seeming more perturbed than relieved. "It's too cold to go out."

"First, I thought I would tell you how your scheme with the rhyming went." Isleen took an empty chair from the table and pulled it out, sat, and smoothed her skirts out around her. "Would you like to know how that went yesterday?"

Isabelle groaned. "You really did it? You teased Simon about his poetry?"

"Oh, better than that." Isleen didn't even try to hide her wicked grin. "I made him speak in rhyme. Until someone else realized it, of course, because then it wouldn't be any fun. But he did it. Without complaint, I might add."

Lord James snickered, then leaned back in his chair. "I knew that would be a jolly good trick."

"Andrew and Simon used to tell that story about the poetry all the time," Lady Rosalind said, an amused smile on her face. "Who caught him?"

"Sir Andrew, of course. He told me all about it at dinner last evening." Isleen picked up a red piece of paper from the middle of the table. "What is this for?"

"Paper chains." Fiona lifted the stack to show her the white underneath. "We were going to make them today, to hang up wherever Her Grace wants them as part of the 'festive decor.' Mrs. Robinson said."

"We hung them on the tree last year," Lady Isabelle put in. "Paper chains, red ribbon, and gingerbread biscuits."

"And the toy soldiers," Lord James put in.

Isleen stood again and went to the shelves. She had spied a small pot with sheers inside. She brought the thing to the table and put it down, taking a pair of scissors for herself. "I still cannot think why anyone would wish to bring a tree indoors."

Rosalind took another pair of scissors. "It is great fun, to see it decorated. And we don't bring it in every year. Three years ago, we had an ice sculpture instead."

"An ice sculpture? I haven't seen many of those." Isleen started cutting a strip of paper.

"It was a swan." The little boy sounded disappointed, even then. "Why couldn't it be a lion or an elephant? We see swans all the time."

Isleen didn't bother hiding her smile. Lord James had such an interesting way about him. He seemed an intelligent child, happy to have a lark, but he was still so young it made moments like this one amusing. "Maybe that makes them an easier subject to chisel from ice." She nodded to the little pot. "Take some scissors, Lord James. Help us prepare the chain."

He did so without complaint. "Will you tell us a story, Miss Frost? Fiona says you have a lot of them."

"And she tells the best stories," Fiona added, somewhat smugly.

"Fi, we mustn't boast."

"It isn't a boast if it's about someone else. And you *do* tell the best stories. They're always interesting."

"Do tell us a story, Miss Frost," Lady Isabelle put in. "Please. It will make the time pass faster."

"Oh, very well. Let me think." She snipped at the paper, once, twice, thrice, and another strip landed in the small pile she had started. "What about the story of Finn McCool accidentally gaining all the world's knowledge? Long ago, when Finn was still young..." She spun out her story, as it had been spun for centuries among the Irish, while the children listened, and their scissors snipped the colorful paper into strips.

The book of poetry Miss Frost had gifted him contained more love poems and satirical pieces about romance than Simon liked. But he'd pick one, as she bid him, memorize it, and give a grand performance. Likely in front of dozens of guests, if she timed his recitation for maximum humiliation.

Not that he thought her unkind, or even the least bit conniving. But she took her role as his challenger seriously. And, though he'd never admit it, he had found her tasks clever, and even enjoyable. Apart from the rhyming scheme.

He put the future worry from his mind and focused on the moment. An afternoon free of the charming Irish woman would clear his head, and his tangle of emotions he hadn't any intention of sorting out. Spending time with his siblings, especially his brother, would ease both his mind and heart.

He had tucked the apothecary's sweets into the pocket of his coat, made his way through the family's corridor, and down the hall to the children's wing. Their bedrooms, nursery, and schoolroom were along one hall, all on the same side, airy and bright. Sometimes, he wished he'd grown up in the castle rather than entering it for the first time at fifteen years old, when his mother judged the renovations complete. His other siblings had spent more of their childhood within its walls, young as they were.

He stopped at the doorway to the schoolroom and prepared to knock, then he hesitated when a burst of laughter sounded through the door.

Mrs. Robinson had seemingly prepared an amusing lesson for the day. Hopefully, she wouldn't mind him interrupting. At least for a short period of time.

He opened the door, knocking lightly on it as he stepped into the room. "Good afternoon, Mrs.—Miss Frost?" She sat at the children's worktable, directly opposite the doorway, a delightful smile turning her full lips upward.

"Lord Farleigh. Welcome." She rose from the table to curtsy, as did her sister, but his siblings remained where they were, snipping at paper with scissors. "I am afraid Mrs. Robinson isn't here at the moment."

"Oh." He looked from her to the bent heads of his brother and sisters, noting the covert glances of the latter. "I came to visit the children. If you do not mind, Miss Frost? I have no wish to intrude."

She blinked rapidly and lifted her hands, opening and closing them as she spoke. "Not at all. Shall I go, then?"

"No. No, you can stay." Why, after he said those words, did he catch a strange expression passing between his sisters? Rosalind even giggled. "You may as well see how I treat my horrid younger siblings."

His words had the desired effect, summoning James to arms. His brother might look to Simon with hero-worship some days and with competitiveness others. Whatever the case, Simon tried to be ready. Though it had been months since the two of them had spent a proper amount of time together.

James leaped up and charged directly at Simon, releasing a battle cry that would make Wellington himself puff up with pride. Knowing his brotherly duty, Simon dipped his shoulder down and caught James, then stood and hefted his little brother up like a sack of flour.

If sacks of flour squirmed and squealed in delight. "No fair, you're still much taller than I am!"

"And stronger. And better behaved, too. Have you ever seen such a wild thing, Miss Frost?" He turned in a quick circle and James laughed again. Then Simon stopped and took in the Irish woman's expression, wondering what he'd see.

Both hands were over her mouth, and her dark eyes had widened to enormous proportions. But she wasn't horrified. She was laughing. "To be sure, he is a frightening creature, attacking you as he did. Without provocation, too."

His sisters and hers watched, eyes wide, but said nothing. "Ladies, I am terribly sorry you had to see this ignoble display."

James struggled, then went limp. "Fine. You win. I give up. Again."

As soon as the boy's shoes hit the ground, he grinned up at his brother. "You won't always be the biggest."

"We have yet to see the evidence of that. Who knows? You may stop shooting upward tomorrow." He put his hand on James's shoulder, pretending to scrutinize the boy's height. "Perhaps I ought to place a yoke on your shoulders, to keep you from growing upward."

Miss Fiona snorted, and James stuck his tongue out at the young miss. Simon ignored the behavior. He hadn't come visiting the nursery to scold. James likely had enough of such things from others.

Instead, he offered an olive branch. "Would anyone here be interested in some sweets?"

"Oh, yes please." Rosalind rose from her chair. "Did you bring enough for our guests?"

"Of course. What kind of man would I be if I left them out? Not a gentleman, surely." He reached into his coat pocket for the small parcel and tossed it to Isabelle, who caught it with a gasp.

"Simon, you mustn't throw things at ladies." She appeared most indignant.

He winked at her. "You caught it, didn't you?"

She stuck her lower lip out at him, then sighed and unwrapped the paper and twine to reveal pastilles in various hues and sizes. James left Simon's side to look down at the sugar-glazed treats, and Miss Fiona leaned closer to get a look at them, too.

Miss Frost came around the table to his side of the room and stopped when she stood beside him. Her eyes held a measure of curiosity, so he was not entirely surprised when she tipped her head to the side and asked, "Do you visit the schoolroom frequently?"

"When I am at home, I try to make a habit of it." He crossed his arms and leaned toward her. "Though it hasn't been as often as I like of late. I cannot let them forget they have an older brother looking after them."

Her dark brows drew together. "I suppose I should have guessed as much after our tour of the castle. You and Lord James seemed thick as thieves."

He shrugged, but didn't hide his grin. She'd been paying attention to him even then? The thought gave him far too much pleasure. He tucked his hands behind his back. "What of you? Have you spent much time in the nursery?"

Isleen tucked a wayward strand of hair behind her ear. "I have come to see my sister every day. I make certain she isn't driving your family's governess to distraction."

Ah, yes. The missing governess. "Where is Mrs. Robinson? Is everything all right?" Not that he minded her absence. Because Miss Frost was present.

Why had he wanted to avoid her? He couldn't remember in that moment.

"Mrs. Robinson is a touch under the weather. I encouraged her to take tea and a nap. I am certain she will feel well again after a little rest." Isleen rocked forward and back on her heels, looking over her shoulder at the children.

"And you are keeping the rapscallions in line in the meantime?"

"As you see." She motioned to the table, where paper had been properly slashed for chain-making.

"They can do this any time." Simon nodded to the table. "Especially if Mrs. Robinson needs them to keep still."

"Have you a better idea for keeping them occupied?" she asked, chin up. "I would love to hear it. Or perhaps you could entertain us."

"Simon can't tell stories like you do," Lord James said, appearing in front of them with a large, cherry-flavored sweet. He popped it into his mouth. "You should hear her stories, Simon. Magic fish, children who turn into swans, swords that talk."

Miss Frost's cheeks pinked; she looked a great deal more innocent and young when she blushed. He liked it. Nearly as much as he liked the more stubborn, confident tilt of her chin when she argued with him.

"They are all old stories from Ireland. Every child knows them where I'm from."

"You tell them the best, though," her sister piped from the table. "You always have."

Simon pressed his hand to his temple. "Let me think on this. Obviously, I don't dare tell stories, knowing I have a master of the art present." He paced away, then back again. "A most complicated difficulty. How does one entertain children—"

"And young ladies," Isabelle said, her fifteen-year-old indignation obvious in her tone. Another year and she'd likely be let out of the school room for their parents' parties, even if she wasn't out in society yet.

"And young ladies," he agreed with an apologetic bow. A game from years ago came to mind. One he had not played since Josephine, Emma, and he had played. Would Isleen take part? When he glanced at her, raising an eyebrow in challenge, she tilted her nose in the air and smirked at him.

Nothing daunted the woman.

He made his declaration with a grin. "We will go on an expedition."

"An expedition?" Miss Fiona sounded incredulous. Her little nose wrinkled in an expression he'd seen her sister wear. "How? We're stuck inside this castle."

"Fi," her sister warned. "That's incredibly ungrateful to speak so to our hosts." She looked up at Simon with a wince. "I beg your pardon—"

"No, she's right." He folded his arms and looked pointedly down at Miss Fiona. "You haven't been nearly anywhere else in a week, with most of your time spent in this room. Even the nicest of places can grow dull." He grinned and gestured to the door. "So we escape."

"How does one play at an expedition?" Isabelle asked, her nose in the air. At fifteen, she likely thought most games beneath her. He certainly had, at her age.

"Everyone picks a feat for us to accomplish. It must be something that sounds adventurous, and we do each of those things. I have obviously begun the game by suggesting an escape from your prison." He went to the door and opened it barely enough to stick his head out.

One of the guards was down at the end of the hall, dressed in servants' livery. Simon pulled his head back in. "Ah, there is a watchman in the hall. We must distract him to make our escape."

Rosalind tittered behind her hand. "Simon, we can't sneak past the guard. Papa wouldn't like it."

Simon caught a pinched expression on Miss Frost's lovely face. The mention of the duke and guards may have perplexed her. He pretended it was part of the game. "I will distract him. The rest of you go down the hall, to the servants' stairs outside Isabelle's room. Go when the guard's back is turned, and make your way upstairs to the library."

Miss Fiona and James exchanged an excited glance, and Rosalind appeared rather curious. Isabelle stood with a put-upon expression.

"Oh, very well. If you insist. Though you are being quite silly, Simon."

"And without any help from me," Miss Frost murmured softly, her lips barely moving. He was perhaps the only one that heard her, and when he looked to see her expression he caught an amused smile on her pretty face.

Was that a gleam of approval in her eyes?

His stomach tightened, not unpleasantly, and Simon had to turn away quickly.

"James, you be lookout. Watch for my signal." Simon opened the door and slipped out, then whistled loudly as he rambled down the hall toward the guard. Tibbs was the man's name. And he remained expressionless until Simon stood directly in front of him.

"Tibbs."

"My lord." He bowed. "Might I be of service?"

In a whisper, Simon explained himself. "Yes. Please turn around and look out the window behind you for a moment. I am facilitating an escape from the schoolroom."

The guard raised his eyebrows and did as he was told. "Do you need anyone to follow you, my lord?"

"No." Simon glanced over his shoulder to see his brother peering out the door. He waved with his hand behind his back, and James slipped down the corridor. The others followed, with Miss Frost bringing up the rear and closing the door behind them. She gave him a curious glance before following the children in their quiet, hurried steps.

He'd wondered, for one horrid moment, if she'd stay behind. Not every woman grown would play such a game with children. Somehow, Mrs. Robinson falling ill had been a great stroke of luck for Simon.

Not that he wished for the governess's poor health.

But he'd certainly take advantage of it.

He turned his grin back to the perplexed guard. "No, we will stay inside the castle. I'll return the children to the nursery in under an hour."

"Very good, my lord."

Simon left the guard, calling over his shoulder as he went, "Thank you. As you were, Tibbs." He strode down the corridor after Miss Frost and his fellow adventurers.

CHAPTER 11

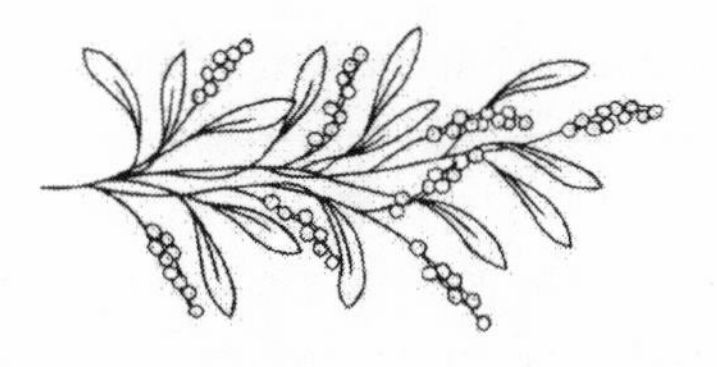

Isleen and the children waited for Simon in the library. James had insisted they keep in the spirit of Simon's game and had them hide behind the furniture. While she felt fairly silly, crouched behind a couch with Fiona, she couldn't deny the look of excitement on her sister's face.

"Do you think they'll show us their secret passages? James says they're everywhere, but that he can't show me a single one."

"I doubt that we will see secret passages." Isleen had to smile at the very idea. "If they do exist, I imagine only the family is allowed to know their locations."

"Bother." Fiona briefly stuck out her bottom lip in an immature pout, but hurriedly pulled it back in. "Tis fun to run around all secret-like, though."

"Indeed, it is." Isleen peered over the edge of the couch when she heard footsteps. And there came Simon into the room, theatrically looking over his shoulder before sweeping his gaze across the library. When he saw her looking, he had the audacity to wink.

She blinked in surprise. Here was an entirely new side to the duke's heir. A playful side she had suspected was buried far deeper than it seemed, given his friends' insistence that Simon never enjoyed himself.

"James," he stage-whispered, and his brother popped out from between a globe and pedestal.

"Here I am, Simon. Are we safely away?"

"Thus far we are. What should we do next?"

James came out into the middle of the room, and his sisters peeked out from behind their chairs. "I think we must have a goal. And I suggest the pastry chef's kitchen."

Lady Isabelle put her hands on her hips. "Of course you would want more sweets. But the pastry kitchen is on the ground floor, and we would have to go through the main kitchen to get there. And past all the servants."

"We could send one person to gather the pastries," Fiona said, surprising Isleen. "After the rest of us get as close as we can."

The idea seemed to please Simon, given the large grin that appeared on his too-handsome face. "An excellent suggestion, Miss Fiona."

Perhaps it was the children who had wrought this change in him. Or at least brought this aspect of his character to the surface. He had entirely devoted himself to their amusement. And Isleen rather liked it.

"If we are going to the kitchen, the fastest way without getting caught would be down to the Earl's Landing, below the gallery, across the Carriage Corridor, and down the ballroom stairs. No one uses those stairs most of the time."

"The Carriage Corridor is right above and open to the Guard Room," Isabelle argued. "We would have to keep quite low to the ground and not make a sound, or the guards would hear."

"Dear me. I had no idea the lot of you were this talented at sneaking about." Isleen grinned when they turned to look at her, then waved them back to the conversation. "Sorry. Didn't mean to distract. Do carry on."

"But the Earl's Gallery stairs are so long," James added. "It will take forever to get down them without being seen."

A bolt of inspiration struck Isleen, and she could not help the wicked smile that overcame her face. Indeed, she narrowed her eyes and focused on Simon as she said, "Not if we use the banister."

He tipped his head back. "The banister, Miss Frost?"

"The banister, Lord Farleigh." She came around the side of the couch and grinned at the young ladies. "We can manage a quick slip down a well-polished stair rail, can we not?"

Lady Isabelle appeared doubtful, but Fiona and Rosalind nodded at once.

"It will be frightfully unladylike. And what if someone below should see?" Lady Isabelle shifted from foot to foot and looked down at her clothing. "I do not think I am dressed for it."

"If I go first, will you try?" Isleen asked. "I know a trick to it for skirts, and we can make your brothers turn their backs at the top of the stairs while we go down."

"Miss Frost." Simon's voice sounded somewhat strangled. "I am not certain this is a good idea."

"Nonsense. I can manage. Can you not?" She whirled around to face him and let the challenge hang between them, her eyebrows raised and her arms crossed over her chest. "Surely, you aren't concerned about being caught."

He glowered at her, but there was no real ill feeling in his eyes. Only surprise. "Is this one of your challenges?"

"Should it be?"

Lord James sighed. "Either way, we need to get moving. Secret expeditions are no fun if you stay in one place too long."

"Come on, Isleen." Fiona took hold of her sister's hand. "We can show them how it's done."

Isleen grinned at Simon, and off she flounced with her sister to the Earl's Gallery. So-called because portraits of the Earls of Montfort (before the king bestowed the title of duke to the first of their ancestors, she'd learned on her tour) lined the corridor which opened to the floor below, accessible by a long, wide staircase.

Once Simon and James had turned their backs to the stairs, Isleen made quick work of showing the girls how to slide down the rail while wearing long skirts. She hadn't done it herself in ages. Years and years, in fact. But she wasn't about to let that stop her from having a little fun.

"You sit sideways," she told them. "As you would on a horse. Or, you gird up your loins." She winked as she gathered her skirt from behind, pulling it up between her legs in the front, making the fabric rise until her knees were uncovered. "To straddle the rail for safety."

Simon made a sound of distress but did not turn around. "If anyone witnesses you with your 'loins girded,' we will all catch a share of trouble."

"Pish." Isleen went to the rail. "Alternatively, you can merely bend over so it is your waist upon the rail. But I don't recommend that." She looked below, to ensure no one was about. And she tried very hard not to notice how high above the ground she stood. Then she sat sideways and leaned toward the rail, riding side-saddle, a hand on either side of it. "I will be lookout once I reach the bottom," she said, and down the banister she went.

The well-polished wood surprised her, and her speed was more than she bargained for. Woosh, she went, right down the steps. And thankful she was, too, that the rail was wide enough for her to keep well-balanced. When she hit the floor below, her feet nearly went out from under her, but she stumbled a few steps and righted herself.

"Bless me," she muttered, her mother's favorite expression of surprise. She'd much rather have used the more colorful terms her brother at times indulged in, but one could only manage so much unladylike behavior at a time.

Isleen peered about and down the hall, and even over the rail to the guardroom. One of the servants looked up at her, a large man she'd heard the duke call *Sterling*. She smiled cheerfully at him, and he went back to staring ahead blankly.

She whisked herself back to the foot of the stairs and looked up. "Come down. I'll catch you."

Fiona came next, straddling the rail instead of attempting to sit sideways. Likely the safer of the two options. Down she came, and Isleen caught her sister around the waist. The two of them giggled and shushed one another.

Rosalind braved the journey next, using Fiona's method, and they helped her come to a soft stop. Then Isabelle, chewing her bottom lip, came to the top of the stairs and stared. She looked back at her brothers, then squared her shoulders and faced forward again. She tried Isleen's tactic and likely was a fine horse woman, given how well she kept her seat.

Her sister helped her land, and the two of them collapsed to the floor in a fit of quiet laughter. They nearly fell all over each other in their mirth. And suddenly, Isleen stopped thinking of them with their titles. They were only children, playing a game together.

"I have never done that before," Isabelle whispered.

"Me neither." Rosalind shivered, then rose from the floor. "It feels dreadfully wicked. Grandmother would faint if she saw us."

"She wouldn't," Isabelle argued. "She'd lecture us in French until *we* fainted from shame."

James landed next and glowered at all of them. "I can hear you all the way upstairs. Hush."

His sisters hid their smiles behind their hands, but their shoulders still trembled with their laughter.

Isleen peered upward, watching as Simon stood with hands on his hips at the top of the stairs. After all of them had slid down the banister, he would do the same. She didn't doubt him for a moment. But she certainly didn't want to miss it.

He heaved a sigh, saluted her mockingly, then threw a leg over the banister and came down at top speed. Isleen had to leap out of his way as he landed, his feet hitting the carpeted floor with an enormous clomp!

She brought her hands together in silent applause. "Well done, my lord."

He gave her an overly dramatic bow, his smile slight and his eyes sparkling. "I could hardly refuse a challenge issued by a lady such as yourself, Miss Frost."

The children had already started making their way across the Carriage Landing, a long open corridor, toward the other side of the house. Isleen slipped closer to Simon as he watched them comically stoop to half their heights, even Isabelle, and slink softly across the carpet, occasionally freezing as though they had heard something and then continuing onward. Giggling softly all the while.

"This is a marvelous game," she whispered.

He looked down at her, one eyebrow arched upward. "Did you think me incapable of providing entertainment for children?"

"Not incapable. I merely did not take you for one who would spend time on such a thing."

"You know little about me, it would seem."

She had to nod her agreement to that. "Every time I learn something new, I like you the better for it." She smiled, then pointed to their path. "We had better get started on this leg of the journey."

"After you, Miss Frost."

"Thank you, Lord Farleigh." And away she went, looking over her shoulder, surprised to find him bent in half like the rest of them. She couldn't deny her pleasure in joining in the game, folding herself over as much as she could and still tiptoe across the floor.

Thus far, every challenge she had given Simon for the wager he had met easily. Even though they had all been things meant to check his pride and provide amusement for others.

Maybe it was time to rethink her strategy. Maybe, instead of trying to make him do things he would not like, she ought to think of things he would genuinely enjoy. Because he wasn't a stuffy Englishman as she had thought when they met.

He had only forgotten what it meant to enjoy himself.

SIMON ADJUSTED HIS CRAVAT USING A MIRROR HANGING above the hearth. The guard room was mostly silent, except for the quiet tap of shoes as a guard-turned-footman walked from one side of the room to the other, lighting candles.

Simon picked up his walking stick from where he'd leaned it against the stone frame. Tonight, they dined with a local gentleman who had been friends with Simon's father for years. A few hours out of the castle would likely be refreshing for their guests. They hadn't left once in the week they had been present. If the children needed a reprieve in the form of their game that afternoon, the adults would certainly appreciate the same.

Somehow, Simon had escaped the day with only that single challenge issued by Miss Frost. Sliding down the banister. A thing he hadn't done in over a decade.

And he had enjoyed it, too.

He gave the stick a twirl in his hands, then tucked it casually beneath his arm. He couldn't help grinning as he thought of Miss Frost sliding down the stair rail. He wished he had seen it for himself. Which was a highly inappropriate thought in need of a quick dismissal.

Taking in a deep breath, he appreciated the notes of cloves and cinnamon mingling in the air, and the softer, sweeter smell of apple. His mother always ordered the medley of dried apples and spices hidden about the room to make for a welcoming scent.

"Faith, am I that early?" a quiet, feminine voice asked from the stairway.

Simon turned on his boot heel. Lady Dunmore descended the steps to the guardroom all alone. He bowed slightly to her as she approached and made her curtsy to him. "My lady. You are not too early. I believe my mother intended everyone to gather in the Regent's Gallery prior to coming down for the coaches. I am here to make certain all is prepared when they descend."

"Ah." She turned and looked at the stairs. "Would it be terrible if I waited with you? The idea of going back up all those stairs is less than welcome." She smiled at him with a gentleness he wouldn't dream of denying.

"Of course. We will send a man to let them know you wait with me." He met the gaze of a footman near the steps and motioned with his chin upward. The footman bowed and went on his way to carry the message to the duchess. "There. Easy as that. Do you wish to sit, my lady?" He motioned to a chair tucked against one wall.

"No, though I thank you for the thought. I am unequal to the task of stairs at the moment because I spent the better part of this afternoon following your mother through the gardens, all the way to the straw hut."

"That is a fair distance." He had spent hours of his life roaming the gardens and woods, following paths artfully grown over with moss or barely visible game trails. The castle's grounds extended around it in large, beautiful swaths of forests and fields. "My mother is so used to the terrain, I imagine she gives the ups and downs little thought."

"The grounds are beautiful. I can see why she treasures them so." Lady Dunmore joined her hands before her, her posture relaxed. She wore a fashionable dress of dark blue, with black and gold feathers in her hair, and long blue gloves on her arms where they peeked out from her evening cape. Her ensemble was simple but certainly appropriate for a woman of her age and status.

She shared her eyes with her daughter, he thought, seeing how dark they were in the flickering light.

Her daughter. Miss Frost. He sighed. "May I ask you an impertinent question, Lady Dunmore?"

She blinked at him in obvious surprise. "Bless me. Can an earl ask an impertinent question? Go on and try, my lord."

He looked down at the black-and-white patterned floor, considering how to best phrase his question. "Your daughter. Miss Frost." He hesitated.

Mrs. Dunmore sounded amused. "She is mine, of course. But I thought we made that clear on introduction."

He looked up, surprised, then couldn't help his chuckle. "Ah, you are where she gets her sense of humor then."

"Perhaps. Isleen is entirely her own person in many ways, yet I cannot deny some influence here and there." Her eyes crinkled at the corners as she spoke. "Before you ask your question, I would like to thank you for treating her so well. I have noted your attention to her, as well as how your friends have brought her into your circle. I must thank you for that, my lord. Isleen makes friends wherever she goes, but she was nervous about doing the same in England."

He hadn't expected a comment such as that. Had he gone out of his way, in any way at all, to make Miss Frost feel at home? Not especially. Even though, after their first conversation, he had found he enjoyed her company. Even her forthright way of speaking. The woman did not mince words, yet she never spoke an unkindness.

"I hope she feels welcome." He shifted uncomfortably. "I realize that not all English and Irish get along."

"Tis a truth," Lady Dunmore said with a sad shake of her head. "They fight as cats and dogs on many a point."

"Yes. Which brings me to my question. Miss Frost seems cautious when it comes to the English. Not afraid, or hateful, but...stand offish. I wonder if she has a specific reason, or if there is something I might do to amend the feeling?"

Simon had the sense that if he could understand the wall

between them, he might find something else behind it. More than a witty Irish woman. More than her pretty face and bewitching, dark eyes. His curiosity had kept him thinking on the feeling that she held back a part of herself. A part he would dearly love to see.

Lady Dunmore's smile faded, and she lowered her gaze to the floor. "I am not certain it is my place to be telling you, my lord. Though I suppose it isn't any great secret." She sighed, the sound heavy with maternal worry.

"I have no wish to pry, my lady." Simon spoke with all the sincerity he felt. "Merely to better understand a guest in my home. You needn't reveal anything."

"It appears to me that you have a kind heart. I will tell you a piece of it." She nodded to herself, then lifted her eyes to meet Simon's gaze. "My daughter had herself a sailor, years ago. An Irish lad who joined the British Royal Navy in 1813. His captain was an Irish man, too, as was most of the crew. After a skirmish, their ship took on water. Another ship saw their distress and sailed on without offering assistance. It was a ship with an English captain who had exchanged words with the Irish. That captain used his personal hatred to justify leaving the Irishmen to their fate."

Dread pooled in Simon's stomach. This would be reason to be suspicious of the English, indeed.

Lady Dunmore turned a little away from him, walking to the hearth to study the fire. Likely taking a moment to collect her emotions. "You can guess how the tale ends."

"Miss Frost's sailor didn't survive."

"True enough. We learned the news a fortnight before Christmas." Her shoulders slumped. "Isleen has a gentle heart, and she dearly loves to be among people. But she's careful now. I imagine as a duke's son, you know how difficult it is to trust another's motives."

He'd told Isleen about his own failings with trusting others, and his suspicions that anyone who approached him wanted an association for their own gain rather than honest friendship. Yes, he understood. But he didn't have the level of pain tied to his distrust that Isleen must.

Isleen. He hadn't thought to call her by that name before. Miss Frost seemed to fit her so much better. But he could not think her cold or distant. Not anymore. Not when he'd seen how she could laugh, her kindness toward servants and children, her eyes bright with curiosity, and now knowing the secret hurt she held in her heart.

The anniversary of her heartbreak approached, too. Would he see evidence of that pain in the coming days? The poor woman.

A hum of voices sounded above, along with laughter and a smattering of footsteps. The others were coming downstairs to leave.

Lady Dunmore raised her gaze to his, her expression questioning, and he nodded once. "I will say nothing of our conversation, my lady. I promise."

She smiled her thanks, and then he offered her his arm as the others appeared on the stairs. "May I escort you to the carriage?"

"Thank you, Lord Farleigh." She took his arm, and he realized she was much shorter than her daughter. The top of her head barely came to his shoulder. Isleen must have inherited her height from her late father.

"It is my honor, Lady Dunmore." He meant it, too. She had honored him with her trust. And he would not break it. But he would watch Isleen with new eyes and understanding.

What would he discover about her next?

CHAPTER 12

"What do you have in store for me today, Miss Frost?"

Isleen looked up from the globe, blinking in some surprise. She hadn't heard Simon enter the library. She stood in the middle of the room, examining the enormous globe the duke kept at its heart. The thing was so large, if it opened on one side, she could likely crawl in and sit quite comfortably.

She had been measuring the distance from Ireland to England, her finger covering and uncovering the channel of water between them, when his question startled her.

"Have you a great desire for torture?" she asked, keeping her expression neutral. "Or is there something else you are after?"

He tipped his head to the side and came deeper into the room, his blue-eyed gaze unwavering. "You haven't asked a thing of me since sliding down the banister. This morning, when I didn't see you at breakfast for the second day in a row, I thought I had better check that I had satisfied that last requirement."

"And what if I said you hadn't?"

He stood on the opposite side of the globe from her, staring over the polar ice cap. "I suppose I would have to make another go at the stair rail."

That made her smile. “Two whole days of nothing from me, and here you are wanting more. I thought you would like the reprieve.”

“It merely makes me anxious. I’m certain you are taking the time to build to something more sinister.”

She laughed and looked down again at Ireland, no more than a green outline on the globe. Her fingers traced a line southward, to the sea where she had lost Sean. She sighed. Old hurts never really went away, even if they became less tender over time.

She gave the globe a gentle spin. “I admit, you’ve left me a bit uncertain. Everything I’ve thrown at you, you’ve taken on as though you liked it. The clothes, the rhymes, acting a bit foolish at dinner. It’s beginning to look like I’ll be kissing a stranger come Christmas Eve.”

He stilled the globe, then turned it the other way round. “It isn’t all that bad, you know. I’ve given a kiss or two beneath the mistletoe.”

“Have you now? And how did those ladies take it?” She didn’t look up at him. She kept her eyes on the continents and oceans rolling away beneath her. “Did they gnash their teeth or swoon at your feet?”

“Swoon at my feet?” He shuddered. “A dreadful thought. No, they batted their eyelashes and flirted, and one of them hinted that I could have more if I followed her out into the dark corridors.” He winced and looked down. “I apologize. I shouldn’t have said—”

“It isn’t necessary. I know about the games people play when they think they can bend the rules.” She shook her head, imagining a person so brazen as to proposition a lord. “It sounds as though I ought to fight harder to avoid that horrible tree parasite you English are all so fond of.”

He stilled the globe again. “It is a harmless tradition.”

“Trees in the house and unwanted kisses,” she murmured, looking up at him, liking the way his dark hair fell across his brow. “Can the English get any stranger?”

"Probably," he admitted with a wry grin and a shrug. "You're a little strange yourself, Miss Frost."

"Am I now? In what way?" she challenged, leaning closer, her dress brushing against the globe. "I've been naught but a perfect guest."

"Very true." He leaned closer too, and suddenly the globe between them did not seem so large. "But you tell stories about children turning into swans and boys gaining all the world's knowledge from a fish."

At that she had to laugh. "Children's tales from my country, Lord Farleigh. They are not all that unusual."

"Perhaps not." He came around the globe to her side, and her laughter stopped at once. He stood so near. Her cheeks warmed despite her wishes to remain calm. "Miss Frost, would you come with me on a ride?"

"Ride? With you?" She stared up at him, hating how breathless her question sounded. They were less than an arm's length apart. And he was especially handsome today, dressed in a silver waistcoat and dark blue coat that brought out the color of his eyes.

He winced and ran a hand through his hair, mussing it more than before. Her fingers itched to reach up and correct it, brush it from his eyes at least. The better to see that beautiful blue...

"Sir Andrew and my sister are coming, too," he admitted. "It wouldn't be seemly for the two of us to ride out alone. Not that I think you would want to be alone with me, that is." He stumbled over the words and stepped back, and she immediately felt as though she had lost something. A moment, perhaps, that could have been more. "Do you wish to come? We asked Emma, and she laughed at us. She's never liked cold weather."

She stopped his rambling as quick as she could. "Of course. I'd like to go riding with you." She took in a quick breath to hastily add the rest. "And your sister. And Sir Andrew. Thank you."

What had happened? They were talking in fits and starts like children. Simon had started it, throwing her mind into a muddle.

Yes, she'd blame him for the sudden awkwardness of conversation.

Except when his smile appeared, slow and somewhat crooked, as though her answer pleased him, she quite forgot what she wanted to blame him for. A smile like that shouldn't be permitted. Not when it had the ability to warm her as though she stood outside on a summer's afternoon. "Excellent. Is an hour from now enough time?"

Enough time? For what? Oh, yes! He'd asked her to ride with him.

"More than plenty."

The answer was easy enough, so long as Darrie hadn't disappeared down the hill like she had the day before. The maid had gone to the village with some of the castle's servants for a shopping trip. It was good of the household maids to invite Darrie, a stranger in their midst, so Isleen hadn't minded the maid's disappearance until the dinner hour.

"Good. Then I will meet you in the guard room in an hour." He bowed and strode away, a lightness in his step that she found quite endearing. Squashing the impulse to giggle, Isleen went to the window. Perhaps she needed a taste of fresh air to rid herself of these strange impulses.

Isleen pushed open one of the windows, and the hinge moved without protest. The moment she put her face over the sill, a gust of cold air stole her breath away.

Quick as a wink, she pulled the window shut again and rubbed at her arms. The cold air shocked her fanciful notions of summer sunshine away. And looking up at the sky, she noted the gray clouds hanging heavily above.

Simon wanted to be out of doors, in *this* weather?

How very odd. Doubtless, he knew the weather in his home country better than she. If Sir Andrew and Lady Josephine were to ride as well, they likely saw nothing wrong with the gray sky and brisk wind. The exercise would do them all a world of good, most likely.

She hurried on her way, planning to layer woolen stockings and as many other layers as she could get beneath her riding habit. Today, warmth was of far greater importance than the figure she'd cut on horseback.

"A RIDE ON A MORNING AS BITTERLY COLD AS THIS ONE IS NOT the best of my plans," Simon muttered to himself.

"Did you say something?" Andrew rode beside Simon, their pace slow as they followed the ladies down the hill.

"Cursing the weather is all." He stared at Isleen's form, noting the jaunty angle of her hat, meant to mimic a man's in shape. Though hers had a rather whimsical holly berry twig and leaf tucked in its band. It seemed her disdain of winter foliage didn't extend to that particular bush.

Andrew snorted, a sound more expected from the horses than a baronet. "This was your idea. People think that *I'm* horse-mad, but I don't go dragging people out of doors when their noses are likely to freeze and fall off."

"You could have said no when I invited you." Pointing out the obvious to Andrew never helped an argument much. Simon ought to know better after all their years of friendship.

"You asked me in front of Josie and made a point of telling us Miss Frost was coming along. You knew that would perk Josie's interest, and I could hardly say no to something your lovely sister asks of me."

"You used to say no to her all the time." Simon tried to sound severe but given how happy his sister and best friend were with their match, he was bickering for the mere sake of bickering.

"That was before I fell in love with her."

Simon cast his most disapproving glare at his best friend. "Love seems a poor excuse for breaking habit. You two once seemed barely tolerant of each other, and now you're in love. I cannot understand it."

"Wait until your turn," Andrew warned with a knowing grin, completely unrepentant. "You will turn your life upside down for the woman who holds your heart. I'd be willing to wager on it."

"No new wagers, if you please. I'm still caught up in the middle of your last game."

Andrew sounded far too smug when he said, "Judging by how intently you stare at Miss Frost at this very moment, it is not an entirely unpleasant way to pass the time."

Simon didn't bother to deny it. That would certainly make his friend suspicious. Instead, he noted, "The holly is an interesting touch to her hat. Think we ought to add a sprig to ours, to appear more festive for the season?"

"Don't be daft. What man would adorn his hat with anything like that? My grandfather put feathers in those blasted tri-corn things you see in portraits—"

"I have a tenant farmer who still wears those."

"Really?" Andrew perked up. "I thought they had all been burnt, as they deserved."

Simon laughed and Isleen looked over her shoulder at him. The way her dark eyebrows were raised, a few black curls loosely framing her pretty face, and the curious smile upon her lips made his heart jump. He smiled back at her, reflexively, and she turned frontward again. He most certainly did *not* sigh. Not with Andrew watching him closely.

"You like her," Andrew said.

Simon's heart raced, but he remained outwardly calm. "Of course I like her. She is an excellent addition to our house party this year."

"So is her brother, but I don't see him invited to ride with us. In fact, I think the only reason Josie and I are here is to keep your intentions less obvious." Andrew nudged Simon's shoulder with his riding crop. "And you know what I meant. You don't merely like her. You *fancy* her."

When the blood rushed to warm Simon's neck and cheeks, there weren't any excuses to disguise the blush. It was too cold for his cheeks to heat for any natural reason. Maybe Andrew wouldn't notice. "That is a strange conclusion to jump to. I have known her for less than a fortnight."

"And I have known you for nearly all our lives," Andrew reminded him. "I can count on one hand, not even using all my fingers I might add, the number of times I have seen you show this sort of interest in a lady."

"You are daft," Simon muttered, ducking his head beneath a low branch. They had made it down the hill and nearly to the village.

"You say that because you aren't sure how she feels about you yet." Andrew smirked. "I can't even venture a guess about her feelings. Besides women being less obvious creatures than men, I don't know her well enough. I must apologize for being little help to you there."

"Andrew." The single word came out as a warning.

The baronet had the gall to put on an innocent expression. "What? If you keep on like this, her brother will ask you your intentions. Or she will. I have the feeling Miss Frost prefers to speak for herself on most occasions."

Simon hunched forward and gave his horse a nudge to outpace Andrew. If he'd wanted advice on his relationship with Isleen, he would've asked for it. As it was, he couldn't say even to himself what he hoped for from their acquaintance. But he did like her. That much he knew.

He'd hoped, foolishly it would seem, to spend more time speaking with her on during their ride. Josephine hadn't given him a chance, keeping Isleen all to herself. And now he had Andrew's suspicions to sort through.

As he caught up to the ladies, on Isleen's side, he slowed his horse and offered her a wan smile. Then he spoke across her to his sister. "Josephine, your husband is tiresome."

"I have always said so, you will recall," she answered with a shrug. "Yet I am glad to see we are finally in accord." Then she grinned and slowed her horse, ostensibly to let her husband catch up to her so they might ride alongside each other into the village.

Isleen's smile brightened as she turned her head toward him. "They have a unique relationship. I cannot imagine what force of nature finally brought the two of them to the conclusion they loved one another rather than the opposite."

"It is still a mystery to me. One day they were as enemies on the battlefield, the next they were announcing their impending marriage." He shook his head over the state of things. His last quip slipped from his lips without his full consent. "Love is ridiculous."

Isleen took no offense, thankfully. She laughed. "I don't know if I agree with that. Though it certainly is nonsensical. Have you never been in love?"

What a question. And a personal one at that. He ought to refuse to answer. He should change the subject. A fortnight's acquaintance wasn't enough for such conversation. And yet, hadn't her own mother told him only a few evenings before of Isleen's experience? That gave him the advantage in the conversation. An unfair one, at that. He settled for the most honest answer he could give. "I don't think I have."

Then they both fell silent until they were through the village. From the corner of his eye, he saw Isleen studying him with undisguised curiosity. On the other side of the village, they came to lands of open meadows. Perfect for riding at a faster clip. For exercising the horses. Or outrunning his own confusing thoughts.

Why had Andrew confronted him with things no one had any business knowing?

Because he *did* fancy Isleen Frost. And knowing she had loved before, so deeply she had seemingly yet to recover enough to find love again, twisted his heart painfully. And it was strange and ridiculous for him to feel this way about her after so short a time.

Spending time alone with her no longer felt wise.

When they left the road for the meadow, Simon looked at Isleen, meeting her gaze directly. "Enjoy yourself, Miss Frost. This may be the last good ride before the weather turns." Then he kicked his horse's flanks, shouting a command for haste, and rode quickly away from his guest.

CHAPTER 13

When Simon had issued his invitation, Isleen had imagined more time spent at his side. The disappointment that had sunk into her stomach when he rode away without looking back worried her.

Why did she care that he hadn't wanted to spend his time with her?

Simon had invited her to be a companion to his sister, so he could spend time with his friend. That made perfect sense. If Isleen had misconstrued his invitation, she had no one to blame but herself.

Josephine stayed at a gentle canter, and Isleen kept her company. Though equal to a more vigorous exercise herself, she didn't wish to leave the other woman's side. The men rode ahead at wicked speeds, until they disappeared over a hill and out of sight.

The cold air whipped around the ladies, and they stayed warm only by keeping their horses moving. Heat from the animals and their own exercise protected them from feeling the bite of the December air. Still, the earth smelled of ice and the only trees still green were the pines.

Squirrels chattered in the trees, and winter birds called to one another as they flew quickly from air into the bare branches.

"The animals seem upset about the weather," she called to Josephine.

"Can you blame them?" The younger woman laughed and tilted her head back to look at the sky. "They haven't a warm hearth to return to after being out."

Isleen grinned at her friend. "Tis true enough. I am looking forward to a hot cup of chocolate when we are through."

They crested the hill that the men had ridden over long before, and finally caught a glimpse of them again. Simon and Sir Andrew were barely within sight but had turned around to gallop back toward the women.

Simon cut a fine figure on his black horse, in his blue coat. He rode like he belonged in a saddle, the movements graceful despite the power in his steed's legs and chest. Her heart fluttered dangerously as she admired his form.

Handsome and charming, it would be easy for any woman to fall in love with such a man as he.

Isleen took in a painful breath.

She'd let her guard down. She had vowed, after Sean's death, to keep her heart open. To look for joy and experience life as he would have wanted her to do. Even if it opened her up to danger or pain.

But that didn't mean she had to like it, especially when she fooled her ownself. Simon Dinard, heir to a duke, didn't have interest in a little Irish nothing like her. If her brother wasn't a politician, their family would never have been invited to the duke's home. They wouldn't even fall beneath his notice.

A baron and a duke were worlds apart. A baron's sister and a duke's son, even more so.

The first drop of rain fell against Isleen's nose. The cold water made her shiver and pull her horse up short.

She looked upward at the clouds, realizing the world around her had grown darker when she had been sure it was only her own thoughts that had dimmed the sunlight.

"Rain," Josephine murmured. "We had better turn back before it gets worse."

As though the sky had heard the lady's words, the droplets fell faster. And faster. And as the men approached, they wore worry on their faces.

Josephine released a tightly held breath, and it came out in a puff of steam. The temperature was dropping, too.

"We need to seek shelter," Sir Andrew shouted when they were within hearing distance. He pointed with his riding crop to the sky behind him. "It's coming down in sheets!"

Isleen looked up and saw what he meant. The rain fell thickly in the distance, and it crept closer to them, turning the world gray. She looked at Simon as he approached, and her heart reacted to the grim expression he wore with an excitable leap.

Completely the wrong reaction.

"I doubt we can outrun the rain if we make for the castle." Simon's horse side-stepped as though impatient to run again. "Not safely. We should go to the Blooms' inn."

"We should hurry, Josie." Sir Andrew's eyes stayed on his wife. "This isn't weather I want you caught in."

"Then let's stop chattering about it and move." Josephine turned her horse about, as did Isleen.

They rode back the way they had come, the raindrops keeping pace with them. Josephine beside her husband, ahead of Simon and Isleen.

Simon said nothing to her as they rode, not until they arrived in the village. The rain fell faster than before, making the skirt of Isleen's long wool riding habit dark with the damp.

The earl dismounted quickly, then held his arms up to help her down. Isleen leaned forward, her hands going to his shoulders, and his on her waist. He guided her from the saddle to the ground, and then the two of them froze.

They stood close. Closer than they had before, holding onto one another. Simon stared down into her eyes, his own dark and uncertain, his lips turned down in a worried frown. "Get inside quickly. Warm up."

Then he took the reins of her horse and disappeared, following his friend. She stared after him a moment, wondering if he'd felt the strange pull toward her that she felt for him.

"Hurry, Isleen," Josephine called, snapping Isleen out of her stupor. Josephine was already at the inn's door, pushing it open.

Following quickly, Isleen realized the inn was also a public house. The sign swinging above the door had a white peacock upon it, the words *The Pale Peacock* written beneath. She hurried through the door, and as it swung shut behind her, she closed the door on thoughts of Simon, too.

Isleen welcomed the warmth of the public house the moment they walked inside. They were shown to a private, upstairs parlor. But Isleen glimpsed the public room full of patrons before they went up. It seems they weren't the only ones seeking out shelter before the storm grew worse.

"I do not usually mind sitting in the public room," Josephine told Isleen, settling in the chair in the quiet room. "But I am glad for a little peace just now. I have always loved visiting the inn. You will love their apple tea and biscuits."

"Do you think I might have stew instead? I think my insides need as much warming as my outer bits." Isleen moved closer to the little wood-burning metal stove in the corner. She rubbed her hands together to try to warm them. "When do you suppose the air developed such a bite to it?"

The thump of boots on the stairs alerted them to new arrivals, and when the door swung open, Sir Andrew and Simon entered the room. They made their way swiftly to the stove, removing their gloves and hats as they came.

Isleen retreated to the table to sit, narrowly avoiding a brush of shoulders with Simon. He barely looked at her. Whatever had caused his strange silence in her presence, she did not like it. It was as though their blossoming friendship had wilted overnight.

"It doesn't look good, Josie." Sir Andrew sat down next to his wife, his forehead creased with concern. "The rain is more ice now, and it's falling fast."

Simon released a weary sigh as he sat in the last empty chair, between his sister and Isleen. "Better we are caught in it here than halfway home. Though I can't imagine the rain will let up anytime soon."

A woman of middling age entered the room, a tray on her hip and a broad smile making her expression quite pleasant.

"Your lordship. My lady. Sir and miss." She curtsied before coming further in, removing plates of biscuits from her tray to the table. She put down a large, hot teapot, too, above a small tea candle. Then she put cups before them. She moved with efficiency and energy.

"Mrs. Bloom." Lady Josephine leaned forward with a friendly look. "It is so good to see you. How are you? How is your family?"

"We are well and happy, my lady. And sure happy to have you here again." She nodded to the large window overlooking the street. "Especially if it means keeping you out of that unpleasantness. What would His Grace say, if you'd have tried to make it up the hill in that?" She tsked and swept to the fire, opening the little door to add in more wood. "What more can I bring to the table for you, sirs and ladies?"

"Have you any hot soup or stew?" Josephine asked before Isleen could. "Perhaps rolls? You have always made such delicious rolls."

"Don't be lettin' your fancy cook find out you like 'em so much," Mrs. Bloom said, her cheeks turning pink. "After word got to him how you felt about my gingerbread, he came down the hill in a huff, wantin' to exchange recipes."

Sir Andrew laughed. "I can understand why you wouldn't want a visit from him again."

"Oh, he's all bluster, but he scares my daughters somethin' fierce." She chuckled. "We've a nice roast beef stew and fresh bread. I'll bring you up a fine, hot meal in two shakes of a lamb's tail."

Josephine nodded. "Thank you, Mrs. Bloom."

Then the four of them were left to themselves, though they heard the sounds of conversation drifting up from the room below. The crackle of the fire, the room growing warmer, gave Isleen reason to relax into her chair.

A gust of wind blew the rain into the window, and it crackled as ice met glass. The daylight dimmed, and Simon and Andrew both frowned at the window.

"I haven't seen weather turn this fast in ages," Simon murmured, pushing his hand through his damp hair. "Do you remember the storm a few years ago? We were stuck up at the castle for days."

Andrew nodded grimly, but Josephine glowered at her brother. "Are you worried we will be trapped at the bottom of the hill instead? Come, Simon. Stop looking so morose. Even if it is a terrible inconvenience, we are warm and safe. We will be fed. And even if it takes a day or two before we can get back up to Clairvoir, we will return unharmed."

"You are too chipper about this, Josie." When Andrew spoke, his tone was strained, and it was only then that Isleen took a closer look at his concerned expression. There was a tightness about his eyes, a tense look to his posture, that spoke of more than worry. There was a protectiveness there, too.

Isleen glanced at Simon, wondering what he made of this exchange. His eyes were averted to the window, his brow drawn down, his lips pressed tightly together. It seemed he was either as worried as his friend or else preoccupied by something else entirely.

To be sure, it was sweet to see a man so protective of his wife. But something niggled at Isleen's thoughts that told her there was more to it than that.

"And you are too dour." Josephine's smile softened. She laid her hand over her husband's on the table. "I am well and unworried, Andrew. I promise."

Mrs. Bloom appeared again, with a much younger version of herself following behind. "Beth, put the cutlery in place like I've shown you."

The girl beamed at her mother before putting on a frown of concentration. She laid out spoons, forks, knives, and squares of linen while her mother came behind her with bowls of thick, meaty stew. Another girl, older than the first, came into the room with a basket full of rolls and a dish of butter. After they arranged the feast on the table, they disappeared again.

Simon moved first, taking the basket of bread and offering it first to his sister and then Isleen, before helping himself and passing it to Andrew. It was the longest Isleen had ever heard him remain silent. Not that he chattered overmuch, normally, but he usually made at least some attempt at conversation.

"Has the weather frozen your tongue, my lord?" Isleen asked, her voice soft even though only the four of them were in the room, and all three of her companions had certainly heard her question. "Or are you unwell? I cannot think why else you would stay so silent."

His lips briefly quirked upward, but the smile died before it truly formed. "I have a lot on my mind."

The unspoken *and I am keeping it to myself* made her heart sink. Had she done something to offend him? Surely, he could not be upset with his friend or sister. Given the look the married couple exchanged, heavy with concern, they didn't understand the reason for his quiet either.

Silly Isleen, she told herself as she spread butter on her bread. *Not everything is about you. If a duke's heir has a lot on his mind, as he says, it's likely to do with his position in the world. Not an Irish interloper.*

Yet his staying quiet continued to prick at her heart, as the freezing rain continued to patter at the window. She finished her stew as quickly as good manners permitted, focused on satisfying her stomach rather than her curiosity.

"I love the sound of rain," Josephine murmured. She had nibbled at her bread and took only a few small spoonfuls of her stew. But she closed her eyes with an expression of contentment, all her features soft.

Her husband's pinched brow relaxed somewhat as he looked at her. Isleen lowered her eyes, surprised at the intimacy one single glance could hold. No one could doubt Sir Andrew's devotion and love for his wife. As exuberant and jovial a person as he was, he had a tenderness for his wife. His heart clearly belonged to Lady Josephine.

Many years ago, someone had looked at Isleen that way. And for the first time in a very long time, the remembrance overcame her good spirits. A burning in the back of her throat warned of oncoming tears. Tears that had no place at this private table, among new friends, and a husband who worried about his wife.

She rose from her chair abruptly, not meeting anyone's eyes. "Pardon me," she murmured, then made her escape through the door and down the stairs.

The noise from the public room hit her at the same time as the added warmth of more bodies in a single place, and the heavy smells of the kitchen's pies, stews, and bread. All of it wrapped about Isleen, and her emotions squeezed her heart tighter still.

She went to the front door, her fingertips brushed the handle, and for an absurd moment she thought the bracing cold would be a blessing. But good sense prevailed when she looked through the window beside the door and saw how dark the world outside had become. Everything had vanished from view—the road, the shops on the opposite side of the street, the trees in the distance—hidden behind heavy curtains of white.

The icy rain had changed again, this time into heavy snowfall.

Isleen left the doorway, but she did not venture up the stairs again. She walked into the public room, where men and women sat at half a dozen tables, and on benches along the walls, laughing and talking as though attending a party.

"Oh, miss. Take my chair, if you please." A man by the fire stood and pointed her to his seat. The person nearest him was a girl, no older than fourteen if Isleen guessed right. "Laurel won't bite, will you, daughter?"

The girl wrinkled her nose up at her father, then smiled at Isleen. "Yes, join us, miss. Have you just come in?"

Isleen didn't hesitate to come forward, a welcome from strangers better than returning upstairs with her emotions as strange and unsteady as the snow whirling about in the wind.

"I did not, thank heavens." She took the man's chair while he fetched another. "I am Miss Frost. I was upstairs with friends until now. I came down to see the state of things. Do storms often come on this suddenly? Or is this a special treat?"

The girl's smile grew as Isleen spoke. "Oh, you're Irish, aren't you? I heard there were Irish guests at the castle, and I've met a few of the servants here in town. I'm Laurel Nelson. My papa's farm is three miles south of town. We came to buy ribbons today, but the weather..." Miss Nelson shook her head. "It caught everyone unawares."

"That it did." Mr. Nelson had returned and sat down in his newfound chair. "I ought've known better. Last time we had a spell like this, Laurel was knee-high. Still. Should've seen the signs."

"Miss Frost is one of the duke's Irish guests, Papa," the girl informed him with a wide grin.

And there, among people who spoke cheerfully of the weather

and farming, Isleen's emotions stopped rippling and she breathed easily once more. Trying not to think of the people sitting in the room above, and what they must think of her hasty and uncalled for exit from their company.

CHAPTER 14

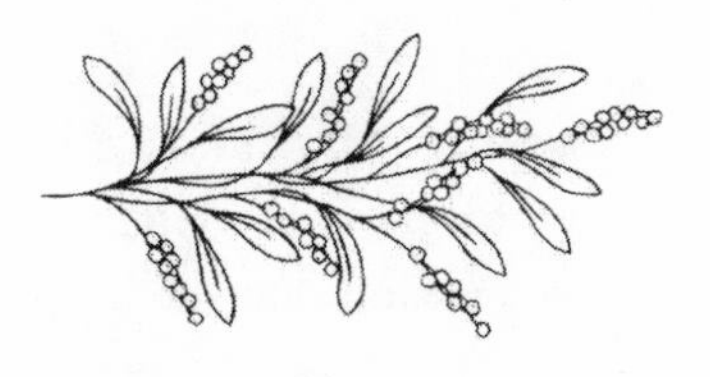

Simon had stared after Isleen in some surprise. She'd disappeared out of the room before he'd even had the chance to rise from his chair. But he did stand up as the door closed behind her, ready to go after her. His sister's words stilled him.

"I think you better leave her be, Simon."

"Are you going after her?" he challenged.

Josephine shook her head slowly. "No. I am going to sit here like a reasonable woman and wait for her to return. Clearly, she did not wish for any of us to follow."

"What's the matter with her?" Simon asked, looking from Andrew to Josephine. "Do either of you know?"

Andrew snorted. "I have my suspicions." He crossed his arms and leaned back. "The fact that you have no idea goes a long way toward confirming them."

Josephine shot her husband a look of warning. "Andrew. No meddling."

"Wouldn't dream of it, Josie-love." He picked up her hand and kissed the back of it. "Should I ask Mr. Bloom about a room for you? I won't say you look tired, as the last time I did you gave me quite a lecture. But I will say that if you want the rest, I wish you to take it."

With a little sigh, Josephine shook her head. "I am fine, Andrew. I promise. But we will likely need a couple of rooms for the night, if they haven't already been claimed. I think it best Isleen and I share one."

Simon stared at them both, incredulous. "Are neither of you concerned for Miss Frost?"

Josephine blinked at him. "Of course we're concerned. Isleen has come to be a friend. I like her very much. But she is obviously out of sorts. I have the impression that she isn't one to easily speak of her emotions, though she makes free with conversation about nearly everything else."

"That she does," Simon muttered, lifting his eyes to the beams in the ceiling. Isleen Frost had spoken to him of politics, religion, botany, love, child-rearing, Ireland, poetry, fashion, and a dozen other topics with great interest. But she did not often speak of herself.

After his conversation with her mother, Simon understood why. At least in part. How could anyone bear to have their heart so wounded and still go on with a smile?

It troubled him that she remained unwed and unattached to another. A woman so full of life as she, with her wicked smiles and bright laughter, deserved more.

Had men tried, and failed, to secure her heart? Perhaps she didn't want to love again. Or couldn't.

He'd brooded too heavily over those questions and had watched her behavior all day in hopes of finding some hint as to the state of her heart. Was it missing? Was it whole? Instead of finding an answer, he'd only succeeded in shutting Isleen out of his own thoughts and feelings.

A quarter of an hour passed, with Andrew and Josephine trying to draw Simon into conversation he didn't feel like having.

Isleen did not return. And Simon couldn't stand her absence from the room a moment longer.

"I will go ask about rooms," he said as he stood from the table, and his sister and best friend looked up at him with startled expressions, as though he had interrupted a conversation. Perhaps he had. He hadn't been paying attention to them for several minutes.

He left before they could call him back and shut the door with a hard snap behind him. He went into the main room, his eyes searching out a dark red riding habit rather than the innkeeper's apron-clad form.

He found Isleen at once, beside a fire, with a small crowd of people around her. Her eyes gleamed happily, and she gestured gracefully with her hands.

He knew that look.

She was telling a story, and her audience listened raptly.

He stayed in the doorway, tucked halfway in the shadowed corridor, his shoulder against the corner. And he watched and listened as best he could. Perhaps she hadn't been as distressed as he thought when she left the room.

Perhaps she had only needed to get away from him.

"Niall of the Nine Hostages wasn't always High King of Ireland," she said in her sing-song way. "But in vision, the bard Torna knew Niall must one day come to the throne. Of course, the king's wife wasn't having it. She had fathered four sons for the old king, and she demanded a successor be chosen. The king had no desire to choose from among the sons he raised and the people's beloved Niall."

"Why didn't the rule go to the first son?" The question came from across the room, but Isleen answered with a wide grin.

"That wasn't always how things were done in the past. The first born wasn't always the most worthy to be king. Think on your Old Testament for evidence of that—wise men were given the task of selecting kings, based on omen and prophesy. Why should ancient Ireland be any different?"

Simon's throat tightened. The first born wasn't always the most worthy. A thing he often wondered about. Many a man in positions similar to his accepted their place as god-given, through right of birth. Yet he grappled with his place in the world. If only a wise man, with the gift of reading portents or prophecy, could pop out of the reeds and tell Simon what to do.

A general murmur of agreement went through the room, and Isleen took up the thread of her tale again.

"The king called for his advisor, Sithchean, though whether the man was a blacksmith or a druid, we know not. But it was his duty to set a challenge for the five men to determine which ought to be king." She narrowed her eyes and looked around the room, theatrically, taking in the faces of her listeners. "So Sithchean sent them into a forge. 'Each of ye make a weapon,' he said, 'and that weapon will tell who among you is worthy.' But as the fifth man walked inside, the old man shut the door behind them and set the forge ablaze."

Gasps went around the room, and Simon's eyebrows shot upward. Had she told this gruesome tale to the schoolroom children? James would eat up every word.

"The men were not trapped long, and as each of them emerged from the smoke, they carried something with them. This was the true test of their worth, for Sithchean could tell what manner of men they were by what they rescued from the blaze." She briefly adjusted her posture, sitting straighter. "Have we any blacksmiths here?"

"Me pa' was a blacksmith," one of the farmers from near the window said.

"Then you will like this end, I think. Here is what happened. The first man to emerge from the burning building was called Brian, the eldest of the king's sons. He came carrying hammers, which meant he was a strong man and a bold fighter, but he would not be best for the people. Fiachra came next, carrying a cask of beer. This meant he would be a father of art and science, but not king. Aillil came third, carrying a chest of weapons. He would be the man who carried out the people's vengeance and justice, but he also would not be king. Fergus was fourth, and the last of the wicked queen's sons. All he carried was a bundle of kindling, worthless, marking him as unsuitable to bear a royal line. And finally, out came Niall."

Isleen paused for dramatic effect, and Simon had to smile to himself. Everyone in the room seemed to hold their breaths, waiting to discover what came next in a tale that had been told thousands of times in Ireland.

"Niall carried the anvil itself, and upon seeing this, Sithchean pronounced that Niall would be High King of Ireland. For what use is a smithy without its anvil? The anvil is how all things are shaped and made. Niall's decision showed an understanding of the people, an understanding of past strengths and future needs. And from that day, the king knew Niall—his long-lost son—would be king." She lowered her voice, as though telling a secret as she finished her tale. "Of course, the wicked queen herself wasn't best pleased, and once again tried to take matters into her own hands. But that is another tale entirely."

Someone started clapping, and then the room as a whole applauded the tale. Simon joined in, impressed with her ability to hold an entire room in her thrall. Isleen blushed and stood, bobbing a quick curtsy; it was when her eyes rose with that motion that she saw Simon standing there, applauding with everyone else.

She bent to speak to a young girl Simon recognized as the daughter of a wealthy farmer, then picked her way across the room, weaving between tables and chairs, to come to his side.

Her cheeks were still red, and her eyes bright, but when she spoke her voice was subdued. "I left quite rudely before. I hope you can forgive me. And Sir Andrew, and Josephine."

"There is nothing to forgive." He looked down into her dark brown eyes, nearly black in the semi-darkness where they stood. "I worried for you." He hadn't meant to admit it out loud. When she lowered her eyes from his to the front of his coat, he felt certain he had said the wrong thing.

"Thank you," she said, her voice low and sweet. "It is a reassurance to know someone cares, even when we behave poorly."

"You didn't behave poorly." He touched her arm lightly, and he saw her swallow with the contact. "Was it I who caused you distress?"

Her lips turned upward, but she did not meet his gaze.

"I thought I had done something to upset you."

"No." She obviously did not wish to discuss anything of importance with him. Not now. And he did not blame her. So he sighed, heavily, and scrubbed his hand across his chin and then through his hair. He needed to change the subject entirely.

"I confess, I expect any moment for you to unleash some new challenge on me, the way your druid-smithy did to those men."

She blinked, her eyes turned up to his again, surprise on her features the instant before she grinned at him. "As we are stuck in this public house for a while, I cannot think what torture might be best for you."

Simon chuckled and his hand slipped from her forearm down to her fingers, quite without his permission or thought, to briefly squeeze her bare hand in his. "I am certain you will think of something."

Her cheeks flamed pink again, but before she could respond, someone behind Simon cleared his throat. They both turned, Simon somewhat apologetically, to see Andrew standing there with his arms folded and a scowl on his face.

"I spoke to Mr. Bloom. We have one room for the night. The rest are taken."

"As there are only four rooms, I am not at all surprised." Simon tried to sound uncaring. "I can sleep on the floor in the parlor upstairs, or down here at a table. Just like when we fell asleep studying in the Cambridge library."

"I can sleep down here, too," Isleen offered cheerily. "There are enough women present that we can find a table to keep to ourselves, and then you needn't worry about Josephine's comfort."

Andrew balked, and Simon had to cover a smile with his hand. "Absolutely not. Josie said the two of you would take the room. The bed is big enough for two, and it's not appropriate for someone of your breeding to sleep in a—in a public room."

She raised her eyebrows at him. "Sir Andrew, I didn't think you cared so much about propriety as that."

"He is right, though." Simon didn't like the idea of Isleen sitting in a chair, head on the hard surface of a table, trying to sleep.

"Oh, very well. But I am not the least bit tired yet. So you ought to see to your wife's comfort for now, Sir Andrew, and I will retire later."

"She is having a merry time of it," Simon told Andrew when his friend seemed perplexed. "Telling stories. Next thing you know, she will have organized a concert for everyone present."

"A concert?" Isleen laughed. "Not at all. Although that does give me an idea for your next challenge, Lord Farleigh."

Her words perked Andrew up, and Simon let himself groan aloud. She wasn't the only one who could act. "What have I doomed myself to this time?"

"A drinking song."

Both Andrew and Simon stared at her with shock. "A what?" Andrew asked, eyes wide.

"An Irish drinking song," she amended. "Come. I'll teach you the words. And it is your duty to get everyone in this public room singing along with you by the end of it." Her eyes glittered up at him. "Come, my lord. It will be quite entertaining."

Before Simon could voice any hesitancy, Andrew did it for

him. For once. "The future duke, singing a drinking song with the people under his watch? I'm not certain—"

"I think it a splendid idea." They all turned to see Josephine standing behind them on the last step of the stairs. She put both hands on her hips. "All of you were taking too long, so I knew you must be having fun without me."

"But a public room, Josie—"

She hopped down the last step and breezed up to her husband. "Sounds lovely. Will you find me a chair?"

Simon moved out of the doorway to clear a path for Josephine and Andrew, which put him nearly on top of Isleen. He gave her an apologetic smile, only to find her staring up at him with an expression he hadn't seen on her face before. Her eyes were soft and sad, but her lips turned up in a smile, and one of her hands rested against his chest as though to keep him from stumbling into her.

The contact of her hand, slim and warm, pressed over his heart, made it hard to remember where they stood. That they were not alone. Because in that moment, standing so close, he wanted nothing more than to dip his head down just low enough to catch her lips with his.

A soft, sharp inhale of breath made him wonder if she had read his thoughts. He met her wide-eyed stare and made himself smile, despite the remembrance of her broken heart. He stepped back, giving her room to smooth down her riding habit. "Teach me this Irish drinking song, Miss Frost. And then tell me exactly how it is a lady such as yourself learned it."

Isleen didn't intend to take so much as a sip of alcohol while she taught Simon one of her favorite songs. And though true enough that it might be sung in a pub by men slinging pints of stout from the glass to the back of their throats, she'd first learned it in the nursery. Folk songs were handy that way. Whether children sang the tune or men stomped their feet along with the words, anyone could enjoy the pleasure of a ridiculous tune.

Simon gave her one harried look from across the table. "How many verses are we at?"

"Eight."

He dropped his forehead into his hand and groaned. "Eight verses of this song? And each time, we sing it faster?"

"Here now, cheer up, my lord. You won't be singing alone."

He lowered his hand to peer over it, narrowing his eyes. "I am not fond of public performance, Miss Frost."

"This isn't a performance. It's a leadership exercise. He who leads men in song can lead them to battle."

"What famous Irish man said that?"

"I don't know that any of them have. I made it up myself, just now." She pushed the large mug of warm cider toward him. Mr. Bloom had served the ladies a spiced cider to warm their insides, but like most beverages served in a public house, there was certainly an extra kick to the drink. Not enough to make someone of Simon's size even so much as tipsy, but Isleen planned to sip demurely at her own mug. "Take your drink and go."

He grumbled as he picked up his mug but went to stand by the large hearth. Everyone in the room talked amongst their own parties, including Josephine and Andrew, who were at a table with a local gentleman and his wife who had been stranded by the storm, too. A storm that continued to drop snow outside the windows.

The drifts would be ten feet deep if they were an inch. Isleen sighed and hoped, not for the first time, that her family wasn't worrying after her. Her mother would be in a state, and Teague would likely curse himself for not coming with her when she invited him on their ride. But it couldn't be helped.

All she could do was make the best of the situation. And that included giving Simon yet another ridiculous task.

He cleared his throat, then spoke in a tone that carried through the room. "My friends, since we are all trapped here together, I thought to offer my services in providing entertainment. I have learned a new song from a friend." He met Isleen's gaze as he said that, and she waved happily from her place along the opposite wall. "And I would like to teach it to all of you. If you want to make things interesting, sing the verses along with me when you've picked it up. And if you miss a word, take a sip of your drink. Oh—and I suppose we should all start with full glasses. Mr. Bloom, if you please? This round is on me. Whatever your choice of drink."

Mr. Bloom went around pouring out drinks, and Mrs. Bloom did the same for those who didn't want anything too strong. Around the room they went, and murmurs of appreciation and thanks filled the air in a pleasant buzz. Josephine and Andrew gave Simon their full attention, too, both of them wearing large, knowing smiles.

"This song is new to me, but I am told it is as old as the hills in Ireland, Scotland, and Wales." Simon cleared his throat one last time. "'The Rattlin' Bog.'" And then he started singing, his voice neither sweet nor sour to hear, but pleasant enough to encourage others.

"Ho, ro, the rattlin' bog
The bog down in the valley o
Real bog, the rattlin' bog
The bog down in the valley o

Well in the bog there was a hole
A rare hole and a rattlin' hole
Hole in the bog
And the bog down in the valley o

Ho, ro, the rattlin' bog
The bog down in the valley o
Real bog, the rattlin' bog
The bog down in the valley o

Well in that hole there was a tree
A rare tree and a rattlin' tree
The tree in the hole
And the hole in the bog
And the bog down in the valley o..."

This time when he reached the chorus, everyone sang along with him. Indeed, the room shook with the clapping and stomping of feet, and laughter filtered through from more than one table. Simon worked them through one verse after another, singing the chorus faster each time. He made it all the way to the nest on the limb, and the limb on the branch, the branch on the tree, the tree in the hold, and the hole in the bog...

But before he finished up the chorus, he made eye contact with Isleen. And she knew he'd forgotten what came next. When he took in a lung full of air and did not immediately expel it in song, the room stilled, a few laughed, and Isleen sprang to her feet and his rescue.

"Well, in that nest there was a bird, a rare bird and a rattlin' bird—" They sang the next line together, and she clapped as she went to stand beside him. His eyes glowed with his thanks, and he did not forget another word.

The bird had an egg, and in that egg was another bird, and on that bird there was a feather... And when they reached the end of the chorus for the last time, Simon raced through the words so fast Isleen could hardly keep up—and burst into laughter the moment they were finished at last. The whole room roared happily, applause came from everyone who wasn't holding a mug, and then from those who had happily finished their drinks down to the last drop.

Simon laughed, too, between gasps for air. He put his hand out to steady himself against the hearth as the cheers around them dwindled into conversation. His eyes focused on hers, and Isleen resisted the urge to check her hair in the mirror hanging over the hearth.

She must look a sight. The weather, the vibrant song...

Her cheeks blazed warm, and she wondered if she looked as wild as she felt at that moment.

Simon's gaze softened. "Thank you. I think that's been the most interesting thing you've yet asked me to do."

"And certainly the most enjoyable to watch." She laughed, her lungs tight and her words too breathless. The song had undoubtedly taken it out of her.

He lowered his voice and stepped closer. "Thank you for not leaving me to make a fool of myself alone."

She attempted to brush aside the compliment. "Ach, I love that song too much to let you ruin it." And she certainly needn't sway closer to him still, but she found herself doing so anyway. Why did her legs feel unsteady? She hadn't imbibed enough to lose her senses. She'd barely taken a sip of her drink!

"Isleen—"

Simon jerked forward as a hand clapped loudly against his back. Sir Andrew had come up behind them. "That was brilliant, my friend. Absolutely perfect. Josie, what did you think?"

Josephine sounded as though she barely held back laughter as she spoke to her brother. "You have a talent, Simon. Next time we have a concert at home, I'll tell Father you must be allowed to lead us all in song."

"Can you imagine what Grandmother's reaction would be to a song like that?" Simon chuckled, then sighed. "I enjoyed myself. Maybe I ought to become a soloist. Or a choir director. What do you think, Miss Frost?"

He had called her by her Christian name a moment before. Isleen had heard it. She wouldn't forget it, either. But she smiled still the same when he addressed her, and the four of them spent the remainder of the dark afternoon and evening in conversation. Until Josephine started to yawn; when her eyes drooped, her husband sent both ladies upstairs to their rented room.

Long after Josephine fell asleep beside her, Isleen remained awake, her mind circling round and round the scene Simon had made, standing at the front of the room, and how it had felt to join him in singing that ridiculous, joyful song.

If only the song were longer. A dozen verses instead of eight. But then, it always had to come to an end. But, oh! How she wished she could have remained at Simon's side for a few minutes more. Just to hear what he had wanted to say when he had called her *Isleen.*

CHAPTER 15

Snow blanketed everything. When Isleen stepped outside the morning after the storm, she had to shield her eyes from the bright white powder reflecting the sun's light. Men were already on rooftops, tied to chimneys, checking their roofs for damages. A small contingent of farmers had arrived at the inn to make certain all inside were safe and well. Then they went on, in a sleigh pulled by one of the largest horses Isleen had ever seen.

Simon stood next to her, and Sir Andrew was on her other side. Josephine had remained indoors, not at all curious about what the world outside looked like after a long night of snowfall.

"The horses can make it up the hill if we stay to the road," Simon murmured. "But only if the whole of it isn't covered in ice."

"The ice didn't last long before it turned to rain." Sir Andrew looked northward, where the hill and trees of Clairvoir rose at the end of the valley. "I can make an attempt for it and come back for all of you if it's safe."

Simon shook his head. "I should go. You stay with Josephine."

"You're the duke's heir. What if your horse slips on a patch of ice and you break your neck?" Sir Andrew demanded, and he sounded rather exasperated with his friend. Isleen wondered, dimly, how many times the baronet must have won their debates with that argument.

When Simon spoke, he sounded dismissive at best. "And you're a married man with a wife—my sister—to care for. My father has another heir."

Isleen winced. Even in jest, Simon taking his value so lightly unsettled her. When he spoke of his place as heir, he seemed to have only two opinions on it. The first was that he existed under a tremendous weight of expectation—whether his own, or his family's, she couldn't say. The second, in moments like this, when he devalued himself as nothing more than a link in a chain, easily replaced by his younger brother.

"I could go," she offered, already knowing what they would say and preparing her arguments.

"We wouldn't send a lady up an icy hill by herself." Sir Andrew scoffed at the idea, but not unkindly. "You must remain here."

She expelled a breath that filled the air before her with fog. "I am an excellent rider."

"Even so, going up a hill covered in ice, riding side-saddle? Nothing about that is safe. Is it, Simon?"

Simon stared into the distance, still as a statue except for the furrowing of his brow. "If she wants to try, let her try. I think we both ought to go. Then if harm befalls one of us, the other can seek help."

Shocked at that answer, Isleen grinned triumphantly at Sir Andrew.

The baronet spluttered. "Then we two should go. Two men have a better chance—"

"Not really," Simon said, interrupting his friend. "Miss Frost is lighter than you are. On a horse or off, she may navigate hazards better. You shouldn't leave Josephine. My sister would never forgive me if something happened to you. Not in her condition."

Sir Andrew's eyes widened. "She told you?"

"I guessed." Simon grinned. "You gave the secret away with your constant worrying. I have never seen you act like a mother hen before."

That explains things. Josephine is with child. Isleen bit her lip and lowered her gaze to hide her smile. Simon must know his friend quite well to determine such a thing when she, a woman, had not picked up on the hints and tells.

"Miss Frost?" Simon's gentle voice brought her gaze upward again, meeting his dark blue eyes and finding them solely focused on her. "Do you truly wish to attempt it? The climb up the hill?"

"I do," she admitted. "I promise I can take the ride safely. I have a good head in an emergency, too. Should anything happen to either of us."

"That is enough for me." Simon looked up at his friend. "And we can send a sleigh or carriage back for Josephine, if we make it to the castle."

Sir Andrew sighed deeply, looking between the two of them, then westward, at the rise in the land leading up and up and up to the castle. "We could all wait here for a rescue party. I am certain the duke will send one."

Isleen did not miss the way Simon's expression changed. He had been all calm focus before, but now his eyes flashed, and his features hardened. Andrew's words had the opposite effect of what he'd intended. "I will get there safely, and I will come back for you and for Josephine."

The earl's best friend knew him well enough to cease his arguing. In due course, Isleen and Simon's mounts were brought to the front of the inn. Simon handed Isleen up into her saddle, which made her feel somewhat silly. How could she claim independence when she needed assistance at the beginning of their journey?

They started along the road in silence, retracing their route from the day before. Up the slow incline, into the trees surrounding the duke's estate. A ride that might take less than a quarter of an hour on an eager mount but would likely take them more than twice as long with the snow and possible dangers ahead.

As soon as Isleen no longer saw the village behind them, she called for a halt.

"Giving up already, Miss Frost?" Simon grinned at her, but the lightness of that expression did not quite reach his eyes. Those merely appeared tired. Had he slept at all the night before? Slumped across a table or in some hardbacked chair?

"Not at all. I am merely adjusting the equipment." She pointed up the hill. "Look away, if you please. This will not be graceful."

He obliged her, facing forward with his mount. "What are you up to?"

The awkward thing about lifting her leg and moving it from one side of the horse to the other was merely that the side-saddle's pommel for this particular saddle held her leg in place on both sides, in a cuff of padded leather. But once she had lifted her leg over and to the other side, she relaxed. Having only one stirrup was an inconvenience, to be sure, but gripping her horse with both legs seemed more desirable than the alternative.

The riding habits of women's wardrobes were voluminous pieces, thank goodness. There was more than enough fabric to ensure her legs were covered nearly to her ankles. She was no more scandalously clad thusly than she would be in a walking-out dress with a shortened hem.

"There. Much better." She gave the horse a nudge with both heels, and forward they went. Simon looked back at her, then down as her horse came alongside his. His lips immediately turned upward.

"Clever."

"The situation merited some alterations, I should think."

"Absolutely." They rode slowly enough that their horses could be sure of each step they took before taking another. The animals didn't seem to mind the snow at all. In fact, Simon's horse seemed delighted when he kicked up powder behind him, and it knickered playfully.

Isleen laughed, and her horse flicked its ears back toward the sound. She caught Simon's smile from the corner of her eye and quickly focused her gaze on the trees ahead of them.

Aside from the sounds of their horses moving through the snow, the world around them remained silent and still, allowing her thoughts to remain at the forefront of her mind. Thoughts about the man who rode beside her, and how much she wished her heart would accept that likely nothing would come of her growing attraction.

Simon glanced at Isleen for what felt like the dozenth time in less than two minutes. She remained silent, her gaze focused ahead of them, her thoughts her own. When she asked to accompany him, he'd given consent in part with the hope that they could talk. Just the two of them. Without worry of anyone interrupting or overhearing.

Now that the chance had come, all he wanted to say jumbled together in his mind. He didn't know where to begin, or how, or what would be best.

He could not blurt out that he found her beautiful, even if that admission circled near the top of his thoughts. Her dark hair and eyes stood out to him, drew him in, and made him wish to know the thoughts behind those eyes. Nor could he admire aloud her wit without sounding like a witless fool himself. Every compliment he sought to pay her either seemed not enough or else far too much for the small amount of time they had known one another.

His father would know what to say. He'd heard the duke speak to the duchess in kind compliments and soft endearments.

Did that sort of thing grow easier with time? Or had his father always known exactly what to say to the woman he most admired?

A better question: Why could Simon not go even an hour without comparing himself to his father?

He sighed, and Isleen's eyebrows rose, though she did not turn to look at him.

"Does something vex you, my lord?"

"Call me Simon." He blurted out the offer without thought. "At least...at least when we're among friends."

She turned, briefly taking her eyes from their path to give him a surprised glance. And a smile that warmed him inside and out. "Thank you. You must call me Isleen among the same."

He'd wanted to call her Isleen for some time. Had thought of her as that for longer than appropriate. "Isleen." It was only the second time he had said her name aloud, and he wasn't even certain she had heard it the evening before, when it had slipped past his usually guarded tongue. What had she asked him? It took him a moment to remember.

"Nothing vexes me." He quickly amended, "Except the snow. Being caught in the storm."

"The most obvious answer, of course." She sounded more amused than understanding, and he couldn't help his grimace. "There. What were you thinking just then?" she demanded with a playful gleam in her eyes. "Perhaps talking about whatever it is will be of some help."

Simon shifted forward in his saddle as they came to a slightly steeper portion of the road, but his horse handled it marvelously. They had yet to find any ice beneath the snow, which meant going back for Andrew and Josephine would take little time, especially in a coach or sleigh.

If he confided his thoughts to her, what would she make of them? Would she think him right to worry about his place as an heir? Or think him ridiculous for questioning something nature had already decided?

"A moment ago, I was thinking of my father." He did not look at her as he revealed his internal struggles. "I wonder, quite often, in fact, if I will ever be half the man that he is."

Silence met that declaration. There was no quick word, no laugh or sigh, only the quiet. His courage took a moment to gain enough strength for him to look at the woman at his side, to interpret her expression if nothing else.

Isleen appeared serene. Her countenance was soft, her eyes gentle as they stared ahead, the corners of her lips tilted ever-so-slightly upward. She caught him staring and turned to face him, her expression unchanged as she spoke. "I think wondering such a thing about a man like the duke, who by all accounts is among the best of men, means you will never stop trying. And that is the most important thing, I think, about being a good person. Whether it is leadership or kindness, courage or gentleness, as long as we never stop trying to be those things, we will succeed."

If he hadn't already been sitting atop his horse, he would have needed to sit immediately upon hearing those words. They were too heavy. Too much to think about. Despite how sincerely and simply she spoke, there were depths to that sort of thinking that he hadn't considered before.

It took him several seconds to realize he'd stopped his horse without meaning to. Isleen had continued forward, so Simon nudged his mount to hurry on at double the speed until he was once again even with Isleen.

Before he could speak, or question what she had said, the Irish woman started talking again, in a light tone that was at odds with her words. "I lost someone very dear to me, years ago. One of the things I have often asked myself since then is whether he would be proud of me. Whether he would see me now and be happy that I am happy. He was full of life and laughter. I promised myself, when the clouds began to clear after I learned he was gone, that I would honor his memory by finding joy in the world around me."

She looked down at her hands holding the reins, and he

watched her shoulders rise and fall on a deep sigh. "Measuring ourselves against the expectations of others, real or imagined, is quite difficult. It creates a weight on our hearts and souls, I think, that we do not always know how to carry."

"Your mother told me something of the sailor—" He stopped himself from saying the rest. From saying, *the sailor you loved.*

A laugh heavily tempered with sorrow escaped her. "Oh dear. Why ever would she do that?" She didn't sound upset at the breach in her mother's trust. Curious. But not angry. "I don't suppose it is secret. His name was Sean Hurst. He was the second son of an Irish gentleman."

"He must have been special, to inspire you that way." Simon turned away from her, his heart stinging as much for her as himself. "I am sorry if speaking of him is painful. That wasn't my intention."

They came to a downed branch, and Simon held his hand up for her to stop while he dismounted. Icicles had formed along the parts of the limb that stuck up into the air. He took the heavy end of the branch, lifted, and dragged it to the side of the path. The snow came up past his ankles on the road, and where it had drifted, the white powder reached nearly to his knees.

He came back and stood beside his horse a moment, breathing heavily. The branch had been heavier than it looked.

"It is and it isn't painful. To speak of Sean, I mean." Isleen adjusted the reins in her hand. "I don't mind thinking of him or speaking about him. It's easier now than it was when the grief was still fresh. Did my mother tell you I'd promised myself to him?"

That pain seared his heart again, and Simon shook his head. He watched her over the back of his horse, his hands on the saddle. He should mount. They should move on. People were waiting. Those at the castle might be worried.

Yet nothing was more important than what Isleen revealed to him that moment. It was a piece of her heart. Something worth treasuring. Worth waiting for.

"She didn't tell me that," he admitted softly, studying the way her dark eyes glimmered. Was she near to tears? Had his prying hurt her still more?

Her smile surprised him. "I loved him very much. We said we would marry after the war. When word came of his death, I grieved deeply. But Sean had a way about him that made it difficult to stay somber. All my memories of him were full of his laugh, his jokes, and all the stories he told. He wouldn't want me to lose myself to sorrow. So, I made up my mind to honor him the best way I could. By finding happiness again."

Simon weighed her words, then nodded once. "And that is how you measure yourself. By his memory." He mounted his horse. "It sounds as though it has worked out well for you, Isleen. You have a cheerful heart. And a gentle one."

"When I am not biting off the heads of Englishmen who think they're better than I am." She grinned at him, and Simon laughed. Her levity broke the somber spell that had befallen them, and they continued their journey up the hill again.

"I suppose I measure myself against my father in a similar way," he admitted, the words no longer weighty. "I wonder how he would speak in a situation, what he would do in another. If he would approve of my words and actions. He was already duke by my age, you know."

"I didn't. I had heard he came into his title quite young, and unexpectedly." She guided her horse carefully around another downed branch, though this one barely protruded into their path. "Do you fear inheriting early?"

"I pray for the opposite almost daily," he admitted. "I don't feel ready. Not to be duke. Not to lose him."

"I doubt he was ready for it, either. No one is ready to lose a parent. Especially when they are good, loving parents." Isleen took in a deep breath. "Oh, I know this place. Past the next bend, we will see the castle."

"We will," he confirmed. They were nearly there. Despite the slow pace, they had arrived quicker than he wished. When would he next have the chance to speak to Isleen like this? Alone and open-hearted?

"I think you should speak to your father."

He blinked and looked over at her. "What do you mean?"

"I think you should tell him how you feel," she stated firmly, then nodded to herself. "I don't think anyone else could possibly ease your mind or heart the way he could. If you tell him your fears, he may know how best to help you move past them. Or perhaps how to accept them. Only he has ever been in your position."

Simon, admit to his father that he didn't think he measured up? It was, in that moment, a horrifying thought. To tell the man he most admired that he feared he fell short of the mark—wouldn't that disappoint the duke? Wouldn't he feel that Simon ought to have more confidence and courage?

He had to gulp back the fear that rose when he wondered, for the briefest moment, if his father might agree with him. Even though the duke had never even hinted at such a thing. What if Simon's doubts gave his father a *new* reason to doubt his ability to fill his future role?

"Perhaps I should. Someday." That was the most he could say.

Isleen did not press him for more. "For what it is worth, Simon Dinard, Lord Farleigh," she said, a gentle curl to her lips. "I think you are a fine man. For more than a few reasons, I might add."

He nearly asked her what those reasons were—but the castle came into sight, along with several servants scuttling about the estate preparing a sleigh. Likely forming the very rescue party Andrew had predicted.

And their conversation came to an end.

CHAPTER 16

Isleen hadn't spoken of Sean to a stranger in a long time. Of course, she couldn't really count Simon as a stranger anymore. He had become a friend and a confidant. In the days since the snow storm, they hadn't spoken alone again. But they'd sat together in the evenings, surrounded by his family and friends, sometimes neighbors, while everyone chatted.

She'd caught him reading from the poetry book she had given him twice and asked teasingly if he'd picked a piece for recitation yet. Simon had raised one dark eyebrow at her and refused to answer both times.

They'd laughed together with the children in the nursery, playing games with them while Mrs. Robinson rested. The poor governess had developed a slight cold that made her tired every afternoon. Doubtless, another servant could've looked after the four youngsters. But Isleen had volunteered, and Simon had wound up in the nursery every afternoon with her.

Today, it had started to snow again. Isleen sat in a window seat in the empty ballroom. Most of what had fallen during the storm had melted in the sunshine, but it seemed winter had decided to come a few days earlier than the traditional change in seasons.

The longest night of the year approached, as did the Christmas festivities, and Isleen didn't miss Ireland as much as she thought she would.

Darrie sat on the other side of the window seat, mending a torn scrap of lace on one of Isleen's shawls. "I cannot help but wonder, miss, how their graces will have a big party with snow falling."

"The rest of their house guests will arrive tomorrow. I'm certain the road will be safe enough for them." Isleen leaned her forehead against the glass. Some of the diamond-shaped pains were red and blue, others clear. It made for a pretty place to sit and look, even if she looked out over the small courtyard in the center of the castle. "And then if it keeps snowing, everyone will be cozy together."

"The servants will miss going down to the village," Darrie remarked with a grin. "The maids go every chance they can, so as to flirt with the farmers and merchant's sons."

Isleen laughed. "I don't blame them. Flirting is a grand way to pass the time." She gave her maid a knowing grin. "Do you do your share of flirting?"

"Sometimes," Darrie admitted. "That gardener we met the day you were painting, he likes to talk to me well enough. And I don't mind the attention."

No, Isleen wouldn't mind that sort of attention either. If she had any. There were moments when she thought Simon flirted with her, but then—no. The man knew how to act the part of a kind host. A good friend. That was all he was. All he could be.

Simon would one day be a duke. And she would always be an Irish nobody, in comparison. Best to just let things be.

A soft, certain female voice called to her. "Miss Frost. Here you are."

The maid leaped to her feet, and Isleen stood quickly, too. They both curtsied, Darrie sinking nearly to the floor, as Cecilia,

Her Grace the Duchess of Montfort, glided across the ballroom floor toward them.

"Good afternoon, Your Grace." Isleen rose from her curtsy and gestured for Darrie to run along. She couldn't imagine a duchess allowing a servant to linger in her presence. "Thank you, Darrie. You may go."

The duchess watched the maid withdraw, a smile on her face. "My lady's maid, Mrs. Larrabee, speaks highly of your family's servants. She says they are obviously quite loyal, well trained, and eager to be of help."

Isleen tried to hide her surprise. "That is kind of her to say."

"Oh, Larrabee is a kitten." The duchess spoke with a hint of humor, the blue eyes she shared with her children sparkling. "She can be all warmth and purrs, or claws and hisses when she's crossed. I tell you that so you know she is not a woman easily impressed."

"Then I am thankful for her approval," Isleen amended, finding it easy to return the duchess's smile. "Were you looking for me, Your Grace?" Surely not. A duchess would never go looking for someone when she could send a servant.

The duchess sank into the spot that Darrie had barely vacated. "Not precisely, though I am glad I happened upon you when I did. I noticed you weren't in the Gallery with your mother for tea. I hope everything is all right?"

"It is, Your Grace. I was with Lady Josephine in the library. She had a new book she wished to show Lady Atella and myself. A book by a new lady author."

"Oh, that new romance. Yes, she gifted me a copy last week. Have you read it yet?" The duchess perked up, as though genuinely interested in her thoughts, as Lady Josephine had been. "I think the author has quite the talent. I cannot help wondering if she will write another. Female authoresses are too few, in my opinion."

"That is what Lady Atella and I said." Isleen slowly returned to her seat. "But I haven't read the whole of it yet. Lady Josephine read the first chapter aloud to us, and Lady Atella borrowed the book first."

"I will loan you my copy, if you wish. Lady Atella enjoys reading, of course, but tends to go quite slow. She isn't one to rush a good book." The duchess's tone was fond as she spoke of her daughter's dearest friend. As though she cared for her greatly. "You must tell me, Miss Frost. Are you enjoying your time at the castle?"

Isleen nearly laughed with relief. That question she could answer easily and without fear for how it might sound to her hostess. "I am. Immensely. Your family and guests are kind, and the castle itself is beautiful and interesting. Apart from that frightful storm, everything has been wonderful."

"And even that storm wasn't too terrible, since no one was hurt. Though I am sorry you were stuck in Lambsthorpe." The duchess crossed her ankles and joined her hands together in her lap. "It was a relief when you and Simon returned, safe and sound, to tell us what had happened."

Was there an emphasis on the way the duchess said her son's name, or had Isleen imagined it? "Your son was adamant that he be the one to return to the castle first, to test the road. I am surprised he let me come along."

Here the duchess laughed, a soft and charming sort of laugh. How did she manage to make even that sound sophisticated? "I cannot say I am. Your mother told me the night of the storm she didn't worry overmuch about you, because she knew you were too smart and stubborn a woman to let a little snow overcome you."

"My mother could say that, Your Grace, because I inherited those traits from her." Isleen folded her hands in her lap and tried her best not to fidget. Why did she feel so young, so uncouth, sitting alone with this woman? Was this how Simon felt around his father all the time? Uncertain and awkward? Poor man.

The duchess leaned back a little, her head against the window casing. "Your family has impressed me. And the duke, I think. He speaks highly of your brother."

"Thank you, Your Grace." What else could she say to that? "Anyone who meets Teague must know how much he loves his country and the people he represents. He has a good head on his shoulders and a kind heart."

"I agree. I am told by my eldest daughter and my eldest son that you are much the same."

Heat raced from Isleen's heart into her cheeks. Josephine and Simon talked about her to their mother? Whatever for?

But that was a silly question. The family would speak of their guests. And she had become fast friends with Josephine. And had spent more than a little time with Simon. Oh dear. She hadn't overstepped, had she?

Something of her sudden panic must have shown on her face, for the Duchess leaned forward and put her hand over Isleen's where it rested in her lap. "Oh, Miss Frost, it seems I have made you uncomfortable. That wasn't my intent at all. Are you all right, dear?"

"I am, thank you," she said, her voice a touch strangled. She cleared her throat. "I beg your pardon. I am merely surprised they spoke of me. That is all."

The duchess's eyes gleamed and one corner of her mouth tipped up just enough to reveal a dimple in her cheek. "They speak of you often, my dear, but it is nothing to worry about. In fact, I must say that I am grateful for it. My children are careful about the friendships they form, in most cases. That they all adore you is quite in your favor."

"They *all?*" Isleen's voice came out as a whisper.

"Yes. Simon, Josephine, Isabelle, Rosalind, and even James." The duchess's nose wrinkled, and she looked easily a dozen years younger when she wore that expression. In fact, it was an expression Isleen had seen countless times on Lord James. "I am impressed that you won James's favor, but he seems to think you an ally in his quest to pester his brother for attention."

Her jaw dropped open, and Isleen had to pop it closed again quickly. "I hope you don't mind, Your Grace. I do not mean to be disrespectful—"

"Oh, tosh. Simon takes himself far too seriously sometimes. It's good that he has James to remind him how to have fun once in a while."

It was so close to what Simon's friends had said about him that Isleen couldn't help the surprised gasp that slipped from her. "You see it, too, then." She hastily added, "Your Grace."

"See what, Miss Frost?" The duchess tipped her head to one side, allowing the curls framing her face to slip elegantly across her cheeks. The woman looked like a Greek statue come to life. "That Simon takes himself far too seriously? Yes. It is something I have noticed of late. I think it started with all the unrest over the Corn Laws. But I could be mistaken. His father would likely know better." She sighed. "He spends far more time with Simon than I do.. I am plagued by these headaches..." She shook her head. "Nevermind. That is surely the result of politics, too."

That his mother knew of her son's struggle eased Isleen's heart. Someone like the duchess wouldn't let her son continue on unhappily for long.

"Besides all that," her grace said, waving her hand as though to bat away the topic of politics, "I have noticed a change in Simon since your family's arrival. And I cannot say it is because of your brother that my son seems more at ease than normal."

The blush came back, full force, and Isleen very much wished for a cup of tea to swallow. Perhaps that would ease the sudden dryness of her throat. Was this the conversation that would end with her being warned away from the duke's heir? Perhaps the duchess would now hint, gently but firmly, that Isleen was not the right sort of woman for Simon? That was what would happen in a novel. Only, the duchess was a far kinder person than Lady Catherine de Bourgh in that novel—

"I am so glad Simon has found a friend in you, Miss Frost."

Isleen forced herself to smile, though it felt more like a grimace upon her face. "I promise that is all we are, Your Grace. Friends, I mean."

At this, the duchess grinned. Her eyes danced. And she lowered her voice to whisper, "Perhaps. For now."

Isleen opened and closed her mouth several times, but only a squeak escaped. This made the duchess laugh, though not unkindly. The sound echoed in the nearly empty ballroom, likely carrying down the stairs and into open corridors.

It was like magic to hear it, and to know the walls the duchess's laughter touched had all been put in place by her mind and will.

"Miss Frost, you seem a very intelligent and compassionate lady. You did not know this, but Emma is something of an expert on those who seek to get close to our family. She acted as Josephine's companion for many years, though we really considered her our foster daughter. Emma can tell in just a few conversations what motivates people attempting a relationship with my children. And she cannot say enough kind things about you."

"I wasn't trying to get close to anyone," Isleen protested, putting her heart into the explanation as much as she could. "I only wanted to be a good houseguest. To help my brother, you know. His position is so important. Everyone was so kind, and it was easy to form friendships. I didn't mean to overstep—"

"Gracious, child." The duchess again touched Isleen, this time on the arm. Her eyes were wide with alarm. "I am not accusing you of anything. Oh, you poor dear. Perhaps I went about this all wrong. Please, calm yourself."

"I am sorry." Isleen breathed deeply. "But you are a duchess, and I am only me."

"Only you?" The duchess moved closer, wrapping her arm around Isleen's shoulders in a maternal manner. The window seat did not so much as creak beneath the woman. "You, Miss Frost, are a lovely person. A person I wish to know better. I might be a duchess, but I wasn't always. And I am also a mother, whose children like you very much. Do not be distressed any longer."

Isleen nodded, hardly trusting herself to speak. "I like your children very much, too." Her blush hadn't gone away, which made it easier to say, "*All* of them."

"But perhaps one in particular?" The duchess hinted with a little smile. "Do not worry yourself overmuch, Isleen. May I call you Isleen? It is such a lovely name."

"Of course, Your Grace. I would be honored." Although she still could not wrap her mind around all the duchess hinted at. Surely, she could not hint at a relationship between Isleen and Simon. No, that would be ridiculous. No one could guess what Isleen had started to feel for the handsome young earl. She had been careful. So very careful not to reveal her feelings. Because she knew how impossible they were.

"I hope we see a lot of you after this house party is over, Miss Frost," the duchess said, her head tilted to the side again as she studied Isleen. "Our home in London will be open to you, as Clairvoir is open to you and yours. It is difficult for my family to find true friends. We count your family among those numbers." The duchess rose, and Isleen jolted to her feet, too.

"Thank you, Your Grace."

"Would you like to come with me to my chambers? That is where the book is. If you would like to read it." Was it her imagination, or did the duchess momentarily seem uncertain, too?

Isleen threw back her shoulders and agreed immediately. "I would, please. The first chapter was enough to catch my interest. I cannot imagine how the meeting of the vicar's daughter and the gentleman might go."

"Lovely." The duchess linked arms with Isleen and led her from the ballroom and down the corridor to the stairway nearest the family's wing. "I think you will love what happens next. I have no wish to spoil it for you, but when you have read chapter six, we simply must discuss it."

"I would like that."

"Miss Frost, I cannot help feeling I would like the author very much. I do wish women did not have to write under pseudonyms. It is patently unfair. First the author of *Pride and Prejudice*, now this new lady writer." As the duchess spoke about her opinions on women and novels, Isleen listened intently, and her heart at last slowed its anxious rhythm.

She shouldn't have doubted the duchess's kindness. Not after coming to know Lady Josephine and Simon, or even the younger children for that matter. They had accepted her into their circles with warmth and enthusiasm.

Maybe the sister of an Irish baron wasn't a nobody. Not to the duke's family. And that thought was comforting. And it made her wonder, in a way she hadn't thought she had the right to wonder, about Simon again.

What if...perhaps...someday, he wanted something more than friendship?

CHAPTER 17

More castle guests arrived as the week went on. Isleen met an entomologist and his wife, the duchess's younger brother and his family, two politicians and their families who helped fill the schoolroom and nursery, and Simon's cousin: the Honorable Mr. Thomas Childwick.

Isleen sat at a table in the Regent's Gallery, a glass lantern before her. She used white paint to create a lace-like pattern of frost along the glass. The other ladies worked on lanterns with her, chatting amiably about how the lanterns would be used as centerpieces for the midnight supper at the Christmas Eve Ball.

Mr. Childwick sat nearby, and she had felt his eyes on her more than once. Not in a way that caused her anxiety or distraction. Thank goodness. He had spent most of his time with Simon, but the duke's son was not in the room at present. Indeed, she hadn't any idea where he might be.

Isleen had sat next to Mr. Childwick at dinner a few evenings before, and he had been well-mannered and solicitous of her comfort. But it had still been Simon who had sat nearest her *after* dinner. Or Josephine or Emma. Which meant she still didn't know Mr. Childwick very well.

Which was why, after completing a fairly complex pattern on her glass, Isleen put down her brush and turned in her chair to face him. "Have you a wish to paint a lantern, Mr. Childwick?"

The others at the table quieted, and Lady Josephine added her voice to Isleen's. "Indeed, cousin. If you would like to practice your artistic abilities, we would not deny you the pleasure."

"I would not mind a turn with a brush," he admitted, "but nor do I wish to deprive any of you ladies of your entertainment."

Isleen motioned to the empty place beside her. "Bring a chair, sir. You are most welcome."

He found a chair that would fit, and the ladies had lantern, paint, and brush settled in the spot before he sat down to it. He went immediately to work, creating a frame of white upon the glass. The talking about the table resumed, and only then did Mr. Childwick speak in a softer voice to Isleen.

"It is good of you to entertain me in Farleigh's absence."

"Are you and your cousin close?" she asked as she painted dots of white on another lantern, then added a lattice along the edge.

Mr. Childwick shrugged one shoulder, and the corner of his mouth came up with it. "For many years, when our families would come together, Simon and I would run off together, usually with Sir Andrew after we were old enough to attend school. He is a good friend to me, even though we haven't seen one another for some time."

"How wonderful that you could come for Christmas."

"Indeed. I am grateful he invited me. My own family has been difficult to be around of late." He looked up from an intricate holly berry design he had created in next to no time. "Everyone but me is either married or actively pursuing a career, you see."

"Ah, that would make some conversations uncomfortable, I imagine." Isleen hummed sympathetically. The women she had gone to school with, as young girls, had all married. It made coming together with them awkward, at times. When all they had to speak on were babies and husbands, Isleen related to them but little.

"Indeed." Mr. Childwick added a sparkle of frost on his holly berry. "Farleigh offered me a respite. We have spoken of many things in the four days I have been here. I find he has a favorite topic of conversation, however, that he returns to again and again."

Isleen had to nod. "His responsibilities as heir?"

The man shook his head, and then he studied her through narrowed eyes. "Is that what he talks to you about, Miss Frost?"

"Sometimes. We also discuss books. And riding. I suppose we mostly discussed history during our conversation last evening, after dinner." She tried to think on what else they had argued about in the last several days. "And then there was the conversation regarding European dances, and whether the *waltz* ought to be named thus, since that is what they call nearly all dances in Prussia."

"Ah. Is that why he demonstrated that odd dance two nights ago? What did he call it. An Irish-something-or-other."

Isleen tried to hide her smile by ducking closer to her lantern. "I am afraid that was something of a dare I issued to him."

"I see." Mr. Childwick studied his lantern, then turned it to paint the opposite side. "My cousin has not visited so many topics with me. Indeed, most often, what he cares to discuss is *you*, Miss Frost."

Her paintbrush slipped, creating a long, thin line that nearly bisected her depiction of a dove. She laid the brush down and picked up the small cloth used for correcting errors on the glass. "He has discussed me?"

"Indeed."

"Oh dear." Imagining what Simon might say about her to others disconcerted Isleen. Immensely. She had thought they were getting along quite well of late. In fact, she had noticed a new warmth in his eyes when they spoke to one another. And she tried, with all her might, not to read into the situation.

Even if Simon's mother seemed to like Isleen, she couldn't hope for more than friendship. Not at the moment. Maybe never. Drat. What was he saying to others about her? She nearly asked. But she clamped her mouth shut instead.

Mr. Childwick took pity on her. That was the only explanation for his next words. "I have never heard my cousin speak with such admiration for a woman, Miss Frost. I think he sincerely likes you."

She nearly said "oh dear" again but swallowed back the words and hastily looked around. After she made certain the others were too busy with their conversation on the subject of their gowns for the ball, she glanced at Mr. Childwick from the corner of her eye.

He grinned, then pointedly bent back toward his lantern.

When Isleen saw his work, she gasped aloud. "Mr. Childwick, you are an artist!" He had painted a scene with trees on a hill, snow falling round about, a star in the heavens, and deer walking across the bottom of it all, antlered heads bent as though they gazed upward.

"I enjoy painting," he admitted. "It is a favorite past-time of mine."

Her berries and snowflakes seemed like children's drawings next to his work. "How did you manage all that with one color of paint? And without sketching it out beforehand?"

He shrugged. "I saw it in my mind's eye, and that was enough."

"I envy your skill, though I imagine I wouldn't wish to devote the hours to practice that you must have. I paint only for personal enjoyment, and on rare occasions at that." She cleaned her brush. "It must give you joy, to have an artist's talent."

His smile turned more sincere. "It does. Though I admit, I prefer a larger palette of colors for most of my work. One of my paintings is hanging in the family gallery, you know. Her Grace, my aunt by marriage, was exceptionally kind when she requested it."

"Which one is yours?"

"The duke's dogs. Have you seen it?"

Isleen thought carefully. "I remember admiring it. Now that I know you have painted it, I must go look again." She started to rise from the table.

"What? Now?" He put his brush down too.

Isleen made their excuses to the other ladies before saying to him. "What better time than the present?"

What poor Mr. Childwick didn't know? Isleen intended to question him closely on all that Simon had said of her. As closely as she could while remaining discreet. Each day she spent in the castle, each moment in the company of Simon Dinard, she wished for another. Another day. Another moment.

The twists and turns in the castle corridors brought them to the family gallery, where the duke had cases displaying important historical finds on the land, including Roman coins and copper cuffs from the days of the druids. On the walls, stretching up perhaps twenty feet, were portraits and paintings by masters, each of them depicting the ducal family members stretching back into previous centuries, with representations of the castle and surrounding lands as well. And above it all, an arched glass ceiling with curtains meant to shield the priceless works from even the indirect sunlight during the summers.

If Isleen had seen this room alone, she would have declared the architect of the castle a genius. Natural light flooded from above, but with the slants and icing of the glass, the paintings were protected from fading. The room, long as well as tall, wasn't the least bit stuff thanks to the way the doors opened into it on two sides, creating a natural breezeway for fresh air to travel through.

"Here we are. The duke's prized dogs, right here." Mr. Childwick stood before a large oil painting of two beautiful dogs at play, leaping through a field with woods in the background. One of the dogs looked to be a common English collie, while the other had thick, puffed-up fur of a breed she could not name.

"They are quite realistic." Isleen leaned closer to peer at the strokes that made up the fur on the larger of the two. "You brought them to life with the expression in their eyes. They seem happy."

"As two dogs frolicking through a meadow ought to be." Mr. Childwick tilted his head and examined his work with a critical eye. "They are Minnie and Winter. The border collie is Minnie, of course. The duke wrote to me last year to say she had died. He adored her. I think Winter is enjoying retirement in the kennels. I painted this five years ago."

"Would you do it differently now?"

Mr. Childwick slowly shook his head. "I try not to look at my completed work that way. As something to be improved upon after I've laid my brush down. Instead, I look for what I did well. I measure myself against it. Am I as pleased with the work I complete today as I was with this painting, the day I presented it to my uncle?" He smiled to himself. "I cannot hold a younger version of myself or my work to the standards I meet now. Though I will hold my present self to the pride and sense of accomplishment as I felt it in the past."

Isleen regarded him with some surprise. Though not as strikingly handsome as his cousin, Mr. Childwick had an appeal of his own in his bearing and the way he spoke. She hadn't noticed it until she stood with him before his painting. "You wish to feel now about your work as you did then." She studied the dogs again, and the sky above them, the trees in the distance.

"I never want to lose the sense of accomplishment, or to lose the joy I feel when I paint." The man nodded once at the painting, then turned on his heel to face her instead of the art. He grinned suddenly, breaking through the moment that had rested with a heavy peace on Isleen's shoulders. "If you are not a dedicated artist, Miss Frost, how do you prefer to bend your talents and time? I am most curious about you, after all my cousin has said."

The opening Isleen had hoped for, at last. "What *has* your cousin said? I must know what misrepresentations need correcting, or what compliments I have already received, before I can list my own."

Mr. Childwick crossed his arms over his chest and paced away from her, a playful smile on his face. "Here we come to the truth. You wanted to speak of Farleigh, not my painting."

Her cheeks flooded with heat. "That isn't entirely true. But... oh, fine. Maybe it was." She sighed and wrapped her arms around herself. "Will you forgive me, Mr. Childwick? I do admire your talent. We can return to speaking of art, if you wish. I have a dozen questions I could ask—"

He cut her off when he spun around, a laugh escaping him. "No, Miss Frost. I apologize. I shouldn't have said what I did. I understand you completely, and I take no offense. In truth, I am relieved you are as preoccupied with my cousin as he is with you."

She lowered her gaze to the carpet, a swirl of black, red, and cream meeting her eyes. "I am entirely too presumptuous about our friendship. When you said he made mention of me, it intrigued me." She sighed and lowered her hands to her side, gripping the fabric of her gown instead, the soft velvet folds of her winter dress grounding her in the moment. "I apologize. Truly. It is none of my business what you and Lord Farleigh discuss."

The gentleman's tone gentled as he stepped closer. "Here now, Miss Frost, don't go turning into a missish puddle. One of the things Farleigh likes most is how often you stand your ground. I cannot have you showing me otherwise when he admires it so."

She hadn't felt capable of standing her ground of late. Her thoughts had been a muddle since the day they returned from the inn. Things she had never worried about crept into her dreams to torment her. Was she too prideful? Unbending? Should she stop debating? Perhaps her storytelling was too childish, too rustic.

Questioning who she was because of her sudden interest in a man made Isleen uncomfortable. When had she last felt so unsure?

She winced. Knowing exactly when. Years ago, when she had

fallen in love with Sean, and she hadn't discovered if he felt the same. The early days of her love had been both a misery and a joy as the newfound emotion took root in her heart.

The carpet beneath her swirled again, righting itself into a pattern of thorns and roses. She released a shaky breath, then drew in another to steady herself before lifting her chin. "There now. I am all right," she said aloud. "Perhaps we should return to painting the lanterns?"

Mr. Childwick studied her, then withdrew a handkerchief from his pocket. "You may wish to dry your eyes, Miss Frost."

She hadn't even known a few confused tears had escaped. She laughed, shakily, and accepted the linen square from him. "Thank you, sir."

"It seems you have a riot of thought and feeling inside you, Miss Frost. I do hope my cousin, if he is the cause, will also be the cure."

Her cheeks warmed as she wiped at them. "I did not expect our interview to be this tumultuous. I hope I have not made you uncomfortable."

"Not in the slightest. If anyone understands complexities of emotions, I hope it would be an artist. We paint with shadow as often as we do with light. But may I make a suggestion? Instead of returning to the lanterns, perhaps we should step outside a moment. It is cold, but the fresh air may help clear your thoughts." He offered her his arm.

"A lovely idea." The shockingly cold air would give her a jolt back to the present. Why had she turned so weepy at the memory of Sean? At the realization that she felt something like love for Simon Dinard, Lord Farleigh?

My heart is letting go of Sean all over again. She shivered at the thought. Was she ready to let her feelings for Sean slip further into the past, making way for something new?

The work of a duke never ended. How was it that so many members of the nobility seemed to fritter away their time in idle pleasure while Simon's father, one of the wealthiest of them, never seemed to have a moment's rest?

Simon left his father's study in a rush he hoped the duke did not notice. He had spent the better part of the morning closeted with the duke, going over accounts for the various properties and estates linked to their family. He hadn't seen Isleen since breakfast.

The eagerness with which he at last sought her out would have disturbed him, if he took the time to examine it. Which he did not.

With his legs taking the longest strides possible, without outright running through the corridors, he made for the Regent's Gallery, where he knew the ladies had begun to work upon the Christmas Eve decorations.

As he bounded across one of the larger corridors, he nearly passed a door which stood slightly ajar, letting in a draft of frigid air.

Simon slowed, looking over his shoulder when something beyond the door caught his eye.

Isleen, standing outside, leaning against a stone railing.

Whatever was she doing there? And how fortunate for him, to catch her. He adjusted his route, though not his speed, and burst through the door out into the open air.

"Isleen, here you are—" She turned, as did someone standing a few feet away. Someone Simon hadn't seen. His cousin, Thomas Childwick. "That is, Miss Frost. Thomas. Ah." He had stopped in his tracks, hardly aware of the cold, focused instead on the wry smile of his cousin. "What are you two doing out here?"

The words had come out more accusatory than he meant, though they were entirely directed at his cousin.

Thomas appeared most amused. "Merely taking a moment to enjoy the bracingly fresh winter air." He glanced at Isleen, who twisted a handkerchief in her fingers. Her cold fingers. What was Thomas thinking, standing out of doors in such weather? What if Isleen caught cold?

Simon took his coat off, leaving him in shirtsleeves and waistcoat. Perhaps not appropriate public wear, but nothing all that inappropriate in the walls of his own home. He draped the coat over Isleen's shoulders. "You should have at least brought out a shawl, Miss Frost. You cannot take ill right before the ball."

Not when he intended to dance with her as often as he could that evening. Or, perhaps, be the one to claim that kiss beneath the mistletoe. If he won the wager. Which he was fairly certain he had. The last several challenges she had given him were far too easily accomplished. Almost as though she wanted him to win.

He had led an evening of charades the night before, at her behest. Helped the children hang their paper chain in the large tree positioned in the Guard Room downstairs, while she continued to express dismay at such an idea of bringing an enormous tree in its pot of dirt into the castle. He'd even smuggled a tray of gingerbread to the school room and the gaggle of children when she suggested it a fit trial for him.

"We only meant to stay out a moment," Thomas said, not sounding nearly repentant enough. "But then we started talking, and perhaps I lost track of the time. Do forgive me, Miss Frost."

"Of course, Mr. Childwick." Then, with a less gentle tone to Simon, "Really, Lord Farleigh. I am perfectly well."

Isleen pulled the front of his coat tightly in front of her, and her large dark eyes stared up at him, her lips slightly turned up as though his reaction had amused her. He reflexively rubbed at the back of his neck and stepped away, shooting another glare at his cousin.

Thomas chuckled, then covered the sound with a hand over his mouth. He coughed. "Beg your pardon, Farleigh. If you'll excuse me, I think I had better return to my lantern painting." He bowed. "Miss Frost. I enjoyed our time together."

"As did I, Mr. Childwick." Simon could detect nothing but sincerity and sweetness from her tone.

The moment Childwick disappeared through the door, leaving it barely ajar behind him, Simon gave Isleen his full attention.

"Would you like to go inside?"

"I imagine you would, standing here in your shirtsleeves." She pulled his coat up around her neck. And did he imagine the hum of satisfaction after she inhaled deeply? He hid his pleasure as best he could.

"I am all right for the moment. As long as you are not cold."

She raised her eyebrows at him, and a little smile appeared at the corner of her mouth. "I find myself cozy at present."

He couldn't help grinning down at her, and it seemed the most natural thing to step closer, to smooth out the overly-large coat across her shoulders. "It looks better on you than it does on me."

She scoffed and lifted her chin upward, out from behind the dark blue wool of his coat. "Of course it looks better on me. I'm a sight prettier than you are. Though it could stand to be taken in."

He laughed, and his hands on her shoulders lowered to her arms, feeling how little they filled the sleeves. "A nip and tuck here and there, perhaps, and you'd turned heads. That's for certain."

"I'd look grand, promenading in Hyde Park, in your coat."

"You'd set the fashionable world on its ear."

"Everyone would wish to know my secret."

"What would you tell them?"

"I haven't the faintest idea," she admitted with a wrinkle in her nose. "I can't have any ladies thinking the best way to add to their wardrobes is to steal coats from *you*."

His hands had fallen farther still, his fingers wrapping gently around hers. Her fingers were warm. It seemed his coat was doing its job. But she reacted instantly to his touch.

"Simon, your hands are freezing." She kept hold of one hand to lead him to the door, pulling him along behind her. The faster she spoke, the thicker her Irish accented each word. "Come inside at once. Silly man. What if *you* caught cold? Ah, that'd be grand, wouldn't it? Me telling their graces that their son stood about in his shirtsleeves like a lunatic, and all the time me talking to him like an addlepated fool."

They were safely inside, the door shut behind them, standing in the quiet corridor. Isleen inspected the hand she held, then covered it in both of hers. She rubbed it, chafing warmth back into his fingers.

Simon laughed, his amusement softened by her ministrations. She looked up at him, her dark eyes narrowed, and her pink lips pursed with irritation.

"Isleen." Gently, he took her hands in his. "I'm fine."

She huffed, and determination lit her dark eyes, but then as she met his gaze, he watched her features soften. The stubborn tilt of her chin changed as she lowered it a fraction, the wrinkle had gone from above her nose, and her cheeks turned a rosy shade of pink. She swallowed, and he realized they stood nearly toe-to-toe. Far closer than was polite.

But he had no desire to step back. In fact, he wanted to do quite the opposite. Tilt his head down toward hers. Put his hand on her waist...

"You ought to take your coat back." Her gentle words interrupted his imaginings.

"I suppose I should."

She slipped free of the shoulders, then the sleeves. Then she held the coat between them by the collar. "It is a fetching color on you, Simon."

He took it from her but didn't put it on. "I think I like it best on you."

Isleen blinked up at him, and he half-expected her to withdraw again in shyness. But that wasn't his Isleen. Instead, she put one hand to her hip and tossed her head back with a flirtatious smirk. "What a thing to say, Simon Dinard, Earl of Farleigh. Shameless flattery, that's all it is."

He laughed and put his coat on, shrugging into it with ease before turning to face her again. "What *were* you and my cousin speaking about? Why did you need air?"

"That's neither here nor there." She waved away his concern. "He's a kind man. I like him."

"Not more than you like me, I hope." Had he really said that out loud? Perhaps Josephine had been right when she'd told him he was out of practice when it came to flirting.

Isleen didn't seem to mind. Her expression remained playful. "That remains to be seen. Though I suppose I *must* like you more, when you've offered me your coat. And sung songs with me in a pub."

"I'll certainly never forget that."

"It seems like you will win the wager you made with Sir Andrew." Isleen shrugged one shoulder, then sighed with dramatic disappointment. "That means I'll have to take part in that ridiculous English tradition. Mistletoe, indeed." Her nose wrinkled again.

Simon offered her his arm, which she took, and he led her down the corridor. Back toward where all the people were working on lanterns and kissing balls, ribbons and greenery. The Christmas ball was three days away.

"Would you rather we put candles in windows?" he asked. "And lay out tables of food, with our doors unlocked?"

"There's no harm in those things," she pointed out. "The latter does a lot of good. Though I can't imagine anyone would climb the castle hill in the dead of night to secret away bread or grain."

He watched her from the corner of his eye. "There is no harm in a mistletoe kiss, either."

Isleen studied the floor as they walked, her brows drawn tightly together. "If you don't mind my saying so, I'd still prefer not to have a stranger's kiss be what I remember about this Christmas Eve ball."

They had arrived at the door to the Regent's Gallery, where they could plainly hear conversation buzzing from within. The footman outside took hold of the handle. Simon had but a moment to see her reaction as he asked, "Who said it would be a stranger to claim that kiss?"

Isleen's head came up, her eyes wide and her lips parting, but she didn't look upset. No, she seemed surprised. Intrigued.

The footman opened the door, and Simon led Isleen into the room full of life, light, and people. In the moment before she released his arm, he felt her hand give him a gentle squeeze. And then she walked away, leaving Simon to interpret the touch as an answer to his question.

He'd never been so happy to win a wager in his life. Because this time, he'd won a prize he couldn't bear to see another have—a kiss from Isleen Frost.

CHAPTER 18

The duke hired sleighs from the village of Lambsthorpe to supplement his party, on December the twenty-third, allowing a fleet of sleighs with bells and horses to sweep across the landscape. Isleen sat next to her brother in the sleigh Teague had claimed for driving. Their mother remained in the castle, with tea cakes and a book.

Fiona had dragged Lord James with her into their sleigh, and the two children laughed and shouted as they went down the hill and to the stretch of empty fields. Sleigh races, the duke had declared, would be a marvelous way to pass the day.

A groom rode on the seat at the back of the sleigh, balancing the vehicle with his added weight, and keeping everything steady.

Isleen kept her hands tucked in her muff, and her eyes on the surrounding snow-covered landscape. White blanketed the hills and valleys, dusted the trees, and turned everything around them into a blank canvas ready for the splash of color a sleigh and its passengers would bring.

"I haven't seen you much in recent days," Teague remarked, leaning close to be heard over the horse's bells. "And whenever I do see you, you're tucked snug as a lamb between Lady Josephine and Lady Atella. Or else arguing with Lord Farleigh in the corner, after dinner."

"And whose fault is that, exactly? You are the one forever locked away with the gentlemen, speaking of politics," she accused with a good-natured nudge to his shoulder. "I'm proud of you for holding your own with them, Teague."

"Thank you. With the duke as my champion, it hasn't been as difficult to be heard as I feared." Teague gave her a crooked smile. "I wonder if the wrong Frost went into politics. You nearly turned the conversation from my point about *you*."

Fiona leaned forward from behind, her grin less than cherubic. "Are we talking about Issie flirting with the earl? I've wagered with James they dance at least twice at the ball."

"Fiona!" Isleen twisted around in her seat, scandalized. "What a thing to do. Young ladies don't place wagers, and certainly do not involve themselves in the business of others." She looked at the boy, to see what he made of the comment.

Lord James shrugged, leaning back in his seat with his fur cap pulled down low over his ears and eyebrows. "My sisters place wagers all the time. Usually with Andrew. We just aren't allowed to gamble with money. I get all of Fi's dessert on Christmas if she's wrong, and she gets my conch shell if she's right."

"A conch shell?" Isleen repeated numbly, looking from the young lord to her sister, barely registering that the boy who had argued with her now called her by the pet name her family used. "You must take back your wager at once, Fi. Or—or I will tell Máthair."

"Best not," Teague said with a wide grin. "Because if you tattle on Fi, I'll have to tattle on you."

"Teague," she whispered, looking over her shoulder. But of course, her sister had heard. Isleen's cheeks blossomed with heat, while Fiona cackled with glee.

Lord James leaned forward, eyes aglow. "What did you bet Simon? What happens if he loses? What happens if *you* lose?"

"I think it has something to do with all the flirting," Fiona sang out.

Isleen glared at her sister. "If there's any more of that sort of talk, there'll be less of it!" It was a typical Irish threat, usually uttered by mothers grown tired of children squabbling, but it did the trick.

Fiona leaned back again, an unrepentant grin on her face, saying no more, even though Lord James tried to wheedle more information from Isleen.

Isleen faced forward, shoulders back and head tilted up. "Good job keeping a secret, Teague Frost."

Teague didn't look any more contrite than Fiona did. "I didn't know it was a secret from Fi. It's all the *conte* and Sir Andrew talk about, when the duke isn't present, teasing Farleigh something awful. And Childwick has since joined in, though none of them ever mention your name directly. They're too gentlemanly for that, I suppose."

She wanted to sink into the nearest bank of snow and not come out again until spring.

There'd not been cause to tease her about a man in years, and Fiona had been a mere babe then. Too young to notice her sister's blushes or stammers. And Teague had been away at university.

The most mortifying thing of all was Lord James's presence. What if he carried the conversation to his brother? His sisters?

"I haven't done anything wrong." She failed to keep the plaintive tone out of her words. "We've been friendly to one another, and that is all."

"Calm yourself, Issie." Teague nudged her the way she'd bumped his shoulder a moment before, his hands still on the horse's leads. "No one thinks you a flirt. I didn't mean to upset you."

She ducked her chin and flicked snow that had fallen from a tree off her coat sleeve. "I'm not upset."

"Good. Besides, if you *were* of a mind to flirt with the earl, he'd be a lucky man. He's a fine fellow and might even deserve you, at that."

"Deserve me?" She bristled. "What do you mean?"

"I mean," he said, voice low so as not to be heard by the little ears in the seat behind, "that I'd give my blessing to it. He's a good man, from a good family." He gave her one serious look before adding, with a wink, "And you'd be richer than Midas, marrying a future duke."

Isleen groaned and raised her muff to hide behind it. "Teague. Don't you dare say a word of this to anyone else. Shameful, scheming man. They'll say we planned it together."

He laughed, and after a moment she forgave him and leaned against his shoulder. Her brother had her best interests at heart. And it eased her mind, at least a touch, that he thought her and Simon an appropriate match for one another.

Not that it mattered all that much what Teague's opinion was. Simon hadn't made any declarations or plans. Wouldn't England's nobility frown on a future duke marrying beneath him on the social ladder? That same ladder they had spoken of, not too many days past.

And yet...her heart continued to hope, to wonder at the possibilities, to examine the matter from all sides.

She knew all the signs of new love as well as those of a broken heart. The symptoms of love were there, calling her attention to the way Simon's smile made her heart flutter, and how his attention made her want to preen and hide herself away simultaneously. But there was every chance she'd end the Christmas season with a broken heart, too.

They arrived at the wide stretch of meadow at last, and the children piled out of the sleighs and ran for the trees, whooping and laughing, scooping up snow and throwing it in the air. Isleen descended from their vehicle with more grace than her younger sister and Lord James. She waved at her brother. "Good luck with your race."

Soon, only men fully grown and their grooms on the rear seats remained in the sleighs. They would drive to the far side of the meadow, then turn and race back to a designated finish line. Sir Andrew waved at Isleen as he passed, and she happily waved back. Then Simon went by in his sleigh, his favored horse not seeming to mind pulling instead of being ridden. The beast was huge and as handsome as his owner.

Simon raised his gloved hand, and Isleen had the urge to blow him a kiss. The very idea made her demure into offering a curtsy instead. He grinned at her and kept going.

Her breath turned to clouds of vapor as she stood still, watching the back of Simon's head and fur cap as he drove away. Had she been too obvious in her growing affection for the man? If Fiona had noticed, when she only ever saw them together in the schoolroom, had others? Had there been gossip about her?

If *Conte* Atella and Sir Andrew were teasing Simon, before her own brother no less, about the wager, it wasn't considered a secret.

Had they bent their heads together over books too often in the evening hours? And what of Mr. Childwick? He had guessed with astonishing speed what her feelings were.

A groom stood in the center of the field and raised a pistol—the starting signal for the race. Isleen, with Lady Josephine, Lady Atella, and other women who had braved the cold, started herding the children toward the tree line to keep them fully out of the path of the horses and sleighs.

Once beneath the bare branches, they formed a line to cheer the men on. Even the duke had decided to participate in the event. Isleen turned her coat collar up and stood between her sister and Lord James.

"I wish they'd let me race," Lord James muttered. "I'm nearly old enough to handle the stripes, you know."

Fiona snorted. "Maybe in a pony and cart race."

"Fi." Isleen glowered at her sister. "Be kind."

She shrugged. "Tis only the truth."

Lord James leaned forward and stuck his tongue out at Fiona. "You can't race at all. You're a girl."

"As though I'd want to," she retorted.

"Children, please." Isleen cast her eyes heavenward and prayed for patience. "Here, look. They're ready to start."

Her last word was overwhelmed by the sound of a gunshot ringing through the meadow.

The race started.

Children jumped up and down, shouting and clapping their mittened hands. The ladies were more demure in their enthusiasm, but were calling out encouragement that doubtless went unheard over the sounds of horse hooves kicking up snow, the runners shushing across the powder and ice, and the jingle of the sleigh bells.

And Isleen shouted, too. As much for Simon as her brother, though she hoped no one else noticed.

Two grooms stood on either side of the finishing line, drawn hastily in the snow with a stick, watching to see who crossed first. Isleen realized the duke and Sir Andrew were even, with Simon and another gentleman close behind. At the last moment, Sir Andrew passed the duke, and Simon crossed at the same moment as his father. The race was quite close, and as the horses slowed and stamped their feet, grooms rushing forward to calm them and pat them down with blankets, the drivers all laughed and called to one another.

"Teague didn't win," Fiona said, leaning forward to smile at Lord James. "But neither did your father or your brother."

Lord James glowered at her, then turned and stormed away.

"Fi, you need to learn more tact." Isleen shook her head at her sister, her eyes on Simon as he shook Sir Andrew's hand and then his father's.

"I only stated the truth. It isn't my fault James is a—" An explosion of snow hit the back of Fiona's head. She shrieked, the sound jarring enough it caused a few of the horses to prance in their harnesses. Isleen turned at the same moment her sister did, and both saw Lord James grinning impudently.

Fiona charged forward, bending as she went to scoop up handfuls of snow, and Lord James took to his feet running, weaving in and out of the trees, laughing.

That was all the other children needed as an excuse to run into the trees, scooping up snow and hurling balls of it at one another. Girls and boys alike, even the duke's two youngest daughters, went hurtling into the trees with laughter.

Teague came and stood next to Isleen, breathing hard and grinning. "I saw it all. Do you think Fiona knows how unwise it is to start a war with the English?"

Isleen shook her head. "I doubt it. But I'm certain she would appreciate her brother sending her reinforcements."

Her brother touched the brim of his hat to her, then bent and scooped up snow. "I'll lend her my support. What about you?"

"Me?" Isleen tilted her chin upward.

His eyes gleamed as he glanced behind her. "I doubt you have much of a choice, Issie." Then he ran off, calling Fiona's name as he went.

"Daft man," she muttered. "Me, in a snowball fight. At my age."

An icy missile hit her shoulder. Her jaw dropped and she spun on her heel, ready to give someone a severe tongue-lashing. What child had *dared*—?

Simon stood ten paces away, already packing together another snowball between his gloves. "Lord Farleigh," she exclaimed. "Don't you dare—"

But he threw the snowball, and she turned just in time to break it with her shoulder. Looking past him, she realized most of the other ladies were now scooping up snow and throwing balls, too. It seemed no one meant to stand on decorum today.

"You'll regret that," she shouted, tossing her muff aside as she picked up snow and charged.

Simon laughed and dodged her first volley, then aimed a snowball at Lady Josephine and caught her in the back of the neck. She shrieked, then spun and pointed at him. "Andrew! Get him!"

"He was my friend first," Simon shouted at her, but Andrew was charging, no snow in hand. Simon laughed and dodged behind a tree. Isleen took the opportunity to form several balls of snow, packing them tight, and glowering. She filled her muff and cradled it to her, listening to the shouts and laughter echoing through the limbs of the trees.

Then she ran into the fray. Using her ammunition wisely, she pelted Sir Andrew and ducked behind a tree before he turned. Then knocked the hat off one of the boys near Fiona's age. She kept running, giggling to herself over the ridiculous battle and her part in it.

She pelted anyone she thought she had a chance of hitting, including Lady Atella and her count, who had taken refuge behind a downed log until Isleen found them. She kept moving, which seemed to be key in avoiding being hit.

Her nose tingled with the cold, but she sniffled and kept onward, looking for Simon. She wove through the trees, dodging snowballs, and finally found Sir Andrew. He had Lord James thrown over his shoulder and allowed Fiona to take free aim at the boy. Isleen ducked behind a tree before any of them saw her, and then she froze.

While she had been searching for Simon, he had evidently been stalking her. Because he stood not six feet away, grinning and holding a large clump of snow overhead.

"Ask for mercy, Irishwoman," he said, his blue eyes light and full of laughter.

She sucked in a breath, her heart pounding more from attraction than fear. The dratted man. He hadn't any idea what he did to her.

But she gave her answer with her chin in the air. "Never!" But before he could charge, Isleen used an old tried and true tactic from her own schoolroom and nursery days. She charged, and with her full might ran straight into him, wrapping her arms about his waist and pushing them both over into the snow.

Immediately, she rolled away. He'd dropped his snow, of course, giving her the chance to scoop up an armful of her own, scramble to her feet, and drop it in his face.

Apparently, her counter-attack had shocked him enough that he did nothing except lay there and take the onslaught. He sputtered and wiped the snow from his face. "Isleen," he growled. "You don't fight fair."

She kicked more snow at him, though it barely reached his face. "'The rules of fair play do not apply in love and war,'" she quipped, quoting an English poet whose name she could not remember.

"Do they not?" he asked, folding his hands over his stomach, fingers laced, as he looked up at her. "And which is this, Isleen? Love or war?"

She took a step back. "I didn't mean—you know that I didn't mean anything by it."

He chuckled and rolled to his stomach, then pushed himself out of the snow with a grunt. He brushed the snow off his coat and trousers, smiling at her as he did. "Didn't you?"

She blinked at him. They'd flirted, of course. But nothing had been said outright. Nothing like this. And when he moved closer to her, one hand outstretched, she had to stamp down on the desire to turn and flee.

Instead, she found herself putting her hand in his, hugging her muff tightly to her with the other arm. "Not really," she whispered. "It wouldn't be ladylike."

"What wouldn't be ladylike?" he asked, pulling her slowly

closer, his blue eyes darkening and his smile warming her from nose tip to her toes.

She came closer to him, tilting her chin upward. Her gaze dropped from his to the curve of his lips. It had been years since anyone had kissed her. Was she too out of practice to attempt it? Did Simon want to kiss her? The draw she felt toward him—he must feel it, too.

Had he asked her a question? "I cannot recall, at present," she murmured, starting to rise on her toes.

"Mm." He didn't seem to mind, as he bent slowly toward her, his eyes lowering from hers to her lips.

He was going to kiss her. And she was going to let him. Let him? She was going to kiss him back!

Then his eyes flickered, as though drawn by movement. Simon stiffened and stepped away from Isleen with the quickness of a startled deer. She blinked up at him, then turned, and her whole body warmed with mortification.

The duke himself stood behind her, several paces away, eyes averted as though the tree he stared up into was the most fascinating thing he'd ever seen. He had his hands tucked behind his back, and he said nothing, nor appeared disapproving.

That was a mercy.

Simon cleared his throat before speaking in a clear, too-loud voice. "May I see you back to your sleigh, Miss Frost?"

She looked at him from the corner of her eye. Surely he didn't mean to pretend the duke had witnessed *nothing*? That nothing had happened between them? Well. She supposed nothing *had* happened. But rather, that it had almost happened. Oh dear. What exactly was the duke thinking?

"Yes, thank you." She took his arm, keeping as much distance between the rest of them as possible. As they strolled past the duke, as calm as though they took a turn about a garden, he lowered his gaze from the tree to smile at them both. A knowing, kind sort of smile.

"I hope you enjoyed the races, Miss Frost."

"I did, Your Grace." She bobbed a curtsy to him, reminding herself that the Duke of Montfort was one of the most powerful men in England. And he had nearly caught her, a lowly baron's daughter, allowing his son to kiss her.

"Excellent. Farleigh? When we return to the stables, I hope you will grant me a few moments of your time."

"Yes, Your Grace," Simon answered at once, bowing. Then they left the wooded area, her cheeks still burning. Simon looked down at her, his eyes wide. "Isleen, I'm sorry. I shouldn't have taken liberties—"

"You didn't," she assured him, keeping her voice low as they approached the line of sleighs. The children were still throwing snowballs at each other in the field, though the adults and drivers milled around the vehicles. "And I will certainly tell your father the truth of the matter, if you need me to. I don't wish to cause you any trouble."

"My father." Simon released a heavy sigh and looked over his shoulder. "He will take me at my word. You needn't worry, Isleen. Your reputation is safe; it will be me he thinks poorly of, not you."

She squeezed his arm gently. "I hope not, Simon."

"I am sorry things were spoiled. Not by my father, but by me." He gave her a most repentant look. "I ought to have known better than to steal away with you, out in the open, where anyone could happen upon us. Forgive me for my indiscretion, Isleen."

How could she not? He had a look about him rather like a kicked puppy. "There is nothing to forgive, Simon." Though she regretted that she might never know the feel of his lips pressed against hers.

What if his father forbade him from spending any more time with her? What if the duke disapproved of young couples exchanging a kiss? The mortification of it all came back, and Isleen had to swallow a groan of embarrassment.

They were only steps away from the sleigh when Simon bent

closer to Isleen and whispered in her ear. "I am sorry, most of all, to have lost the chance to kiss you."

A whirling wind spun about in Isleen's stomach while her blood sang in her ears.

Her lips parted, and she turned to him with a quiet gasp of surprise. He only smiled, then handed her up into her sleigh, onto the seat next to her brother, who was distracted calling for Fiona and Lord James to stop their play and return.

Simon withdrew, and when Teague turned to look at her, amused and exasperated, she had composed herself somewhat. "Can you believe those children? It's as though they'd rather play in the woods forever than come back where it's warm."

"I cannot say I blame them," she whispered. Because she, too, rather wished she had just a little more time in the woods.

SIMON HAD LEARNED, LONG AGO, TO MIMIC THE WAY HIS father raised a single eyebrow when the duke wished to make a point. It was a trait all the children had worked to learn, and that James had nearly mastered. Sometimes, the single raised brow indicated humor. Other times, disbelief.

Today, when the duke folded his arms, leaned against the base of the tree, and raised that eyebrow at his son, Simon read neither of those things. His father's green eyes were dark, his mouth a flat line betraying neither joy nor sorrow, and his posture was relaxed.

The duke had lingered at the stables while everyone else went up the hill, and Simon remained with him. When they were the last two remaining, His Grace had led Simon out of the cobbled stable-yard and to a tall evergreen, where he had taken up his relaxed position.

"Well?" the duke said, his deep voice kind. "Are you going to explain what I saw today?"

Heat crept up Simon's neck even while his stomach dropped. "Miss Frost and I were only talking, Your Grace."

The duke raised one hand. "Father. I am your father in this moment, not the duke. A father who is concerned for his son, and for the people under his care."

Simon stared at the duke, somewhat surprised. "You are always the duke."

"Unfortunately, I always bear that title." His father smiled, the expression tight and perhaps a little sad. "But right now, the duke comes after the father. And you had more than a conversation on your mind with Miss Frost."

"That is true," Simon admitted softly. "But I did not act on my desire to kiss her."

The duke's forehead wrinkled as his eyes narrowed. "You wished to kiss her?"

Simon straightened his shoulders. "More than that, Father. I hope you will grant me your leave to offer Miss Frost a courtship, with the goal of marriage in mind, should we suit."

Father stared, his expression unchanging. "You haven't even known her a month."

Simon had nettled himself with that truth for nearly a fortnight. How could he possibly know what he wanted after such a short time? And yet, he'd never felt more certain of anything in his life. He answered his father with complete sincerity, keeping his voice even and his shoulders back, his answer full of confidence.

"Which is why I wish for a proper courtship. But if what I know of her to this point holds true, there is no woman of my acquaintance who would suit me better than Miss Frost."

The duke studied his son, still leaning against the tree. Still unmoved. "And what about your suitability for her, Simon? What makes you worthy of this woman you hold in such high esteem?"

Simon's confidence withered. The fear of falling short of his father's expectations built again. "What do you mean? I am your heir. An earl—"

"A chance of birth, though a good one." The duke nodded his understanding. "But hardly a qualifier for a happy marriage. In fact, looking at previous histories, one could argue that a high rank would make such a marriage difficult."

His father didn't think Simon could make Isleen happy? Though the heir might doubt his place as duke, he'd never doubted that his parents loved him. Or that they had instilled in him the desire to find a love of his own, to cherish and care for his future wife and family. He'd learned from *them*. How could his father doubt *that?*

"Yet it is precisely because I am your son that I have a better chance than most at making her happy, if I am her choice," Simon stated with a clearness of mind and heart that gave his words added weight. "She will be first in my heart and in my life. How could she be otherwise? If I am fortunate enough to have her heart, I will devote my life to her happiness and security. Have you not done the same for my mother?"

The duke's shoulders relaxed. "And what of her low birth? The daughter and sister of a baron, and an Irish baron at that."

"Low birth?" he repeated, incredulous. "Isleen carries herself as well as the ladies at the highest point of society. Beyond that, she is kind, witty, and intelligent. One day—far in the future, I hope—she would make a wonderful duchess. Isleen—"

"Miss Frost," his father corrected, and Simon caught a twinkle in his father's eye that nearly distracted him from his purpose.

"Isleen Frost," Simon amended, "is strong and capable. Her rank is of no matter to me. As you said, rank is a matter of chance. Not of choice or examination. She has been raised in the home of a politician. That will give her the experience she needs to begin in her position, and I will help her. She can do it, Father. I know she can."

A pause followed his words, and his father sighed heavily. He pushed away from the tree, approaching Simon, the two of them eye-to-eye. The day that Simon had matched his father in height, it had felt like an accomplishment of some kind. But since then, he'd learned that matching his father in form was not at all the same as matching him in wisdom and capability.

Father put his hand on Simon's shoulder, holding his gaze. "Simon. You were always a stubborn boy, and you have grown into a determined man. It is an honor to be your father."

Every tangled emotion within Simon untwisted itself, and he stood still, dazed by his father's simple declaration. "Thank you, Father."

The older man nodded once, and that single eyebrow hitched upward. This time, accompanied by a smile and his father's good humor. "If Miss Frost welcomes your attentions and your suit, she will be most welcome in our family. I have faith that you will choose well for yourself, and for your future duchess."

Simon's knees nearly buckled in relief, but instead he gave his father a grin. "If she'll have me, I think Miss Frost will be a wonderful addition to the family."

"Your mother certainly likes her," the duke said, surprising Simon with that piece of knowledge. "And I am predisposed to agree with anything your mother says. Keep me informed of where you stand with Miss Frost. I want to be among the first to wish you happy." His father's words warmed Simon through and through. Had he guessed his father had such faith in him? "Now. Let us continue up to the castle. There is much that remains to be done for our Christmas Eve ball."

"Thank you, Father."

The duke blinked at him. "For what?"

"For having faith in me."

At this, the duke's smile turned to something else. It became gentler. Fatherly. "Perhaps I don't say it enough, Simon. So listen well, because what I say now, I have always felt in my heart. I am proud to be your father, because I am proud of you. You have become a man of sound principle. I hope I have many years left to watch you, to share everything that I wish my father had had time to share with me. But if that wish is not granted, the family and our title will be well cared for in your capable hands."

Simon's eyes burned, but he nodded once, sharply. Then his father surprised him by pulling Simon into a strong embrace. Despite his age, the duke was still a strong man. Something Simon felt in his father's arms that he had not felt in ages.

When they parted, Simon saw the duke's eyes glitter with tears held back. He gave Simon one last squeeze of the shoulders, the layers of winter clothing between them not diminishing the feel one wit. "I love you, Simon."

"Thank you, Father." Simon grinned. "I love you, too, sir."

He hadn't expected such a moment between them. Not when he'd climbed into the sleigh that morning, not when his father had held him back for conversation. But he couldn't imagine a better way to begin Christmas than with the gift his father had given him.

When the time came for Simon to step into his father's role, he'd know he did so with his father's approval and blessing. Hopefully, when that day came, it would be with Isleen at his side. As his duchess. His companion in all things, and his wife.

CHAPTER 19

The comings and goings in the castle had slowed with the return of the sleighs and riders. Simon went to his quarters, as everyone else had, to change into dry clothing and twirled his walking stick in one hand. He studied himself in the mirror while his valet flitted about, straightening up the closet where Simon had dressed.

"What do you think?" Simon asked, turning to his loyal servant. "Stick or no stick?" He tucked it beneath his arm, then held it behind his back.

The valet blinked at him. "I hardly see the need for the walking stick about the castle, my lord."

"It's less about need, and more about cutting the right figure." Simon turned to the mirror again. He'd never worried so much about his appearance in his life. And he wasn't even *proposing* to Isleen. He just wanted to walk with her, speak to her alone, and ask if she would allow him to pay court to her.

He probably should speak to her brother first. Yet he knew Isleen would prefer to have both the first and last word on the matter. He grinned at his reflection as he recalled how she'd tipped her lovely face up to his as they stood in the snow, ready to accept his kiss.

An incredible woman.

"Then carry about the stick, my lord, if it makes you feel the more dashing to do so." The valet closed the bureau drawer. "Will you return to dress for dinner?"

Simon looked down at his clothing. "This is appropriate evening wear, I think." He wore a black coat over a light blue waistcoat. Isleen had commented on the color of his eyes on occasion, and he well knew any shade of blue he wore would bring out the shade favorably.

Any advantage he could take in this important moment, he would take.

Which meant carrying the walking stick. If only to bolster his courage. There was comfort in carrying the concealed blade, as much for the physical protection it offered as the sentimental value it held for him.

With this final thought on the matter, Simon resisted looking in the mirror again and left the dressing room with purpose. He would find Isleen, and he would ask her to consider him as a suitor.

And he would spend the coming weeks at the castle coming to know her, and the months of the social Season in London taking her about Town, to museums and galleries, parties and balls, and anywhere else her heart desired.

She'd likely enjoy visiting Oxford, too. He could show her the library, and they could compare it to Dublin's University library.

He turned the corner, going toward the main staircase that would take him from the second floor to the first, where the guest rooms with Isleen's family waited.

A man stood in at the corner when Simon came around it. A man dressed in browns and a shabby hat. Someone who didn't belong indoors. Startled by the sight, and the familiarity of the face, Simon froze. The gardener, Whorton.

Holding a pistol.

Simon slowly raised his hands. He spoke slowly, and quietly. "Whorton. What are you doing?"

Not a single guard disguised as a footman was in sight. They must be elsewhere in the house.

"Move yer feet, lordling," the gardener snarled. "The door to the secret stairs. Now."

Simon kept his hands up and shuffled to the side. "What secret stairs? Do you mean the servants'? That's down the hall." He took a step backward.

The deranged gardener smirked. "Not the servants' stair. The secret stair. Behind that rug on the wall."

Simon looked at the tapestry, one which depicted a maiden in a field with a white peacock resting its head in her lap. How had the man found out about one of the family's secret passages? That particular stairway led beneath the ground floor, to a hidden tunnel under the castle. A tunnel that had been there since the fifteenth century. Simon shuffled slowly to the wall.

"What is the meaning of this, Whorton?"

"Shut yer mouth, and drop the stick. I won't have you swingin' it at me head."

Simon winced but lowered his only weapon carefully to the ground. Pointing the tip of it to the tapestry. What else could he do?

"Is it money you're after?" Simon asked. "Because kidnapping a duke's son won't get it for you."

"Quiet," the man snarled again, stepping closer but keeping the gun at his hip. Smart of him. He'd keep control of it that way. "Down the stairs. Be quick about it, too."

Simon clenched his jaw, refusing to show any fear, and went to the door. Down the stairs he went, Whorton following behind him.

This was not how Simon had envisioned his afternoon going.

Isleen leaned as far out her window as she could without fear of toppling out. She pulled in one lungful of air after another, trying to cool the heat in her cheeks and calm her racing heart.

"Miss, you're going to fall or catch cold, and I'll be the one your family blames for it." Darrie scolded as well as any upper servant, for all that she was younger than Isleen.

"I'm trying to breathe." Isleen didn't realize how odd that sounded until her maid laughed.

"You can breathe just as well with both feet on the ground and the window closed. Come along, miss. Here are your gloves for dinner."

Isleen lowered herself from toes to heels, then swung the window shut. She didn't dare tell Darrie about the duke, catching her and Simon in the woods. Had it been someone less kind or invested in Simon's future, scandal surely would have followed.

Her cheeks blazed again. Darrie, approaching with elbow-length gloves, paused. "You haven't fallen ill, have you? Playing in the snow today, as though you weren't a lady, couldn't lead to anything good." Darrie raised her hand and placed it first on Isleen's forehead, then on her cheeks. "Your brow is normal. Are you blushing, then?"

"Nevermind that." Isleen took the gloves. "I'm not ill. There is nothing to worry about." She drew the gloves on one at a time, then let Darrie button them above her elbows. They were a lovely set, but not entirely practical for meals. She would have to strip them off for dinner, then put them on again to mingle with the other guests afterward.

"You're sure you want to be ready this early?" Darrie glanced up through her lashes. "How exactly will you pass the time?"

Isleen smoothed the material over her arms, then picked up a fan from her dressing table. "I'll wander about the castle and find something to do. Perhaps I'll have a conversation with someone. Or read a book."

Darrie smirked but said no more. Given the maid's romantic turn of mind, she likely suspected Isleen had a gentleman she planned to meet.

The maid confirmed Isleen's suspicions when she turned the conversation down a similar path. "Did you know the servants meet in the halls with their sweethearts? In secret passages and such. They don't know all of 'em, of course, since the duke's family must keep some things to themselves. But they arrange their schedule to bump into one another, right inside the walls."

"Really?" Isleen shook her head. "It cannot be that difficult when they all work together in the castle, I suppose."

"Oh, it's even the outdoor staff." Darrie's grin grew larger. "Remember that gardener we met? He's got a sweetheart in one of the upstairs maids. He's been trying to surprise her with a Christmas present for days, sneaking up here to meet her in secret."

"Poor man. I hope he doesn't lose his position. I cannot think the duke would want his gardeners poking about inside the walls." Isleen nodded at her reflection. She was as presentable as she'd ever be. "I shouldn't need you until late, Darrie. You're welcome to enjoy the fire here or in the servants' hall. I'll ring for you if you aren't here when I come back."

"Yes, miss. Thank you."

Isleen left her room to find the corridor empty of all save a footman at one end. She nodded to him with a smile, then went on her way around the corner and toward the main stairs that would take her to the second floor and the formal dining room. If she happened to pass by near the family wing, and perhaps glimpsed Simon, she could find out exactly how much the duke saw, and if she needed to prepare herself for a lecture on propriety from her mother.

Isleen hesitated at the intersection of two corridors and looked at the servants' stairs. Dare she take the shortcut upward? She bit her lip, then decided she could at least peek inside. If no one was using the stairway, perhaps she could.

Her hand hovered briefly over the hidden indent that acted as a handle, then she gave it a tug. The wall swung open, and she smiled to herself as she climbed up the tightly wound stairway. How often did Simon, the proper duke's son, slip in and out of servants' hidden passages?

She came out on the second floor to find the corridor empty again. No one else seemed in a rush to dress for dinner after their adventures in the snow. Yet she could not imagine keeping still. She had to restrain herself from skipping down the hall, such was her pleasure, and she very nearly tripped over a stick left in the middle of the carpet.

Isleen bent down to pick up the cane but stopped the moment her gloved fingers brushed the finely polished wood.

Simon's walking stick. She knew it was his even before her gaze flicked to the end with his silver-pressed letter "S." But what was it doing in the middle of the corridor? Where was its owner?

She wrapped her hand around it, her eyes following its length with curiosity. Simon wouldn't leave this gift from his father lying about. Not when it concealed a dangerous weapon inside, especially.

She looked at both sides of the corridor, trying to find some hint or explanation for its presence there, or some indication of where Simon had gone. And her eyes noted something. A small, almost imperceptible, line between the wall and floor where the stick had pointed.

A passage? Here?

Isleen went to the wall and put her hand against it, pushing gently, feeling for a seem to open. Her gloves made it difficult, and she stripped one off rather than give up. Her fingers slid behind the tapestry, one she had admired often for the beautiful white peacock in its center. And that was when she felt the smallest waft of air.

Her fingers caught an indentation. She had to use her nails to tug at it, but the door slid open at last.

This stair wasn't lit by stained glass windows. Nor did it feel as welcoming as the other. She swallowed and peered downward into the dimness.

Grasping Simon's stick in one hand, she used the other to feel her way along the wall as she went down, down, down. A sinking feeling in her stomach made her hesitate. Perhaps she should fetch someone. Her brother. Or a footman.

What if Simon hadn't even come this way?

She gripped his walking stick tighter, took in a deep breath, and found her courage. She was an Irish woman, from a land where children turned to swans and kings fell in love with fairy queens. She could manage a dark staircase. And she'd have a story to tell after.

Isleen kept going down, her slippered feet making little sound.

She had descended for some time, had gone lower than even the ground floor. Was she at the level of the cellar? Ahead, dim light filtered through the dark. And it had grown cold—as cold as the outdoors. Her skin prickled, bumps raising along her arms and legs.

And then she stilled, holding her breath.

Were those voices?

Yes. Men's voices.

She gripped the cane tighter. Oh dear. Why hadn't she taken up fencing when Teague had offered her lessons? Instead she'd learned archery, a more ladylike pursuit.

She crept down the dark corridor, one hand still along the wall, her eyes finally adjusted to the dimness. A flickering light ahead made her blink. Had someone brought a lantern into the darkness?

"You cannot be serious." Simon! That was his voice. "What do you hope to gain, forcing me through this passage in the middle of winter? Leave now, man, and I'll give you a head start before I report you."

"You won't be reportin' nothin'," a harsh voice growled out. "This passage takes us both to the cart, where you'll sit still and quiet like I told you."

Simon's voice didn't sound any less bold as he said, "You cannot think it possible to kidnap the duke's son right from under his nose? And for what purpose? Money?"

"I don't give a damn about money. Stop talking and get moving."

Isleen covered her mouth to keep the startled gasp from escaping. Her heart drummed a frightened beat in her ears, drowning out whatever Simon said next. What did she do? Did she run back the way she had come to find help? But four flights of stairs in a dress, and then finding someone and explaining—what if they were too late to help Simon?

What if the horrid man holding him captive lost patience and hurt him?

She looked down at the stick in her hand. What could she do? A woman, alone, armed with something she couldn't possibly wield.

What would the heroes of her stories do?

She took the stick in both hands, holding it as she'd seen her brother hold a cricket bat. Except she meant to swing at something higher. She peeked around the corner. Simon's captor held a lantern. And a pistol. His back was to her, as was Simon's, as they went to a stone-framed doorway.

It was now or never.

On quick, silent feet, Isleen darted forward, stick in the air to bring it down on the man's head. But her slipper made a sound, a scuff, and the man started to turn. She brought the heavy cane down anyway, hitting his shoulder.

Everything happened in the moment between two heartbeats.

The pistol went off, the sound loud and echoing again and again through the stone passage, deafening her. The man dropped the lantern, too, and it went spinning and sputtering, the flame nearly extinguished. He sprang at Isleen, missing her when she fell to the side. Simon lept forward, and she shoved his stick toward him, ramming the tip into his thigh without meaning to.

He didn't stop his forward momentum but grabbed the stick from her hand, twisted the handle, and drew out the blade just as the other man turned, expression enraged and hands curled into fists.

What remained of the light reflected against Simon's steel blade, pointed as it was directly at the other man's throat.

From her place pressed against the wall and the ground, Isleen saw the entire scene unfold. Simon, in his dust-covered finery, looked every bit the way she imagined a warrior would look when facing down his enemy.

"Isleen." He did not turn to look at her, his entire focus on the man he held at his mercy. "Are you injured?"

Her arms and legs shook as she righted herself, first sitting, then coming to a crouch before standing. "I am well."

"Good. You found your way down here. Can you find your way back?"

"I can, Simon."

"Pick up the pistol. Don't be afraid. It's already fired. The lantern, too. Then lead the way upstairs. I'll follow behind with Whorton."

"Whorton?" she repeated, then studied the other man, his face contorted with rage. "The gardener?"

"Hurry, Isleen."

She shook out her arms, then slid along the wall to keep as far from the man as possible. She stooped down for the handle of the lantern, which burned brighter once she had it turned aright.

Then she picked up the pistol, shuddering as her grip tightened around it.

"Isleen?"

She paused, looking over the horrid man's shoulder to where Simon's eyes all-too-briefly flickered to meet her gaze. "Thank you."

She shivered, but smiled, then turned and led them back the way they had come.

Isleen did not have to lead them far. A man in the duke's livery came down the stairs as they arrived there, holding his own pistol out and wearing a dark frown.

"Sterling," Simon greeted him, and Isleen stepped back against the wall, allowing the men a better view.

For a terrible, frightening moment, she wondered if the footman was in league with the gardener.

"My lord. What goes on here?" the footman asked, voice commanding. "I found the passage open and came to investigate."

"Whorton took it into his head to invite me, at the end of a muzzle, on an evening jaunt. I'm still not certain of our destination. Lucky for me, Miss Frost is dreadfully curious and found us out."

The gardener cursed, his words ugly, against both Simon and Isleen. The liveried footman nodded once. "You can assist the lady if you wish, my lord. I'll take this one the rest of the way up."

"A fine suggestion." A quiet hiss of metal into scabbard, the blade sheathed, preceded Simon stepping around Whorton. He came toward Isleen, a comforting smile in place. "Up we go, my darling."

She almost missed the endearment, as his hand took the fired pistol from hers. He tucked it into the back of his trousers, then offered her his hand.

Isleen took it, twining her fingers through his, then followed him. Up, up, up. She looked over her shoulder again and again, Whorton glaring up at her, and Sterling the armed footman coming along behind them all. She shuddered and turned forward.

"Ground floor?" Simon asked, then pushed open a section of wall that didn't look as though it ought to open. There *had* been exits to the other floors of the castle. She'd been in too much of a hurry and a fright to notice them. And without clear light.

They emerged in a servant's corridor, and the sounds of pots clattering and the French chef shouting filled the air, along with the scent of bread and roasting meat.

Simon tugged Isleen to the side, pulling her close. He stared down into her upturned face, his brow drawn down. "Are you certain you are unharmed?"

She nodded once and released a heavy sigh. "You should return to your room. I want to take you, but—" He looked to where Sterling and Whorton stood in the shadows.

"You have something important to handle. I understand."

He frowned at her. "Wait here a moment." Then he made some sort of signal to Sterling, who forced Whorton to follow. They walked toward the sounds of the kitchen, which quieted after a moment.

Isleen wrapped her arms around herself and realized, with a shaky laugh, that she had lost the glove she removed ages and ages ago. She had dropped it. But where? And did it even matter?

Simon returned, and he took her hand again, stilling her worries. "Let me take you upstairs to my father's study. He'll need to be informed of all this, and I doubt you wish to be alone."

"I could manage." She stuck her chin out, but felt it wobble without her permission.

"Of course you could, love. It's me who needs the company." He squeezed her hand and led her out of the dark, into the Guard Room.

She didn't know if it was his continued use of endearments or the shock of her adventure that left her felling dizzy, but she kept up with him without a word, going up stairs and across landings until he brought her through the library, knocked on another hidden door—this one looked like bookshelves—and led her into an elegant study of greens and golds.

The duke stood behind his desk, speaking to a grizzled older man dressed as an upper servant but with the bearing of a general.

"I just received word," the duke said, not bothering with a greeting as he came around his desk in a few quick strides. He looked from Simon to Isleen. "You are both unharmed?"

How had that man arrived before them? And how had he known what had happened? The duke's home was a mystery to her, despite her weeks spent as a guest within its walls.

"Yes, Father." Simon hadn't released her hand, not even to speak to the duke. Nor had either of them paid proper respect with bows and curtsies. But Isleen couldn't quite bring herself to care. Her knees wobbled. "And we owe a debt of gratitude to Isleen." Simon looked down at her, seemed to read her thoughts in her eyes, and immediately brought her to a large, comfortable couch turned to face a small fireplace. He placed his hand upon her shoulder and kept it there. The warmth from his palm seeped through the cloth of her gown to her skin, calming her.

"Tell me everything," the duke demanded. "Sterling is getting answers from the abductor, who will spend the night in our holding room. I think you and I will have a conversation with him tonight, too."

The older man had gone to a shelf, moving a book aside to reveal a glass bottle. While Simon spoke of being taken by Whorton, the servant poured a small glass of amber liquid and brought it to Isleen.

"A mite stronger than tea, miss, but it will calm your nerves," he promised.

She took the glass and sipped, the amber liquid sliding down her throat with a burning sensation that made her wince. How did men sit about drinking such things? She much preferred a glass of wine, or tea with lots of honey. She thanked him and held the glass, one sip enough for the moment.

Simon had finished his tale with speed. "And then I heard a crack, I turned around, and Isleen was there. Throwing herself at the ground and my stick into my hands."

The duke, who'd been standing across from Simon, lowered himself to one knee before her. "I am grateful to you, Miss Frost. And sorry you found yourself in that situation."

"Thank you, Your Grace." Isleen put her bare hand over Simon's where it remained on her shoulder. What more could she say that wouldn't sound foolish or trite? Only the truth. "I would do anything to help Simon, or any member of your family."

The duke's expression softened into a fatherly sort of fondness. "I believe you."

A knock on the door heralded Isleen's mother, who someone had thought to summon. With much clucking and cooing, the baroness bundled Isleen off to her room. Darrie was there, eyes wide but tongue silent, and the three of them soon had Isleen dressed for the night and tucked up into bed, with tea and a tray of hot soup.

It was rather glorious to be cared for in such a way.

"We didn't think you'd want to have to speak of this over dinner, or pretend nothing had happened," Máthair said, settling into a chair beside Isleen's bed. Darrie bustled about, setting up a pallet on the floor. "Even though it's all come off all right, you've had a fright. Just rest until morning, Issie. And then everything will be sorted out."

Sinking into her pillows after indulging in the tea and simple meal, Isleen thanked her mother and closed her eyes. Despite all that had happened, her last thought was not of the dark stairway she'd climbed, nor of the foul words Whorton had snarled.

Instead, she thought of Simon, and how he'd sounded when he'd called her "love."

CHAPTER 20

Christmas Eve morning dawned with a blue sky and a landscape of white. Simon stood in his bedroom, looking out over the lands that had been in his family for hundreds of years. The Montforts had held their castle home and the lands round about in trust, for the crown and their descendants, and while he'd thus shouldered some of that responsibility, one day it would all fall to him.

And he would work to prove, every day, his worthiness of that trust.

All while people like Whorton and his friends worked to tear apart what they didn't understand. Their interview with the man the night before had revealed a small network of men, each of them with friends or family who had been present the day of the St. Peter's Field riot. Whorton had lost a friend to one of the hussar's sabers.

Anger and jealousy had stirred the men to act, and three of them had decided the best course of action would be to steal from the duke—a powerful and politically active noble—the life of his heir. Nevermind that His Grace had nothing to do with the riot, the deaths, or any of the rest of it. Or that he was a loud voice in favor of change that would better the lives of the working class.

The men had hatred in their hearts. And Simon had been their intended victim, with the duke their target.

If Isleen hadn't stumbled upon his cane, if she hadn't followed him into the darkness, he didn't know if he would have escaped. He owed her his life, and he meant to make good on that debt. In fact, he very much hoped she'd accept his courtship.

Something else the evil intended Whorton had ruined was Simon's plan to speak to Isleen about their future.

Would she want him still, after the previous evening's nightmare?

Simon left the window and its grand view, making his way out into the halls with determined steps, hardly aware he'd left his coat on the back of his chair.

He needed to know. Before anything else interrupted them.

He went directly to Isleen's room, ignoring Sterling, who shadowed him the moment he stepped out of his quarters.

Simon knocked lightly on the door, then he waited. He raised his hand to knock again, and the door swung open, revealing Isleen's maid. Immediately, she went into a deep curtsy. What was the girl's name?

"Darrie," he said. "Is Isleen available?"

"She left her room an hour ago," the maid said. "I think she went to the schoolroom, to take breakfast with Miss Fiona."

"Thank you," he said over his shoulder, already walking that direction. He took another flight of stairs back up to the third floor where he'd left his rooms, and pressed on to the schoolroom.

He arrived at the door and stepped through it without knocking only to find the maids tidying away the breakfast things. There were no children present, except the very smallest in their chairs being fed by their nurses. He looked about, not seeing the governess for his siblings or any of them.

"Where has everyone gone?" he asked the room at large.

Everyone froze and looked up at him, then several lowered their heads and dropped into deep curtsies.

"The children went outside," someone finally said, a nurse he didn't know. "Miss Frost and Mrs. Robinson took them out for fresh air. To the front terrace."

Simon nodded and left in a hurry. Down two flights of stairs, through corridors, and out through the carriageway he went, to the large front terrace that appeared more suitable for staging a battle plan than for children to romp about. Again, Sterling followed.

"My lord, what about a coat?" he asked.

Simon waved away the question. What did coats matter when he had to find Isleen?

And find her he did, standing with James and her sister, lifting one large ball of snow atop another, building a snowman.

Simon didn't even feel the cold as he strode through the ankle-deep snow, making directly for Isleen. He didn't notice the other children playing. Or the incredulous stare of his siblings' governess. He only saw Isleen, dressed in her warm winter coat, her black hair partially obscured by a dark green velvet hood.

"Simon," James shouted. "What are you doing out here?"

Isleen's head came up, and she turned to see him when he was but three strides away.

He didn't slow. In fact, he came all the way to her, taking her in his arms. "Isleen." There wasn't another moment to waste. No time to explain his thoughts or apologize for the manner in which he presented them. Even though her lips parted, and her eyes widened, he had to know her answer. "Isleen, may I court you?"

Her hands had come up to his chest the moment he'd touched her. They stood there, staring at one another, unaware of anything else outside the circle of their arms. And she did not repeat his question, nor ask for clarification. Instead, she spoke two words with absolute surety.

"You may."

And he would have kissed her in that very moment. Except

that someone loudly cleared their throat. Mrs. Robinson, perhaps, thinking of impressionable young children.

"I win the wager," Miss Fiona said, hopping up and down in place.

James groaned.

And a cold breeze whipped around Simon, reminding him that he stood outside, in the snow, in his shirtsleeves.

Isleen's lips curled upward. "You're going to catch cold, my lord."

He narrowed his eyes at her, still tempted to steal that kiss. "I think it worth the risk."

She laughed and stepped away from him, her cheeks pink. "And I am quite sure I have lost our wager. I can think of nothing more ridiculous to ask of you than to parade about outside without your coat on."

Simon grinned back at her as his hands fell, empty, to his side. "And who do you think will catch you beneath the mistletoe?"

Isleen gave him her most haughty stare. "Some horrid Englishman, I suppose."

Simon bowed, ruffled James's hair, and went back into the castle with a lightness to his step he hadn't had in years.

THE CHRISTMAS EVE BALL AT CASTLE CLAIRVOIR WAS THE event of the year. Nobility and gentry for miles around had arrived in sleighs and carriages both, dressed in their finest. A large tree stood inside the Guard Room, covered in ribbons and paper chains, with paper dolls and tin soldiers marching through its branches. Green boughs adorned stair rails, hearths, and twisted artfully around columns. And in the open ballroom, with music playing softly from the musicians in the small balcony above, silver and gold gleamed and reflected the light of the chandeliers.

Kissing balls waited, above doorways and in high corners, for both the unsuspecting and the most calculating of lovers to find them. Isleen knew the location of each and every one and stubbornly avoided them.

Josephine and Emma, her two newfound friends, stood on either side of her, watching as the duke and duchess prepared to open the ball themselves. They had linked arms, giggling together as though they were girls newly out in society, instead of the mature women they were.

"It isn't the fashion," Josephine whispered to Isleen. "But Father always has a first dance with Mother on Christmas Eve."

"I don't think a duke or duchess need worry overmuch about fashion," Isleen murmured back.

"I quite like when they set this example." Emma smoothed the front of her gown. "Because it grants me at least one dance with my husband, too."

Sir Andrew materialized at that moment, his hand extended to Lady Josephine. The ambassador was but a step behind, and he held his hand out to Emma, who grinned broadly at Isleen before accepting it.

Isleen looked down at the dark red of her gown, her white gloves a stark contrast to the color. She'd put rubies in her ears and a red ribbon through her hair, along with holly berries sewn artfully into her braided crown. For the first time in a long time, she felt the warmth and joy of Christmas both inside and out.

She brought her gaze up again as the duke called for attention and the musicians quieted.

Married couples did not dance together, as a rule. But who better to break society's rules than a ducal couple, within the walls of their own castle?

"Before we begin our ball," the duke said from his place at the center of the room, "I extend my welcome and warm wishes to all of you, friends and family both. Thank you for spending your Christmas Eve at Castle Clairvoir. May there be many more nights such as this one to come."

Simon didn't appear among the dancers. Where had he gone? She had spied him across the room only minutes ago. Did he mean to sneak up on her and ask for a dance?

She wasn't about to step out with him while all the married couples swept onto the floor. What would people say? And they hadn't even begun their courtship proper. No, she'd best retreat. There wouldn't be any dancing with that man until later.

Teague appeared at her side before she could withdraw, standing next to her with a happy smile on his face. "Isn't the duke's family grand?" he asked. "You cannot deny they have a true affection for each other."

"No one could," she agreed with a nod.

Her brother offered her his arm. "Walk with me a moment? Along of the edges of the room, I think would suffice."

She looped her hand through his elbow and let him lead her safely away from the dancing. They walked along the long row of windows at one side of the room.

"Lord Farleigh has asked to court you," Teague said. "He wanted my blessing, and our mother's. He also informed us you'd already agreed." He chuckled, then winked at his sister. "Smart man, knowing he had to ask you first."

"He's learning more every day," she quipped.

"Does this courtship make you happy?" He looked down at her, his voice soft so none but her would hear. "It has been a long time since you've given a man permission to show you favor."

She dropped her gaze to the beautiful wooden floor beneath them. "I think my heart needed that time to heal. I am happy. And I hope..." She let her voice trail away as her brother stopped their progress, his expression curious. "I hope it is so much more than courtship, Teague. I well and truly want to give Simon my heart."

Her brother's posture relaxed, and he took her hand to bow

over it. "That is precisely what I hoped to hear. Good luck, Isleen. I have the feeling he's a match for you in more ways than one." He winked, and then withdrew. Leaving her where she stood.

Isleen glanced about herself, and then upward, and scowled. "That dirty traitor," she muttered.

She stood in the corner, tucked neatly beneath a sprig of mistletoe, and when she lowered her gaze again, it was to see Simon approaching. Never would she have predicted this moment between them when she first met him those several weeks ago.

He bent his head toward her but did not claim his kiss at once.

"I've been reading an Irish poet," he said. "Thomas Moore."

She could only reply to the nonsensical comment by raising her eyebrows. "I have heard of him."

His smile turned crooked. "Have you? A woman of my acquaintance suggested I memorize one of his poems. It took me ages to pick one. Would you like to hear it?"

Her pulse raced warmly through her veins, and she wanted to shake him. She'd prepared for a kiss. Not for a discussion on poetry. "If you feel you must share."

"I will spare you most of it." He bent a little closer, and the sounds of the ballroom seemed to soften, as though a curtain fell between where they stood and everyone else around them.

"'The time I've lost in wooing,
In watching and pursuing
The light, that lies
In woman's eyes,
Has been my heart's undoing.'"

"Wooing?" she echoed. "If you were wooing, Lord Farleigh, then there would be a lot more kissing—"

He bent the rest of the way, and she stopped talking altogether as her lips met his in their first kiss. Soft. Brief. Only the barest sample of what she knew was to come.

Because they were in a ballroom.

And people were cheering as they parted.

She looked over Simon's shoulder, and there stood Josephine and Sir Andrew, Emma and her *conte*, and Isleen's own traitorous brother, all of them applauding.

"About time," Sir Andrew said, his voice carrying all too clearly to Isleen's ears.

Emma and Josephine both elbowed him in the ribs, then Josephine fluttered forward to kiss Isleen upon the cheek, the token of affection quite sisterly. "Congratulations, Isleen. You've now partaken in one of our favorite English traditions."

For a moment, Isleen's heart pricked with pain amidst her joy. Would marrying Simon mean giving up all she loved of her Irish heritage? What of her own traditions?

She looked up at him, her hand in his, and the truth was a gentle pressure on her heart. Even if she had to give it all up, loving Simon would be worth those sacrifices and more.

Emma looped her arm through her husband's. "This is one of the most wonderful Christmases we have had in a very long time."

"All of you owe me a forfeit," Sir Andrew stated, surprising Isleen. He pointed to his wife, Emma, and the *conte*. "I told you it wouldn't be until Christmas Eve that they admitted their feelings."

"How do you know it was today?" his cousin Emma argued. "It may have been yesterday. Or the day before. Or—"

It was the ambassador who took pity on Isleen. He took his wife by the hand. "Come now, let the two of them alone. We can sort everything out later, yes?"

Teague appeared ready to lose the battle with his laughter, and Isleen heartily wished them all on the other side of the castle. Mistletoe, while presenting a pleasant opportunity for a kiss, was far too public.

Simon leaned close to whisper in her ear. "Will you step outside with me a moment?" Simon asked, and Isleen wondered if he'd read her thoughts once more. "Just for a moment."

They slipped away amid the others' excitable chatter, and Isleen's cheeks cooled at last. Simon had kissed her. Beneath the mistletoe and where anyone could see—and everyone had, in fact, witnessed that moment.

She followed him down a corridor strewn with guests, to a glass-paned door that opened onto a small balcony. They stepped outside, the cold air dancing across her mostly bare shoulders. He shut the door behind them, and Isleen narrowed her eyes, wondering if he had given up on propriety. She wouldn't blame him if he had.

His arm came around her waist, and she forgot everything she ought to say. "Look." He drew her to the stone rail and pointed downward with his free hand.

A wagon pulled by two large horses waited in the quiet below, with servants carrying crates and baskets to fill its bed. She peered through the dim evening light, trying to make out what happened below.

"Loaves of bread," Simon whispered in her ear. "Rounds of cheese. Barrels of apples. Gingerbread. And anything else the kitchens could prepare to go down to the village."

She stared, her heart beating faster. Had he done this for her?

"It isn't the same as leaving our doors unlocked with food on the table," he added, sounding less sure of himself. "But as you said, who would make the climb up to the castle on a snowy night like this? The vicar said we could use the churchyard. All of that will be laid out for anyone who has need to come and take whatever they wish. And here." He gently turned her around and pointed at one of the windows, where a single candle burned. "The candle in the window, to let the Holy Family know that there is room for them here."

Her eyes burned with tears that fell in silent tracks down her cheeks. "Simon. I don't know what to say."

"Perhaps next year, we can go down to the village, too. I am sorry things didn't work out where you could have a part in it this time, but—"

"It's perfect. And beautiful." She looked up at him, and the light coming through the curtained door softly touched upon his features. "Thank you."

"If you put up with our Christmas traditions, the least I can do is honor yours, too." His gloved thumb wiped away the tears on one cheek. "I would do anything for the woman who holds my heart."

Isleen stood on her toes and kissed him. A true, deep kiss. Her hands went to his shoulders for balance, and his arms wrapped around her waist and drew her closer against his chest. He tasted of gingerbread and sugar, and of all the good things she had ever known.

Their lips parted, and she lowered herself back to the ground, though she leaned her cheek against his chest. He turned his head to rest his lips against her forehead. "Merry Christmas, Isleen."

"Merry Christmas, Simon."

Neither one of them even felt the cold.

EPILOGUE

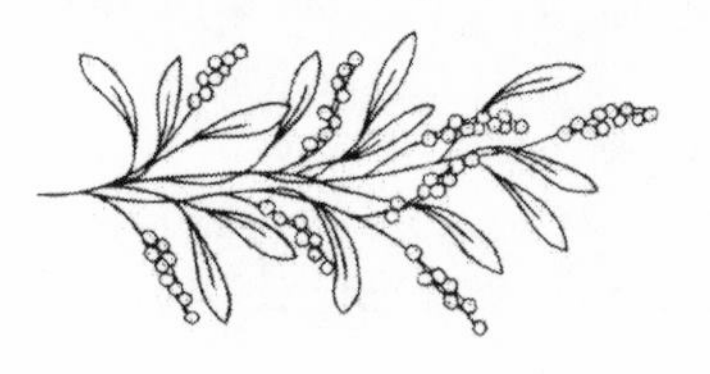

Isleen looped her arm through Simon's as they walked together through the garden. April had come, and with it were days made up equally of sunshine and storms. Which made the gardens rather dreary, if one only liked gardens when they were dry, colorful things.

But Isleen didn't walk through the castle gardens for flowers. She walked for the fresh air, and for the company of her new husband.

Simon had given her the courtship of her dreams when they went to London for the beginning of Parliament. They rode through Hyde Park, visited museums and libraries, attended concerts and plays, all while arm in arm. Sometimes even hand in hand.

Together, they had met Thomas Moore in person and talked of Dublin and poetry. They had gone to Gunter's for ices, even though the day they went it had snowed. Simon had showed her off to anyone and everyone, with a pride that had made her blush.

When he'd finally asked for her hand in marriage, she'd agreed, but only if they returned to Clairvoir for a quiet ceremony. Family and closest friends, only.

And when everyone else had returned to London and their homes, Isleen and Simon had remained. Taking the time to be alone together, at last.

"I am grateful your mother didn't mind leaving us behind," Isleen said, pausing to examine a rose bush that hadn't yet put out buds. They would bloom soon enough, the groundskeeper had promised. "I thought for certain she'd want me to attend a thousand parties."

"I'm certain those are still in your future." Simon stole her hand and raised it to his lips, placing a gentle kiss on her knuckles. "But I will be there, too. Keeping you company for as long as you wish."

Isleen sighed happily. "Considering how ill-suited you are at poetry, my love, you still say the most wonderful things."

"You never did say how you found out about my weakness." He drew her along to the edge of a fountain and sat there, guiding her to sit beside him. "The poetry, the ridiculous fashion, making a fool of myself in front of others. I still say it was Andrew, but he denies it."

"As well he should." She leaned her head against his shoulder. "It was your sisters and brother. Well. I suppose it was mostly James."

"James?" Simon couldn't have sounded more shocked if she'd claimed Sterling, the guard, had given him away. "That little troublemaker."

"He adores you." She looked up at her husband. "Almost as much as I do."

He sighed and kissed her forehead. "I suppose I'll have to forgive him, then. After I even the score. But how? That boy knows no shame."

"I'm certain Fiona will have ideas."

"Your sister is a keen strategist."

"You will have to ask her before she returns to Ireland for the summer." Isleen traced the lines of the castle towers with her eyes, noting which had windows and which did not. Simon had given her a tour of the secret rooms and staircases the evening before, taking special care in showing her how to find her way out of each one.

The secrets of Clairvoir belonged to those who lived within its walls, to the family who kept it standing in honor and loyalty to the crown. And now, she was one of those people.

"Isleen?"

"Hm?"

"Is it too much?" Simon sounded uncertain, and so gentle.

Isleen looked up at him. "The castle? I've certainly never lived in anything its size before. But I think I'll manage."

He narrowed his eyes at her. "The responsibility."

"I will manage," she assured him, and not for the first time. "As will you, when the time comes. Until then, we will learn from your parents. Who are the very best duke and duchess I have ever heard of."

He relaxed again and leaned his forehead against hers. "There's one more thing I need to tell you."

"Really? Are you also a prince? Or perhaps there is another castle I need to be aware of? Or are the maids assassins to match the company of footmen guards?" She had nearly forgotten what they were talking about, as she focused instead on his rather delightfully close lips.

"Assassin maids? That's not a terrible idea. Would Darrie train them?"

Isleen lifted her chin, her lips barely brushing his as she said, "Get on with it, Simon."

"I'm taking you with me to Ireland this summer. To tend to our estate there."

She pulled back, looking up at him with wide eyes. "Truly? We can go together?"

"As soon as Parliament adjourns, we will accompany your

family to Dublin. And from there, to my family's estate. If you wish it."

"I very much wish it." She took the opportunity to prove just how much by sliding her arms about him and drawing him to her in a most delicious kiss.

AUTHOR'S NOTES

These author's notes are always tricky things to add. For this book, what it really comes down to are two things.

1. I did the best I could with my research. And yes, that includes the Christmas tree, which was 100% present at Castle Belvoir during the Regency era (they have historical records of this) and Belvoir is what I've loosely based Clairvoir upon.
2. This series of books is meant to be light, in feel and in emotion. So while events such as the Peterloo Massacre are touched on in brief, the primary focus is our couple and their happily ever after. They were written for enjoyment without undue anxiety. I feel that Isleen and Simon continue that lovely tradition of gentle romance.

Reader, you may have noticed that I didn't include a sneak-peek at the end of this book as I did the others. You have no glimpse into the mind or heart of my next hero or heroine. Never fear - there will be more Clairvoir Books! I just can't decide which story I want to tell next. I have three to choose from.

Now, for another important part: Thank you so much to my family and my friends, who listened to me talk through plot points and listen to Christmas music in September. Thank you to my editor, who worked with my (ridiculous) schedule and my missing of deadlines. Thank you to my friend, Shaela, who loves Christmas and loves talking to me about my books. (She also makes the pretty covers!)

Thank you to my critique group for helping me iron out the details, and this includes Laura Beers, Laura Rollins, Mindy Strunk, and Anneka Walker. They are incredibly talented authors. You should go read their books, too.

Thank you to my four incredible children. Thank you to my kind and generous husband. I'm so glad y'all are there for all my adventures!

Until Next Time,
Sally Britton

P.S. Don't forget to either join my newsletter on my website (authorsallybritton.com) or come check out my audiobooks on YouTube!

ALSO BY SALLY BRITTON

Castle Clairvoir Romances:

Mr. Gardiner and the Governess | *A Companion for the Count*

Sir Andrew and the Authoress | *Lord Farleigh and Miss Frost*

The Inglewood Series:

Rescuing Lord Inglewood | *Discovering Grace*

Saving Miss Everly | *Engaging Sir Isaac*

Reforming Lord Neil

The Branches of Love Series:

Martha's Patience | *The Social Tutor*

The Gentleman Physician | *His Bluestocking Bride*

The Earl and His Lady | *Miss Devon's Choice*

Courting the Vicar's Daughter | *Penny's Yuletide Wish*

Stand Alone Regency Romances:

The Captain and Miss Winter | *His Unexpected Heiress*

A Haunting at Havenwood | *Her Unsuitable Match*

An Unsuitable Suitor | *A Mistletoe Mismatch*

Hearts of Arizona Series:

Silver Dollar Duke | *Copper for the Countess* | *A Lady's Heart of Gold*

ABOUT THE AUTHOR

Hello Reader! I would love for you to sign up for my newsletter to keep up with my new releases!

Just a little about me: I, along with my husband, our four incredible children, and our house full of pets, live in Oklahoma. So far, we really like it there.

I wrote my first story on my mother's electric typewriter when I was fourteen years old. Reading my way through Jane Austen, Louisa May Alcott, and Lucy Maud Montgomery, I decided to write about the elegant, complex world of centuries past.

I graduated in 2007 with a bachelor's in English, my emphasis on British literature. I met and married her husband not long after and we've been building our happily ever after since that day.

Vincent Van Gogh is attributed with the quote, "What is done in love is done well." I love those words so much that I've taken them as my motto, for myself and my characters, writing stories where love is a choice.

All of my published works are available on Amazon.com and you can connect with me and sign up for my newsletter on my website, AuthorSallyBritton.com.

Made in the USA
Las Vegas, NV
27 August 2024